Forget-Me-Nots and Forgotten Graves

FORGET-ME-NOTS AND FORGOTTEN GRAVES

Mitchell R. White

Published by White Jade Publications LLC
April, 2025; Revised May, 2026

FORGET-ME-NOTS AND FORGOTTEN GRAVES

Cover Art and Design by M R White.
Interior Text Design by M R White.
First Electronic Edition: March, 2025
First Paperback Edition: April, 2025

ISBN 979-8-9927943-4-2 Electronic
ISBN 979-8-9927943-5-9 Paperback
ASIN B0F22CQQBB Electronic
ASIN B0F32SMBGX Paperback

To all those who served with honor, bravery and dedication. I appreciate each and every one of you.

“The bitterest tears shed over graves are for words left unsaid and deeds left undone.”

— *Harriet Beecher Stowe*

Table of Contents

Chapter One — Fresh Beginnings

Morning Excitement at Bloomers

Aileen Brannigan balanced her travel mug of coffee while unlocking Brannigan's Bloomers' front doors. The early June morning carried hints of the scorching Texas heat to come, but for now, the air held a pleasant freshness that made her smile. She'd arrived earlier than usual, eager to prepare for what promised to be an exciting day.

Inside the door, she reached to the left and flicked on the lights, illuminating the rectangular sales floor. The familiar scents of potting soil, fertilizer, and blooming flowers welcomed her. Her eyes scanned across the red hibiscus that had arrived the day before. She imagined the blooms had been carved from jade, like the infamous missing Red Jade Cat. She paused at the checkout counter, fishing reading glasses from her canvas work apron, and reviewed her morning checklist.

A rhythmic scratchy-whirring sound from the parking lot caught her attention. Through the front windows, she watched Rick Malone glide up on his well-worn skateboard, neatly sidestepping onto the sidewalk without breaking stride. He flipped his road board up with a quick tip of a toe, catching it with two fingers of his right hand. His blond crew cut bright in the morning sun as he tucked the ride under his arm.

"Morning, Mrs. B!" Rick's voice bounced around the shop, his usual reserve replaced by a grin that painted his whole face. He wore cargo shorts and a faded Keating Koalas t-shirt that had seen better days.

"You're early," Aileen said, yawning as she checked her watch. "Everything okay at home?"

Rick's smile faltered, his gaze dropping to his skateboard. He kicked at a loose pebble on the floor, the movement abrupt. "Dad's working a temp job this week. Makes mornings easier." He didn't elaborate, and Aileen didn't press. She knew too well about Forrest Malone's demons.

"Perfect timing, then. The site contractor's coming at nine to start planning the greenhouse expansion." Aileen gestured toward the back lot. "Want to help me walk through the area one more time?"

Rick's face lit up with a wide grin. "Two new greenhouses, right? That's going to be amazing."

They made their way through the entry display area, past shelves of gardening tools and chemical treatments, down the hallway past the break room and loading bay. Aileen's ice-blue eyes scanned the greenhouse, pausing on a wilting fern, a stack of unsorted pots, a dripping faucet. Her fingers tapped a silent rhythm against her apron as she made a mental list.

The morning sun streamed through the first greenhouse as they entered, creating prisms in the water droplets from last night's automated misting. Aileen paused to adjust a hanging basket of purple petunias. "These need to go out front today. They're at their peak."

Rick nodded, already making mental notes. "Those should sell nicely, right?"

Aileen smiled at the pleased look on his face as Rick examined the automatic sprinklers he'd worked overtime on after Easter. They continued through the second greenhouse and out the back door, where the true challenge lay. The three-quarter acre lot stretched before them, overgrown with Texas scrub and littered with years of accumulated debris. The barely-standing wooden back fence held a mix of Coral honeysuckle and crossvine, bees already laboring in the rising early summer heat.

"Hard to believe this'll be cleared by the end of summer," Rick said, kicking at a rusted bucket half-buried in weeds.

"That's why we're starting early." Aileen pulled a folded paper from her apron pocket: the preliminary layout from the contractor. "Two new greenhouses, right here." She pointed to spots on the paper, then gestured to the corresponding areas. "And a proper storage building back there."

"The team's going to flip when they hear about the summer jobs," Rick grinned. "Even if half of them say no."

Aileen raised an eyebrow. "Already figured out who'll accept?"

"Darwin will say yes just to have something to analyze, and to avoid any family boating trips. Verona..." He blushed slightly. "Well, she usually shows up anyway."

"And you?" Aileen asked, though she already knew the answer.

"Try and stop me, Mrs. B." Rick's quiet confidence made her smile. He'd been her rock since she bought the struggling garden center three years ago.

"You know you don't have to work on the clearing and construction. You've always got a job in the front and greenhouses."

"Yeah, but," he started. "I think it'll go smoother with me helping the others keep on task and out of trouble."

Aileen smiled at Rick's actions. He did this every time, taking initiative.

The sun climbed higher as they discussed placement options. By the time they headed back inside, Aileen's travel mug needed refilling and her mind raced with business possibilities. Fresh beginnings, indeed.

"Time to open up properly," she said as they reached the front. "Ready for an interesting summer?"

Rick hid his skateboard behind the counter. "Always ready, Mrs. B. Always ready."

Teen Team Meeting

The door chime, so lively during the early rush, gave only an occasional, lazy jingle. Aileen heard the first arrivals for the team meeting. Darwin Henslee's precise diction carried down the hallway, explaining some mathematical concept to Verona Aspen, who responded with her typical mix of interest and impatience.

"But if you consider the Fibonacci sequence in nature..." Darwin was saying as they entered the break room.

"Later, Brain," Verona interrupted, her frizzy espresso-colored hair bouncing as she shook her head. "Mrs. B's got news!"

Aileen smiled at the pair from her position near the new coffee maker. At twelve, Darwin looked even younger in his pressed khakis and polo shirt, while fourteen-year-old Verona had opted for shorts and a tank top more suited to the June heat.

Jessie Mae Burnsides arrived next, her blonde hair tucked under a practical work cap, properly dressed for manual labor. She carried herself with her usual quiet confidence, though a subtle shadow had crept into her blue eyes, a flicker of unresolved tension. Aileen winced; she knew that look. Even on an exciting day like today, Jessie wasn't fully present yet.

"Hustle's ready for work," Gloriano commented as he sauntered in, noting Jessie's sleepy look. Ryan Ruggle followed Glory, wearing designer shorts and a crop top A few weeks ago, that outfit would have signaled trouble. Now, it just meant Ryan had expensive taste.

Garrett Herbers completed the group, guitar case slung over his shoulder. Aileen knew that if he didn't have his instrument she should worry. "Sorry if I'm late, Mrs. B. Had to help Mom with chores."

"You're right on time, Garth," Aileen assured him, using his nickname. "Everyone grab a seat. Rick's minding the front while we talk."

They settled into their familiar positions: Darwin perched nervously, Verona relaxed, the others clustered nearby. Aileen's eyes swept the room before she started.

"As some of you may have noticed, we had surveyors out back last week." She paused, enjoying their anticipation. "Brannigan's Bloomers is expanding. Two new greenhouses, plus a proper storage building."

"That's awesome!" Verona exclaimed, sitting up straighter.

"It also means summer jobs," Aileen continued. "Part-time, flexible hours. The contractor needs help with site clearance and basic construction. Later, we'll need help setting up the new spaces."

Darwin's silver-blue eyes lit up. "Will we be applying geometry to the greenhouse layouts?"

"Among other things," Aileen smiled. "So, who's interested?"

The responses came quickly. Garrett's "Count me in, Mrs. B" overlapped with Darwin's detailed explanation of his summer availability. Verona nearly bounced off the couch with enthusiasm, while Jessie offered a measured "Yes, but I'll need to work around my hours at Lendon's."

Ryan examined her manicure. "Sorry, Mrs. B. I've got... other commitments."

Aileen paused, giving Ryan a considered look.

"It's okay, Aileen. I'll be with my grandparents in New Hampshire. I only hope I don't get bored," she added with a slight pout.

"Gloriano?" Aileen fixed him with a stern look. "Are you turning me down again?"

The teen shifted, uncomfortable under her gaze. His dark eyes darted around the room before settling back on Aileen. "Actually..."

"Go on," she encouraged, knowing what was coming.

"Judge Canton got me a summer internship with the City," he admitted. "Working with the Parks Department. I get to design and run programs for teens at the community center!"

The room erupted in congratulations, with even Ryan looking impressed. Gloriano's tough-guy facade cracked into a genuine smile.

"That's wonderful news," Aileen said warmly. "Though I expect full reports on any interesting city business."

"Yes, *Doña* Aileen," he grinned, relaxing into the praise.

"Alright then," Aileen checked her watch. "Those who are working today, go change. Remember, long sleeves, jeans and a big hat. And sunscreen! I'll supply gloves. The contractor will be here in an hour. Jessie, you're all set, want to help me with some preliminary planning?"

While her teammates discussed summer adventures, Aileen noted sharp edge of melancholy cutting through Jessie's forced smile. The girl's usual energy seemed muted, her wan smile not reaching her eyes.

She opened her mouth to ask as Rick's head popped into the doorway. "Mrs. B? The Masters crew just called. They're running early. Twenty minutes."

Aileen's eyebrows rose. Twenty minutes, eh? Excellent. Jessie, shall we get started?"

✧ ⌑ ✧ ⌑ ✧

Jessie Remembers

Aileen sat at her desk in the business office, reviewing the contractor's paperwork. A burst of laughter from the break room caught her attention, Rick's low chuckle followed by a quieter response from Jessie. She glanced at her calendar, and her heart sank as she noticed the date. June 2nd. Dana Mitchell would have turned twenty-one today. Aileen made a mental note to check on Dana's mother Tamryn after work.

The sound of Rick and Jessie's conversation drifted down the hallway again, but this time Aileen heard strain in Jessie's voice. Setting aside the papers, she stood and walked to the break room.

Rick sat at the table, a clipboard of site plans in front of him. Jessie stood by the window, absently turning a water bottle in her hands. Her blue eyes lacked their usual spark, showing a deep sadness instead. Her voice had gone soft and breathy, uneven and husky.

"Time for a break," Aileen announced, heading for the mini-fridge. She pulled out two sodas and grabbed a fresh coffee for herself. "The contractor won't be back from the supply run for at least thirty minutes."

Rick accepted his soda with a nod, but Jessie remained by the window. Aileen set the second soda on the table and pulled out a chair.

"Want to talk about it?" she asked.

Jessie turned, wiping quickly at her eyes. "I'm fine, Mrs. B. Just... thinking."

"About Dana?" Aileen kept her voice gentle.

The question broke something loose. Jessie sank into a chair, tears flowing freely now. "I saw Mom's social media post this morning. 'Happy birthday in heaven, sweet niece.' I wasn't... I wasn't prepared."

Rick moved to get up, but Jessie shook her head. "Stay. Please." He settled back, his face showing concern for his friend.

"She used to come over all the time," Jessie continued, her voice wavering. "Every Friday after school, she'd help me with my homework.

She made math fun, if you can believe it. Always had some silly song or story to explain things."

"That sounds like Dana," Aileen said, remembering the bright young woman in old photos in Tamryn's office, described by friends.

"And then one day, she just... vanished. Her and that teacher both." Jessie's hands clenched around the water bottle. "Nobody ever found out what happened. How does someone just disappear?"

Rick leaned forward. "Hey, remember that time Dana convinced you to enter the talent show? You were what, eleven?"

A small smile broke through Jessie's tears. "She made me dress up as a mad scientist. Had my hair standing straight up with static electricity."

"Did you win?" Aileen asked.

"Third place," Jessie laughed softly. "Dana was so proud, you'd have thought I won Olympic gold."

The break room door swung open, revealing Darwin decked out in what appeared to be full safari gear: knee socks, cargo shorts, a khaki shirt with multiple pockets, and a wide-brimmed hat with a chin strap. All that was missing was the backpack and walking stick.

"The contractor has returned!" he announced importantly. "I've calculated the optimal entry point for their equipment based on soil density and..." He trailed off, noticing the room's atmosphere. "Is this a bad time?"

Jessie wiped her eyes one final time and stood up. "No, it's perfect timing. Let's go hear about these optimal entry points of yours."

As they filed out, Rick hanging back to walk with Jessie, Aileen watched them go. It never failed to amaze her, young people showing such resilience in the face of loss. She gathered the empty bottles, straightened the chairs, and followed her team outside, where the future of Brannigan's Bloomers would soon take shape.

Tamryn Has News

The afternoon sun streamed through the front windows of Bloomers, catching dust motes stirred up by Aileen's broom. Without Rick to mind the counter, she'd fallen behind on the day's routine tasks. The bell above the door chimed as she propped the broom against the wall.

"I was hoping you'd be free," Tamryn Mitchell called out, looking perfectly put together despite the Texas heat. The mayor carried a small notepad and wore her usual professional attire. a light blue blazer over a cream blouse that matched tailored slacks.

"For you? Always." Aileen smiled at her friend. "Though I warn you, I'm a bit short-handed today. Rick's out back with the contractor."

"The expansion project?" Tamryn's eyes lit up. "How exciting! But first, I need some blanket flowers for that sad corner of my garden."

"Gaillardia would be perfect there," Aileen agreed, leading the way to a display of native plants. "I have some gorgeous specimens that just bloomed."

Ephron Dewitt, one of Aileen's regular customers and maybe the best gardener in the county, approached with a basket of potting supplies. "Mayor Mitchell! Just the person I wanted to see. Is it true about the new supermarket?"

Tamryn straightened, shifting into what Aileen thought of as her 'mayor mode.' "News travels fast in Silvergrove, doesn't it? Yes, we're in talks with a major developer. Nothing's final yet, but it's looking promising."

"Well, it's about time!" called Miss Betty from near the chemical treatments. "That old Piggly Wiggly lot has been an eyesore forever."

"Now hold on," Ephron protested, setting his basket on the counter. "Some of us liked the Pig just fine. Not everything needs to be all modern and fancy."

Aileen moved behind the register. "Let me ring you up, Ephron. Anything else? And would you like some coffee to go? I just made a fresh pot."

"Thanks, Miz Brannigan." He followed her to the coffee maker near the checkout. "It's not that I'm against progress, mind you. But that Piggly Wiggly, it was where folks met up, talked about their days. My

Eleanor used to say you couldn't get through the produce section without three good conversations."

Tamryn joined them, still holding her chosen plants. "I remember those days, Mr. Dewitt. But times change. We need to look to Silvergrove's future."

"The future, hah!" Ephron accepted his coffee. "What's wrong with things the way they are?"

Miss Betty approached with her own purchases. "What's wrong is driving forty-five minutes to get decent groceries. My daughter says the new place could have one of those fancy coffee bars inside. And who knows what all else!"

"Coffee bars?" Ephron shook his head. "In a grocery store? What's next, putting a bank in a Walmart?" He gathered his bags and receipt. "Mark my words, all this progress is going to change Silvergrove, and not all for the good either."

After he left, Betty leaned in closer. "Don't mind him, Mayor. Some of us are looking forward to having more options in town."

Tamryn smiled diplomatically. "Change can be difficult, but I believe this will benefit our community in the long run."

As Aileen rang up Betty's purchases, more customers drifted into the conversation, splitting predictably between excitement for the new development and nostalgia for simpler times. Tamryn handled each comment with practiced grace, neither promising too much nor dismissing concerns.

Manville Beadle jumped into the conversation from the corner where he was eyeing some petunias. "Is that why those big limos have been visiting?" he asked.

Customers looked at Manville like he'd just grown another head.

"Well, I have a friend who saw them. Yesterday." Manville began to mumble to the small flowers around him.

The mayor gathered her plants and receipt. "I should get these home before the heat wilts them. Walk me out, Aileen?"

At the door, Tamryn paused. "I'll need your support on this one, old friend. The town council meeting next week could get... interesting."

"You know I'm always in your corner," Aileen assured her. She watched Tamryn walk to her car, noting the slight stiffness in her friend's shoulders. Whatever was coming, it wouldn't be as simple as just building a new supermarket.

Aileen chose to broach the difficult question now, rather than after work. "Speaking of support, is there anything I can do for you? I know how important this day is."

Tamryn let out a long sigh. "Yes, I barely slept last night. I appreciate your offer, but unless you have some bottled snooze somewhere, I'm good."

"Anything, anytime. You call. I've got the cell by my bed."

Tamryn turned her chin down, holding back tears, and turned to leave without a word. She held her head high, back rigid, until she got into her car and drove away.

Inside Bloomers, the remaining customers had broken into small groups, their animated discussions about Silvergrove's future filling the shop with energy. Aileen picked up her broom again, smiling to herself. Some days, running a garden center felt more like managing a town hall.

Closing for the Day

The setting sun painted stretched shadows on Bloomers' front parking lot. Aileen looked up from her closing paperwork at the sound of footsteps in the hallway. Darwin appeared in her office doorway, his safari outfit considerably worse for wear. The boy's normally bright blond hair was plastered to his forehead, and his face glowed an alarming shade of pink despite the sunscreen she'd insisted everyone use.

"Mrs. Brannigan?" Even exhausted, Darwin maintained his precise diction. "I believe I may have miscalculated the optimal physical requirements for site clearance work."

Rick appeared behind him, carrying Darwin's abandoned sun hat. "He did great, Mrs. B. Just maybe not cut out for the heavy lifting part."

"Perhaps," Darwin agreed, wincing as he shifted position, "I could contribute more effectively from an organizational standpoint? Inside? With air conditioning?"

Aileen bit back a smile. "I think we can arrange that. Your calculations for the greenhouse layouts were spot-on today."

"They were rather elegant solutions, weren't they?" Darwin brightened, then immediately regretted the enthusiasm as his sunburn made itself known.

The bell over the front door chimed. "Darwin?" Mrs. Henslee's voice called. "Are you ready, honey?"

"Back here, Mom!" Darwin called out, then lowered his voice. "Would it be possible not to mention the sunburn? She tends to become... excessive in her concern."

"Your secret's safe with us," Aileen assured him. "Go on, we'll see you tomorrow, inside."

After Darwin left, Rick helped Aileen with the final closing tasks. He moved more slowly than usual after the day's work but maintained his quiet efficiency.

"You did well with Jessie today," Aileen said as she counted out the register. "Sometimes people just need someone to listen."

Rick moved to straighten a display of hand trowels. "She's strong, but Dana's birthday hit her hard. I didn't know they were cousins."

"This town has more connections than a spider's web," Aileen said. She locked the cash drawer and gathered her things. "Need a ride home? Bell has air conditioning."

"Thanks, Mrs. B, but I'm good." Rick retrieved his skateboard from behind the counter. "Mom's working late shift at the diner. Better if I'm home when Dad gets in."

Aileen watched him roll the board between his hands, knowing what he wasn't saying. "Call if you need anything. Any time. If your dad gives you grief, you come sleep at my place."

"Yes, ma'am." He managed a tired smile. "It'll be fine. He's usually better when he's working."

They walked out together, Aileen setting the alarm and locking up. The evening air still held the day's heat, but a slight breeze offered hope of a cooler night. Rick placed his skateboard and pushed off, his form silhouetted against the sunset as he headed home.

Aileen climbed into her blue Hyundai, lovingly nicknamed Bell. As she pulled out of the parking lot, her mind wandered over the day's events – the excitement of the expansion project, Jessie's grief over Dana, Tamryn's news about the supermarket, and the undercurrents of change running through her adopted hometown.

"Well, Bell," she said aloud, patting the car's dashboard, "looks like Silvergrove's in for an interesting summer."

The Hyundai hummed in response as they headed home, leaving Brannigan's Bloomers to rest until another Texas morning dawned.

Chapter Two — Progress and Politics

Midday at Bloomers

The June sun beat down on Darwin's safari hat as he consulted his clipboard. "According to my calculations, the debris removal is seventeen percent ahead of schedule."

"That's because Rick's doing most of the work," Verona said, perched on a stack of empty plant containers. She watched Rick and Garrett wrestling with a rusted metal frame, her eyes following Rick's movements.

Aileen smiled at her team's dynamics while checking items off her own list. The Masters crew had cleared a surprising amount of the back lot in just a few days. A promising start, even with the occasional odd looks Mr. Masters gave the teens.

Her phone buzzed. Tamryn's name on the display.

"Aileen?" Tamryn's voice sounded tight, each word clipped. "You're coming to the council meeting this afternoon, right?"

"Wasn't planning to. We're making good progress here, and —"

"Please." The word came out sharp, almost desperate. "I need... I mean, the council needs to see business owners supporting progress. Vanstone's presenting his supermarket proposal."

Garrett and Rick approached, carrying the metal frame between them. Aileen held up a finger for them to wait.

"Tamryn, what's wrong? You sound —"

"Nothing's wrong. Everything's fine. Just... please come? Two o'clock sharp."

The call ended abruptly. Aileen stared at her phone, troubled by her friend's behavior.

"Problems, Mrs. B?" Rick asked, dropping his end of the frame into the growing pile of scrap metal.

"Maybe." She tucked the phone away. "I need to attend the council meeting this afternoon. Think you can manage here?"

"We've got this," Garrett assured her, strumming an air guitar. "Though Darwin might need another sunscreen break."

"I merely suggested a scientifically appropriate reapplication schedule," Darwin protested from beneath his hat.

Aileen gathered her things, mind already turning to Tamryn's strange call. In six years as mayor, her friend had never sounded so uncertain.

"Rick's in charge," she announced. "Darwin, please take over at the sales desk. If you need help, call Rick on his phone rather than leave the desk, he'll send someone in. Verona, actually help instead of just watching. Garrett, no impromptu concerts until after closing."

A chorus of "Yes, Mrs. B" followed her as she headed inside to change. Whatever was happening at city hall this afternoon, she had a feeling Silvergrove was in for some interesting times.

Council Showdown

Aileen slipped into the back of the council chamber just as Kenyon Vanstone approached the podium. His expensive suit and practiced smile suggested success, but something in his eyes reminded her of a certain used car salesman she'd known.

"Members of the council," he began, "Mayor Mitchell, distinguished citizens of Silvergrove. Today marks an opportunity for progress."

Vanstone's polished presentation poured across the large display: architectural renderings, economic projections, promises of jobs. The supermarket would be modern, efficient, environmentally conscious. As he spoke, Aileen studied the council members' faces.

Raymond Patton rose from his seat in the audience. "If I may, Mr. Vanstone?" At Tamryn's nod, he continued. "As a lifelong resident and investor in Silvergrove's future, I fully support this project. The Patton family has always believed in progress tempered by tradition."

Vanstone spoke up. "Madam Mayor, if I may, I'd like to invite Mr. Patton to come up here with me." Patton's surprise showed he had no idea what Vanstone might want. After Tamryn's curt nod, Patton strode carefully up next to the podium.

"Mr. Patton, what were you offered when I asked you to invest?"

Raymond looked around the crowd before answering. Aileen noticed a mix of smiles and skepticism. "I was offered a fair return on my money."

"That's all, nothing else?"

Raymond nodded slowly, curiosity clear on his face.

"I would now like to make you another offer. Would you consider being our community liaison? Your respected standing in the community would be invaluable to this project's success. What do you say?" Vanstone paused, smiling widely.

Raymond stood still, too shocked to speak. The crowd erupted in applause and hoots of derision in equal measure. Tamryn tapped her gavel for order.

Councilman Elmer Sellers cleared his throat and waved for attention. "That's all very nice, but where's the money to build this big place coming from? Last I checked, these fancy stores cost real dollars, and I know Ray couldn't cover it all."

"Financing is secured," Vanstone assured him. "Major investors, including Mr. Patton, plus —"

"What about traffic?" Councilwoman Dahlia Bresslin interrupted. "Adding a supermarket, no matter which property you choose, would make it worse."

"Our traffic study indicates —"

"Studies can say anything," Councilman Sven Eidbo cut in. "Depends who's paying for them."

Meghan Cacciatori waved for attention, then spoke up. "Which property did you say you would build on, Mr. Vanstone?"

Ken cleared his throat, waiting for the furor to die down a bit. "We have examined several properties, Ms. Bresslin. There are four that are our 'short list,' including the open area south of the Big Rig Truck Stop, and the old Piggly Wiggly store and adjacent field."

"So which one?" Dahlia insisted.

"The final choice will wait until we have general approval from the council to proceed."

More hoots and hollering from the crowd made further talk impossible. Tamryn tapped her gavel. "Let's maintain order, please. Mr. Vanstone deserves a fair hearing."

"Fair?" Councilman Abel Morales leaned forward. "What's fair about pushing out local businesses? We've got three family groceries that barely survive now. This monstrosity will hurt the Latino community too!"

"Actually," Vanstone smiled, "we've approached all three of the current operators about running specialty departments within the new store. Fresh opportunities for them."

Councilman Weldon Durrell grinned his approval. "That's thinking ahead. We need this kind of innovation."

"Innovation?" Eidbo scoffed. "Sounds like corporate takeover to me."

"I'd like to hear from some business owners," Councilman Basil Mossberger said. "Mrs. Brannigan? You're expanding your garden center. What's your take?"

Aileen stood, choosing her words carefully. "Change is inevitable. The question is whether we guide it or let it guide us."

"Exactly!" Basil said. "We can't stay stuck in the past."

"Nobody's suggesting that," Meghan Cacciatori countered. "But there's change and there's changing too fast, too much."

The debate circled for another twenty minutes. Finally, Tamryn called for the vote.

"All in favor of approving the initial development proposal?"

Weldon's hand shot up first, followed by Basil and Meghan. Tamryn raised her hand last and waited for any others.

"Opposed?"

Sven and Elmer raised their hands together, with Abel and Dahlia right behind.

"Four to four," Tamryn announced, tension evident in her voice. "As mayor, I have the authority to break this tie in either direction. However, given the significance of this project, I believe we need stronger consensus. Motion fails for lack of majority. We'll reconvene for further discussion next week."

The crack of Tamryn's gavel caused the chamber to erupt in mixed reactions. Vanstone maintained his smile, but his knuckles whitened around his briefcase handle. Raymond Patton's face darkened as he watched the developer leave.

As the room cleared, Tamryn approached Aileen. "This is a disaster," she muttered. "We need this project. The tax base, the jobs, the future of Silvergrove – it all depends on growth."

"The opposition seems pretty determined," Aileen observed.

"They're stuck in the past." Tamryn's low-throated growl carried unusual bitterness. "Sometimes I think half this town would rather see those empty lots stay empty forever, ghosts and all."

"Ghosts?"

Tamryn waved the word away. "Figure of speech. Listen, I've got another meeting. Dinner tonight? Casa Sol? Andy mentioned he'd like to come, and I thought maybe Judge Canton..."

"Sounds good," Aileen agreed, watching her friend hurry away without her usual closing hug. Something was definitely off with Tamryn, but what?

Bad News at Bloomers

Aileen pulled into her parking space behind Brannigan's Bloomers, her mind still churning over the council meeting. The setting sun turned the oak in Miss Betty's yard a bright gold. The partially cleared back lot, where Rick and Garrett were gathering tools from the day's work.

Darwin perched on an overturned wheelbarrow, safari hat askew, making notes on his ever-present clipboard. "Mrs. Brannigan! We achieved another thirteen percent clearance today, despite the unexpected discovery of what appears to be a pre-1960s septic system."

"More like a cesspool," Verona added from her safer position near the back door. "You should have seen Darwin's face when Rick figured out what it was."

"I maintained scientific objectivity," Darwin protested, though his cheeks pinked.

Mr. Masters' truck pulled in, and Aileen's stomach dropped as she saw his expression. The contractor killed his engine and climbed down, nodding to Rick and Garrett as they approached.

"Mrs. Brannigan, got a minute?"

"Of course." She gestured toward the break room. "Kids, finish up out here, please."

Inside, Masters removed his hard hat and ran a hand through his thinning hair. "There's no easy way to say this. We're bidding on the supermarket project."

"I see." Aileen kept her voice neutral, though her heart sank.

"If we win the bid I'll need to pull our resources from here. And with our local presence, we probably will." He gestured vaguely toward the back lot. "I can recommend some other contractors, but with the size of the supermarket project..."

"They'll all be bidding too," Aileen finished.

"Yes, ma'am. I'm sorry. You've been good to work with, and those kids of yours..." He smiled. "Well, they're something else."

Movement in the hallway caught Aileen's attention. Rick stood just outside the break room, tool belt in hand, his face carefully blank. Behind him, Darwin clutched his clipboard like a shield.

"How long?" Rick asked.

"We'll finish the week," Masters said. "Get the septic situation sorted at least. After that..." He shrugged.

Garrett appeared behind the others, guitar case slung over his shoulder. "Mrs. B? Want me to write a song about corporate greed?"

That broke the tension. Even Masters chuckled. "Nothing personal, kids. Just business."

"Of course," Aileen agreed. "We understand."

After Masters left, the teens gathered in the break room. Verona perched on the counter, swinging her legs. "So what now?"

"Now," Aileen said, "we adapt. Darwin, please start researching alternative contractors. Rick, we'll need to revise our timeline. Garrett, hold that song about corporate greed, but maybe write us a song about persistence?"

"Already got a chord progression in mind," Garrett grinned.

"What about the septic tank?" Darwin asked. "I've outlined the optimal removal procedure —"

"Let's save that for tomorrow," Aileen interrupted quickly. "For now, help Rick and Garrett put the tools away."

As the teens filed out, Rick hung back. "We'll figure it out, Mrs. B. Like you always say, there's more than one way to solve a puzzle."

Aileen watched him follow the others, his quiet confidence steadying her own uncertainty. She had forty minutes to get home and change for dinner at Casa Sol. Plenty of time to worry about contractors tomorrow.

Not a Date at Casa Sol

Andy Burrell stood on Aileen's porch at precisely 7:48 PM, both watches confirming he was early. He adjusted his bow tie twice before ringing the bell.

"You're early," Aileen said, opening the door. She was still fastening an earring, her silver-streaked brown hair falling loose around her shoulders.

"Better than late," Andy offered, then immediately regretted the banality. "You look... that is... the color suits you."

Aileen smoothed the dark blue dress she rarely wore. "Thank you. Though I'm not sure why Tamryn insisted on Casa Sol. The Classy Cook would have done fine."

"Judge Canton's idea, actually." Andy held the car door for her. "Something about proper ambiance for important discussions."

"Important discussions?" Aileen raised an eyebrow. "What aren't you telling me?"

"I, uh..." Andy turned the wrong way out of her driveway, caught himself, and made a three-point correction. "That is... oh look, we're here!"

Casa Sol's entrance glowed with warm lighting, its modern interpretation of Spanish colonial architecture a stark contrast to Silvergrove's usual practical buildings. Tamryn and Judge Canton waited in the foyer, the judge's elegant gray suit making Tamryn's conservative dress look almost dowdy in comparison.

"Perfect timing," Judge Canton said, though her slight smile suggested she'd noticed Andy's discomfiture as he stood next to Aileen, fiddling with his tie.

The maître d' led them to a corner table with a view of both the vineyard and the sunset over City Lake. Andy pulled out Aileen's chair, nearly bumping the server in his eagerness to help.

"The council meeting was interesting," Judge Canton observed once they'd ordered. "Quite the performance by Mr. Vanstone."

Tamryn's hand tightened around her water glass. "Performance? He's trying to bring progress to Silvergrove."

"Progress comes in many forms," the judge replied. "Some more transparent than others."

"Speaking of transparency," Andy jumped in, "did anyone see the new documentary about migrating butterflies? Fascinating stuff about... uh... wings..."

Aileen hid her smile behind her menu. Andy's face showed a mixture of confusion and embarrassment.

"Butterflies aside," Judge Canton continued, "I'm curious about Raymond Patton's sudden involvement. That family hasn't shown interest in local development since the Reagan administration."

"Ray's a respected citizen," Tamryn said, her tone unexpectedly sharp. "His support matters."

"Of course it does." The judge's tone stayed neutral. "Just like it mattered when his father blocked the hospital expansion in '89. Old money talks, but what's it saying in this case?"

Aileen sipped her wine while she formed a question. "What's Vanstone trying to pull, surprising Ray like that? His presentation was so smooth, and then an impromptu switch in the middle."

Their appetizers arrived, saving Tamryn from responding. Andy launched into another nature documentary synopsis, this time about penguins, while Aileen watched Tamryn's fork circle her plate, food untouched.

"Raymond looked dumbfounded. Either he's Academy Award grade, or that was an epic sideswipe." Judge Canton took another bite.

"And was that a deflection from Vanstone about the property?" Aileen asked. I find it hard to believe he doesn't know exactly which land he wants."

Andy joined the talk with gusto, on point this time. "Maybe some Patton land is involved?"

"The property choice will be crucial," Judge Canton said during a pause in the conversation. "Some locations carry more... Let's say history than others."

Tamryn's fork clattered against her plate. "History is just that. The past. We need to look forward."

"The past has a way of surfacing, complicating things," the judge mused. "Especially in small towns."

"Sometimes the past should stay buried," Tamryn snapped, then immediately looked stricken. "I mean... some things are better left alone."

An uncomfortable silence fell. Andy opened his mouth, probably to discuss another documentary, but Aileen touched his arm gently. Like a rare astronomical event, his social awareness finally aligned with reality, and he wisely kept his thoughts to himself.

"Well," Judge Canton said, "whatever surfaces, I'm sure the truth will serve justice. It usually does."

Tamryn stood, looking stricken. "Excuse me. I need some air."

As she hurried toward the patio, Aileen moved to follow, but the judge's hand on her wrist stopped her. "Give her a moment. Sometimes people need space to compose themselves."

"Or decompose," Andy offered helpfully, then wilted under their combined stares. "Sorry. Wrong word choice. More wine?"

Through the window, Aileen watched Tamryn pacing the patio, phone pressed to her ear. Whatever was eating at her friend, it went deeper than just a tied council vote.

The judge caught her watching. "Interesting times ahead, Mrs. Brannigan. I hope the pressure of this small crisis doesn't break our esteemed mayor."

Late Night Plans

The Classy Cook's neon sign buzzed and flickered in the growing darkness. Inside, Kenyon Vanstone sat in the corner booth, studying a spreadsheet on his tablet while picking at a chicken-fried steak.

Raymond Patton slid into the opposite seat, his weathered face showing fatigue. "Ken. Wasn't expecting another meeting today."

"Ray." Vanstone's practiced smile appeared. "Thanks for coming. Coffee?"

"It's late for coffee." Ray ordered water instead, waiting until the waitress left before continuing. "That was quite a show at council. Could have warned me about the liaison position."

"Spontaneous inspiration. Your family name still carries weight here."

"Weight we earned through generations of honest dealing." Ray's eyes narrowed slightly. "Let's keep it that way."

Vanstone set his tablet aside. "Of course. Speaking of honest dealing, we need to discuss our council situation."

"Four-four split's not ideal."

"No." Vanstone leaned forward. "But splits can be... adjusted. Let's look at our No votes."

"Sven Eidbo's old guard," Ray offered. "Traditional values, suspicious of change."

"Elmer Sellers?"

"Follows Sven's lead mostly. Those two won't budge."

Vanstone tilted his head, making notes. "Dahlia Bresslin?"

"Too vocal in her opposition. Makes it personal." Ray shook his head. "She'd rather die than change her vote. Besides, her supporters would skin her alive if she dared." Raymond chewed slowly on a corn chip.

"Why is that?" Vanstone asked.

Ray wiped his lips with a napkin. "Her followers, and she's got quite a gaggle of them, would start yelling about corruption. They're all crazy."

Vanstone made a note. "Which leaves Abel Morales." Vanstone's smile widened slightly. "A man with... financial considerations."

Ray stiffened. "What exactly are you suggesting?"

"Oh, nothing improper. But someone in his position might appreciate... additional opportunities. Contract opportunities."

"You mean bribes." Ray's husky monotone trembled with quiet danger.

"No, no!" Vanstone held up his hands. "You misunderstand me completely. I meant legitimate business arrangements. His family farms, don't they?"

Ray relaxed slightly. "Yes. Brothers grow produce east of town. Good people."

"See? That's exactly what I mean. The store will need local suppliers. Premium contracts, fresh and high quality goods, fair prices..." Vanstone spread his hands. "All completely above board."

"Abel's honest," Ray said slowly. "But he does worry about opportunities for the Latin community."

"Exactly. Construction jobs, permanent positions, supplier contracts – all things that could benefit his people." Vanstone's smile turned conspiratorial. "Sometimes opposing progress actually hurts those we're trying to protect."

Ray studied his water glass. "Maybe. But Ken? Keep everything clean. My family name means something here."

"Of course, of course. Just business opportunities, nothing more." Vanstone's fingers drummed the table. "Though if you happened to mention these possibilities to Abel..."

"I'll think about it." Ray stood. "But remember – my support depends on everything staying legitimate. One hint of anything shady, I'm out. And I'll take my investment with me."

"Understood completely." Vanstone watched Ray leave, his smile fading. Alone, he pulled out his phone, scrolling past names of contacts, until he stopped. "Insurance." He stared at the screen, and his eyes narrowed in resolve. After a moment's hesitation, he put the phone away.

Cathy Mueller appeared with his check. "Anything else, sir?"

"No." He glanced at her nametag. "Thank you, Cathy. Just... sometimes progress needs a little push, doesn't it?"

"Above my pay grade, sir." Cathy's practiced smile matched his own. "Have a good night."

Vanstone gathered his things, leaving a generous tip. Ray Patton's principles were admirable, but principles didn't build supermarkets. Sometimes progress needed more than just a push – it needed a shove in the right direction.

Chapter Three — Shifting Ground

Clearing Troubles

The morning sun hadn't burned away the dew when Aileen arrived at Brannigan's Bloomers. Only one Masters crew truck sat in the lot, where three had worked the day before. Rick and Garrett were already moving debris, while Darwin consulted what appeared to be architectural drawings.

"Mrs. B!" Darwin waved his papers. "I've developed alternative approaches given our reduced resources. If we optimize our efforts according to this grid pattern —"

"We'd still need more muscle," Rick interrupted, wiping his forehead. "Masters pulled Miguel and Jose for the supermarket bid prep."

Verona appeared from behind a stack of old pallets. "I could help more."

"You could help now," Garrett suggested, earning an eye roll.

Aileen's phone buzzed. Cathy Mueller's name surprised her – the Classy Cook usually called for plant advice closer to lunch.

"Aileen? Got a minute?" Something in Cathy's tone stopped her: tight, careful, the kind of voice a person uses when they're choosing words.

"Of course. Plant problems?"

"Not exactly. Had some interesting customers last night. Ken Vanstone and Raymond Patton."

Aileen watched Rick struggle with a particularly stubborn root. "The developer and our new community liaison? Not unusual after the council meeting."

"Maybe not. But they sure acted strange. Kept checking who was nearby, shutting up when I approached. Asked for the corner booth specifically."

"Lots of business folks prefer privacy, Cathy." Aileen frowned, surprised at her own words. Why *was* she defending them?

"Privacy's one thing. Paranoia's another. Ray Patton's been coming here for years, never acted like this before."

Aileen frowned. "Why tell me? Shouldn't you mention this to Tamryn or Chief Couch?"

"Please." Cathy's laugh carried through the phone. "Everyone knows you're the one who figures things out. Like with the missing girl last month, and the jade cat business."

"That was different. There's nothing to investigate here," Aileen said, the words flat even to her own ears. "But thanks for letting me know."

After hanging up, Aileen watched her teens work. Rick and Garrett had the root halfway out, Darwin was sketching something elaborate, and Verona... was actually helping. Aileen surveyed the scene, a small smile playing on her lips. Progress, of sorts.

She pushed Cathy's call aside. Aileen frowned. On paper, the supermarket project was perfectly legitimate. Some of the players, though… Besides, she had enough puzzles to solve right here in her own backyard.

"Mrs. B?" Rick called. "Think we found another septic tank."

"Cesspool," Darwin corrected, consulting his clipboard. "Based on the construction style and depth, probably circa 1958."

Aileen sighed. Sometimes the past refused to stay buried, no matter how much you wished it would.

Changed Minds

Whispers ricocheted off the council chamber's marble walls like angry wasps. Chief Couch had stationed two extra officers near the doors, watching the growing, restive crowd peering in. Abel's brothers clustered near the front, their pressed shirts and serious expressions marking this as more than casual attendance. Vanstone's assistant set up a tripod-mounted camera while the developer worked the room, shaking hands and smiling.

"Quite a turnout," Judge Canton murmured from her observer's seat. "Amazing how quickly word spreads in small towns. The whispers started before the gavel fell."

Meghan Cacciatori leaned toward Basil Mossberger. "Think anything will change?"

"Progress always wins," Basil replied, loud enough to draw glares from Dahlia's supporters.

Tamryn's gavel cut through the noise. "I see we have a quorum. Before we proceed with new business, I'll ask: has any council member reconsidered their position on the supermarket development proposal?"

In the strained silence that followed, even the smallest cough echoed like a thunderclap. Aileen watched Abel Morales shift in his seat, his normally confident posture tense. Finally, he raised his hand.

"Councilman Morales?" Tamryn's voice remained neutral. "You wish to change your vote?"

"*Sí.*" Abel stood, facing his fellow council members. "I vote Yes."

The chamber exploded into chaos. Dahlia Bresslin shot to her feet. "You can't just —"

"Order!" Tamryn's gavel crashed down. "Councilman Morales has the floor."

"Abel, what happened?" Sven Eidbo demanded. "Last week you said —"

"I said what I believed then." Abel's tone suggested authority born of conviction. "But I talked with *mi familia.*" He gestured to his brothers. "We discussed opportunities. Real ones, not empty promises."

"Sold out is what you did," Dahlia spat, her face flushed.

"*¡Cállate!*" Abel's youngest brother Marco called from the gallery. "Let him speak!"

"*Señora* Bresslin, you listen!" Abel's passion filled the room. "My brothers grow the best produce in three counties. My cousins need construction work. My nephew Miguel just graduated technical school."

Abel's voice strengthened. "This project means contracts for Latino farmers, jobs for our young people. Not just minimum wage stockers – real careers!"

Vanstone bobbed enthusiastically from his seat. Aileen noticed his smile seemed a shade too pleased. Meghan Cacciatori's shoulders dropped like a marionette with cut strings, while across the room, Basil indulged in a silent victory lap, mouthing "told you so" with the self-satisfaction of a cat who'd just knocked over a very expensive vase.

"The vote is now five to three in favor," Tamryn announced. "Pending any legal challenges, the initial development proposal for a new supermarket in Silvergrove is approved." Her gavel's bang sounded like an artillery round going off. "Meeting adjourned!"

Dahlia stormed toward the exit, pausing only to jab a finger at Abel. "You'll regret this." Abel's family closed ranks around him, rapid-fire Spanish drowning out her exit.

"Interesting how quickly hearts can change," Judge Canton said as she passed Aileen. "Almost like magic."

Aileen followed Tamryn toward her office, catching glimpses of various reactions: Vanstone accepting congratulations, Patton watching from a corner, Abel's brother Eduardo already discussing produce contracts.

Inside the mayor's office, Tamryn slumped in her chair. Her phone buzzed; she glanced at it and hit ignore.

"Finally."

"You don't seem happy about winning," Aileen observed, noticing a new photo on Tamryn's desk – young Dana in her softball uniform.

"Just tired." Tamryn turned the photo face-down. "Once the details are settled, I'm taking some time off. Maybe a few weeks."

"Tam, what's really —"

"Not now, Aileen." Tamryn's smile looked forced as her phone buzzed again. Her hard gaze softened. "Sorry, Aileen. I don't mean to be sharp with you. I have calls to make. You'll stay for the site selection, right?"

Walking back through the chamber, Aileen watched Abel with his family. His reasons made perfect sense, but Vanstone's smug smile nagged at her. The developer caught her watching and raised his water glass in a mock toast.

Outside, protesters were gathering with hastily made signs. Progress, Aileen reflected, rarely came quietly to small towns. And sometimes, like Judge Canton suggested, changes of heart happened just a little too quickly.

Site Selection

Aileen entered the conference room to find Judge Canton in a chair, studying the portrait of Mayor Thaddeus Blevins from 1932. Tamryn stood at the head of the polished oak table, spreading site photos and maps. The small window cast lines across the wood-paneled walls, making the past mayors' faces seem especially stern.

"Quite a gallery," Judge Canton remarked. "Though I notice they get progressively less diverse as you go back in time."

Vanstone arrived with Raymond Patton, both carrying leather portfolios. "Shall we begin?" Vanstone asked, not waiting for Tamryn's response before taking his seat.

"Let's review our options," Tamryn said, her voice carrying the same strain Aileen had noticed earlier. "Four potential sites for the new development."

"The Highway 96 location," Vanstone began, "adjacent to the Big Rig Truck Stop."

"Too far out," Patton said quickly. "Town needs this closer to the center."

Judge Canton made a note. "And the traffic study suggests increased accident risk with two major entries so close, and the high speeds of highway traffic."

"Fine." Vanstone crossed it off his list. "The Highway 21 tract, east of that peculiarly named doughnut shop?"

"Doughnut Stop Believin' is a local institution," Tamryn said sharply. "But that land's mostly wetland. Environmental studies alone would take months."

Aileen watched Tamryn's fingers drum nervously on the table as they eliminated the second site. The mayor's reflection in the window seemed ghostly against the gathering clouds outside.

"The Hiawatha lot near Keating High?" Vanstone suggested.

"Possible," Patton allowed. "Good access, fairly level."

"School traffic could be problematic," Judge Canton observed.

"Which leaves the old Piggly Wiggly site," Vanstone said, watching Tamryn and Patton carefully. "Plus that empty field next door."

Tamryn's fingers stopped drumming. "That property has issues."

"Such as?" Judge Canton asked.

"Drainage problems," Patton said quickly. "And old foundations to deal with. And hoodlums, vagrants. They sleep there."

Aileen remembered one evening as she passed the abandoned grocery. She would swear she saw ghosts in the broken windows, in the gloom.

"Every site has challenges," Vanstone replied. "I'll need to walk both remaining properties with Masters and our surveyor before deciding."

Aileen noticed how Tamryn and Patton exchanged quick glances at the mention of walking the Piggly Wiggly site. The portrait of Tamryn's father, Mayor Trenton, seemed to stare down at his daughter with particular intensity.

"We should schedule those walk-throughs soon," Vanstone continued. "Unless there are other concerns about either location?"

"None that can't be addressed," Tamryn said, though her voice lacked conviction. "I'll have my office coordinate schedules."

"Excellent." Vanstone gathered his materials. "Coming, Ray?"

Patton followed Vanstone out. Their satisfied smiles reminded Aileen of yesterday's council meeting.

"Tamryn?" Aileen started, but the mayor was already heading for her office.

"Sorry, conference call in five minutes. We'll catch up soon."

Judge Canton watched them leave. "Interesting reactions to the Piggly Wiggly site, wouldn't you say?"

"Very," Aileen agreed. "Almost like they're afraid of what might be found there."

"Or who might be displaced," the judge added. "Scruffy and his veterans have been using those old offices as shelter since the building closed."

"The town turns a blind eye because they keep the vandals away," Aileen said, absently rubbing her hip where she'd been bruised during that the near-fatal encounter. If Scruffy hadn't organized his veteran friends to stop that Mercedes... "He looks after things in his own way."

"Including stray kittens," Judge Canton smiled. "I noticed the new tabby under your desk at Bloomers yesterday. Scruffy's latest rescue?"

"Third one this year. He has a gift for finding the ones that need help most." Aileen thought of the scarred veteran sharing coffee with her last week, lucid and focused while discussing the kittens, then drifting into confused muttering about desert patrols.

"In my experience," the judge said, studying Mayor Blevins' portrait again, "people don't fear what might be found nearly as much as they fear what will be found." She turned to Aileen. "But that's just speculation, of course. Though I imagine Scruffy sees quite a bit from those broken windows. When he's having good days."

Outside, the gathering clouds began to pour big drops, sending people scurrying for cover. Aileen wondered if the rain would wash away whatever secrets the old Piggly Wiggly site held – or expose them. And what would happen to Scruffy and his friends when progress inevitably marched forward?

Goodbyes and Notes

Aileen's breakfast nook offered a perfect view of her garden, now silvered by moonlight. Ryan's empty chair across the table emphasized the weight of their earlier goodbye.

"You're my second mom, you know that?" Ryan had said, fierce determination in her amber eyes. "After everything... I mean, you literally saved my life."

"You saved yourself," Aileen had reminded her. "I just helped you see the way."

"Still." Ryan's hug had been tight, desperate. "I won't mess up again. I promise. No more bad choices."

Now, sipping Andy's gift of chamomile-lavender tea, Aileen pulled out a fresh notebook. The blank pages seemed to demand answers to questions she hadn't even properly formed.

She wrote: *Abel's vote change – too convenient?*

Below that: *Vanstone's satisfaction – like he knew it would happen.*

The tea's delicate fragrance reminded her of Andy's awkward presentation of the gift set after the jade cat case. Such a sweet gesture, though his bow tie had been crooked the entire time.

Tamryn's behavior, she added to her list. *Exhausted? Guilty? Afraid?*

Raymond Patton – why so invested? Why so nervous about the Piggly Wiggly site?

The moon cast light and dark bars across her notes, like nature's own attempt at redaction. She remembered Judge Canton's words about fear and certainty, about what will be found rather than what might be.

Cathy's observation of V & P at dinner – secretive, watchful.

Her pen hesitated over the next entry. *Dana's photo on Tam's desk – why display it now? How often does she change them?*

The list grew, connections forming like the delicate tendrils of her morning glory vines. Each item seemed minor alone, but together they formed a pattern she couldn't quite grasp. Like one of her puzzle books, but with real lives at stake.

Speaking of which...

Aileen closed the notebook and reached for her latest puzzle book. The familiar weight felt comforted her as she headed upstairs. Tomorrow would bring new challenges – the continuing work at Bloomers, the site walk-throughs, more town rumors to navigate.

But tonight, she'd let her mind rest with crosswords and cryptograms. The other puzzles, the ones involving her friends and her town, would wait for daylight.

As she drifted off, puzzle book sliding from her fingers, her last thought was of Ryan's promise. Sometimes the hardest mysteries weren't about finding truth, but about keeping it once you had it.

Chapter Four — Cracks Appear

Walking the Sites

Aileen pulled into the Keating High parking lot, finding Vanstone's Mercedes already there. The developer stood with Raymond Patton near the proposed site, both men gesturing at the empty field where morning glories climbed a rusted chain-link fence. Aileen watched as Patton paced faster, his gestures short and abrupt, until he shoved his hands deep into his pockets.

Tamryn's Subaru arrived moments later, kicking up dust from the gravel access road.

"Perfect timing," Vanstone called out. "Shall we begin with this location?"

The late morning sun cast eye-watering brightness and heat across the sixteen-acre plot. Wild sunflowers dotted the eastern edge, their faces tracking the morning light. A mockingbird scolded them from atop a scraggly tupelo tree.

"Isn't this a big space?" Aileen asked.

"Nah, it's on the lower end of what we need." Vanstone stared into the distance at the fence lines.

"Really? Why so big?"

"Store's planned at about 130,000 square feet. That's five acres, about. Then parking needs another eight acres to meet standards. Add in access roads, and just like that you're up to fifteen acres or more." Vanstone took a pair of opera glasses from a pocket and scanned around.

"Good drainage slope here," Vanstone said, consulting his tablet while describing his vision. "The building would face east, taking advantage of the natural grade. Parking wrapping around north and south. Loading docks on the west side, away from school traffic."

"What about that low spot?" Patton asked, pointing to where cattails grew thick in standing water. "This corner floods during heavy rain. Always has."

"Nothing our engineers can't handle." Aileen saw how Vanstone's confidence irritated Patton. "Though it will add to costs. We'd need to bring in stone and fill dirt, establish proper runoff channels."

"The school board will want assurances about traffic patterns," Aileen noted, watching a grounds crew mowing the baseball outfield beyond the fence.

"Already modeled," Vanstone replied. "We'll offset peak hours."

Tamryn stayed quiet during the inspection. Only the rapid tapping of her fingers on her phone revealed her distraction. When Aileen caught her eye, the mayor's lips pulled into a thin smile.

"Time for the Piggly Wiggly site?" Vanstone suggested after twenty minutes.

The four-car caravan moved across town, tires crunching over broken asphalt as they parked in the cracked lot of the abandoned store. Broken letters on the building's facade cast ghost-like shadows.

"More space here," Vanstone noted, spreading his arms. "Nearly nineteen acres with the adjacent field. And relatively flat already."

"Except for that old storm cellar," Patton muttered.

"What cellar?" Vanstone asked sharply.

"Nothing... I'm remembering wrong," Patton said, mopping his forehead despite the mild temperature.

Aileen studied the building while the others discussed setbacks and easements. Broken windows in the old store gaped like missing teeth, plywood covers long since torn away. Morning glory vines, different from the ones at the school site, had colonized the western wall. Movement in one dark opening caught her eye – Scruffy's weathered face appeared briefly, then vanished into shadow.

"Should we look inside?" Vanstone asked.

"Probably not safe," Patton said quickly. "Structure's compromised. Look at that corner there, falling down. Those support beams —"

"We've blocked most entrances," Tamryn added. "Liability issues."

But Vanstone was already heading for a partially open door. "Just a quick peek. Need to assess demolition challenges."

Inside, dust motes danced in rays of light piercing the gloom. Empty shelving units cast skeleton shadows across stained linoleum. Aileen saw signs of habitation – a swept corner, a folded blanket quickly hidden behind a counter, an ancient coffee maker still bearing a price tag from 1992.

"Homeless camp," Vanstone observed. "We'll need to clear them out before work starts."

"There's a veterans' shelter opening next month," Tamryn said. "We can coordinate timing."

Aileen caught another glimpse of Scruffy through a broken window, his face uncharacteristically stern as he watched their invasion of his domain. She made a mental note to visit him later with coffee and news.

"Well!" Vanstone clapped his hands, stirring more dust. "I think we've seen enough. I'll have my decision by tonight's party."

Outside again, Patton lingered, staring at the empty field next door. His hands trembled slightly as he lit a cigarette. A crow landed on the old store's sign, calling harshly.

"Ray?" Tamryn called. "We have that budget meeting."

"Coming." He crushed out the barely-smoked cigarette. "Just... remembering things. Before they changed everything. The Pattons owned all this land, once."

Aileen watched them drive away, wondering what memories could make Raymond Patton's hands shake like that. Behind her, in the abandoned store, a shadow moved from window to window, keeping watch over secrets both old and new.

Cat and Mouse

Back at Bloomers, Aileen found her teen crew sprawled in various poses around the break room. The approaching storm had driven away customers, leaving them time to play with Bosco, who had discovered the joy of counter-surfing.

"No, no, down!" Jessie lunged as the kitten batted her water bottle toward the edge. "Ms. B, he's getting worse."

"Getting better at being bad," Rick corrected, rescuing a box of paper clips before it joined the growing collection of items on the floor.

"Maybe we can distract him?" Darwin asked. He waved a strip of plastic from a package of cookies. Bosco jumped up and hooked the fluttering toy and ran under the table. "There! He'll leave us alone now."

Within seconds, the frenetic feline was back on the big table, chasing Rick's cookie toward the far corner. "You little pest!" Rick yelled, rescuing his snack before it slid onto the floor.

Thunder rumbled outside as Bosco, undeterred, launched himself at the coffee maker. Verona caught him mid-leap. "Maybe we should rename him Chaos."

"Too late," Aileen said, watching the orange tabby squirm free. "He already answers to Bosco. Sometimes. When he wants to."

Rain began pelting the greenhouse roof as Bosco discovered Darwin's backpack. "Hey!" Darwin protested. "My laptop's in there!"

"Cabinet time," Aileen announced. "Everything that can be knocked over needs to go behind doors. Otherwise, His Majesty here will continue his reign of terror."

The teens began clearing surfaces while Bosco supervised from atop the refrigerator. Each time they finished an area, he would inspect their work by attempting to find new things to disturb.

"There," Rick said, closing the last cabinet. "Nothing left to —"

Bosco streaked past them all, making a break for Aileen's office.

"Oh no," Aileen groaned. "My desk..."

They found the kitten proudly seated atop a scatter of papers, one paw resting on her favorite puzzle book. His expression clearly said, "Look what I found for us to play with!"

"That's it," Aileen decided, watching the rain sheet down outside. "We're not getting any customers in this weather, and you can't work outside. Go on home, all of you. I'll deal with Hurricane Bosco here."

As the teens gathered their things, Bosco curled up in Aileen's desk chair, purring innocently as if he hadn't just created bedlam in two rooms.

Jessie helped Aileen reclaim her work space. Aileen wondered if she'd ever find the order forms she'd need the next day. She couldn't help but smile at the now indolent little purr-monster.

"Scruffy sure knows how to pick them," Jessie said, scratching the kitten's ears. "This one's got personality plus."

"Just like his rescuer," Aileen agreed, thinking of the veteran's watchful presence at the Piggly Wiggly site that morning. Both Scruffy and his latest rescue had ways of seeing things others might miss.

Party Crasher

The community center sparkled with white twinkle lights strung across exposed beams. Gloriano and his crew had transformed the utilitarian space into something approaching elegance, with cream-colored tablecloths and centerpieces featuring local wildflowers. A small crowd of protesters marched outside, their signs visible through the windows: "LOCAL BUSINESS MATTERS" and "SAVE OUR TOWN."

"Nice turnout," Cathy Mueller said, joining Aileen near the punch bowl. "Though I notice most of the No voters didn't come."

"Abel's here," Aileen motioned toward where the councilman stood with his family. "And Elmer Sellers, though he's talking to himself again."

Andy appeared at Aileen's elbow holding two cups of punch. "This is nice," he said. "Gloriano and his bunch sure did a fine job."

Aileen took a test sip, then gulped the tasty liquid. She didn't realize how thirsty she was.

"Where did they get the big bowl and these nice cups? I expected paper at best."

"I think it's an antique they found in an old storeroom of the courthouse," Andy offered.

"No," Cathy corrected, "I think it belonged to the Patton family before moving to the museum. I heard it was stored for nearly a century in some back room of their mansion down near City Lake. You know, the one that caught fire a few years back?"

The room hummed with conversation as more guests arrived. Aileen counted about sixty people, mostly project supporters dressed in their small-town best. Judge Canton entered, elegant in a navy pantsuit, and made her way to where Andy Burrell was attempting to straighten his bow tie.

"Ladies and gentlemen!" Vanstone raised his voice to carry across the room. "Thank you all for coming to celebrate this milestone in Silvergrove's development."

He stood on a small platform, champagne glass raised. Raymond Patton hovered nearby, looking uncomfortable in a suit that seemed a size too large. The miniature supermarket display commanded the table, while Tamryn hovered nearby, her customary grace fraying at the edges. She's so pale and thin these days, Aileen thought. I need to see her more often, be sure she's getting a good dinner. I could be a better friend, at least.

"As you know, we've secured all necessary funding and approvals. The plans are complete, pending only final site selection." Vanstone paused for effect. "But first, I'm excited to announce a community contest!"

The crowd murmured with interest.

"The new store needs a name," Vanstone continued. "Something that reflects Silvergrove's spirit. We're offering spectacular prizes for the winning submissions."

He detailed the contest: grand prize of a year's worth of groceries, four runner-up prizes including a week-long cruise for two out of Galveston. Excited chatter filled the room as people began discussing potential names.

"And now," Vanstone said, raising his hand for quiet, "the moment you've been waiting for. After careful consideration of both properties, I'm pleased to announce we've selected the old Piggly Wiggly site and adjacent field for our new development."

The crash of breaking glass cut through the beginning of applause. Raymond Patton stood rigid, his dropped drink shattered at his feet.

"You promised!" he shouted, face ghostly white. "You said... you promised it would be... you can't! You can't!"

The room fell silent as Patton stumbled backward, still shouting incoherently. "The school site! It had to be... you don't understand... oh God, oh God..."

He turned and fled, slamming through the double doors into the rain-soaked night. His last wild-eyed look reminded Aileen of Scruffy during one of his bad episodes.

In the shocked silence, Aileen noticed Tamryn gripping her chair's arms, knuckles white. The mayor's face had a gray cast, and she appeared to be fighting for composure.

"Well," Vanstone said with forced cheerfulness, "seems our friend Ray had a bit too much punch! Now, about those contest entries..."

The mood in the room shifted. People gathered in small clusters, speaking in low voices. Judge Canton caught Aileen's eye and raised an eyebrow.

"Interesting reaction to a simple site selection," Andy murmured, appearing at Aileen's elbow. His bow tie had surrendered to gravity again. "Almost like he was afraid of something."

"Or someone," Aileen replied, watching Tamryn finally stand, steadying herself against the wall. The mayor made her way to the door, moving like someone marching underwater.

Outside, the protesters had gone home, their abandoned signs drooping in the rain. Someone had written "PROGRESS = DESTRUCTION" across one in red paint that ran like blood in the downpour.

Aileen thought of Scruffy watching from the shadows that morning, of Patton's trembling hands, of Tamryn's forced smiles. The Piggly Wiggly site held secrets, that much was clear. But were they secrets worth killing – or dying – to protect?

Connecting Dots

Aileen's living room glowed with a single lamp. The TV murmured in the background; an excitable weather reporter droning on about storms moving east; but she hadn't really heard it for the past hour. Her notebook lay open on the coffee table, surrounded by colored markers and her latest puzzle book.

She studied her growing mind map. At the center, she'd written "Piggly Wiggly Site" in blue. Red lines radiated out to "Patton's Meltdown" and "Tamryn's Fear." Green connections linked "Scruffy's Territory" and "Homeless Vets." Black lines led to question marks: "Storm Cellar?" and "What Changed?"

Bosco batted at her pen as she added another note: "Before they changed everything" – Patton's exact words from this morning.

"What changed, little one?" she asked the kitten. "And when?"

Wild-eyed, Bosco took off on a full-power zoom, bouncing off the walls to increase his speed around corners.

She drew a timeline below the map. The Piggly Wiggly had closed nearly fifteen years ago. Scruffy and his veterans had moved in about five years back. Dana disappeared... she paused, remembering Jessie's pain... four years ago.

The timing nagged at her. She circled the four-year mark twice.

Thunder rattled her windows as she added another branch to her map: "Abel's Vote Change." It didn't seem connected to the site drama, but her instincts said to include everything unusual.

A final note at the bottom of the page: "Watch Tamryn tomorrow – cancelled meetings = avoiding something?"

Bosco curled up on her puzzle book, purring. Like his rescuer Scruffy, the kitten had a way of claiming spaces that others had abandoned. But unlike the Piggly Wiggly, her puzzle book wouldn't hold dark secrets.

Would it?

She closed the notebook, deciding some riddles were better faced in daylight. She popped off the television, picked up the dozing Bosco and her puzzle magazine, and moved to her bedroom in the back of the house.

Sleep would be long coming, with tomorrow's questions already forming in her mind.

Chapter Five — What Lies Beneath

Dawn Breaking

Orange-gold sunrise painted the abandoned Piggly Wiggly's weathered walls as three massive earth movers rumbled onto the adjacent field. Morning mist curled around their treads, the machines' diesel growl drowning out early birdsong. A crew of workers in yellow safety vests gathered near the site office trailer, checking clipboards and plans.

Kenyon Vanstone stood beside his silver Mercedes, hands clasped behind his back, rocking on his heels with barely contained excitement. "Beautiful morning to break ground, wouldn't you say, Ray?"

Raymond Patton didn't answer. He paced the gravel lot, pausing every few steps to stare at the field. Sweat darkened his shirt collar despite the cool morning air. He stopped to light another cigarette from the stub of his previous smoke, then went back to his fretful pacing.

"Those Masters boys know their business," Vanstone continued. "Top-notch equipment, experienced crews. We'll have this site cleared and leveled by end of week."

"What's the rush?" Patton asked.

"In this business, time's money. Lots of money."

"Maybe..." Patton's voice cracked. He cleared his throat. "Maybe we should do one final survey. Just to be sure."

"Already done." Vanstone checked his Rolex. "Everything's marked and logged. Utilities, drainage, the works."

The first earth mover revved its engine, blade lowering to bite into the tall grass.

"Wait!" Patton called, then lowered his voice. "I mean, shouldn't someone stay and supervise? Watch for... problems?"

"That's what the site foreman's for." Vanstone's lips tightened, a flicker of annoyance crossing his face as he watched his associate. "Ray, you don't look well. Getting cold feet about our venture?"

"Must be something I ate," Patton said. He rubbed the front of his shirt.

"Or drank," Vanstone said, clearly amused at his underling's discomfort.

"No! No, I just..." Patton wiped his forehead. "I know this property. Been in my family forever. I should stay, make sure everything goes smooth. For the project's sake."

Vanstone studied him for a moment, then shrugged. "Suit yourself. I've got meetings in Tyler all morning anyway." He opened his car door, then paused. "Just don't interfere with the crew. Let them do their jobs."

"Right. Of course." Patton was already walking toward the field, hands clenched into fists.

The Mercedes purred away as the machines began their work in earnest. Patton paced the perimeter, muttering to himself, stopping whenever a blade cut too deep into the earth. The sun climbed higher, burning away the last wisps of ground fog, as Patton's nervous circuit of the field grew faster and more erratic.

He checked his watch: 7:45 AM. The day had barely begun, but Raymond Patton already wore the haunted look of a man who knew it would end badly.

Scruffy's Warning

Aileen looked up from her inventory sheets at the sound of boots on the garden center's wooden floor. Scruffy stood in the doorway, more disheveled than usual, his hands working the edge of his frayed field jacket.

"Morning, Sergeant," she said, recognizing his agitated state. "Coffee's fresh."

He jerked a nod but didn't move. Through the back windows, Rick and the teens were clearing brush, their laughter carrying faintly inside.

"They're taking it, Ms. B." Scruffy's voice rasped. "Big machines. Yellow vests. Just like... just like..."

"Sit down," Aileen Aileen held up a hand., pulling out a chair. "Coffee first. Black, three sugars, right?"

His hands steadied slightly as he took the mug. A tiny mew came from his jacket pocket.

"Brought you something," he mumbled. "Found her this morning. Had to get her away before..." He blinked rapidly. "Before they tear everything up."

Aileen watched him extract a tiny Siamese kitten, blue seal-point markings beginning to show on her cream-colored fur. "She's beautiful, Scruffy. Thank you for thinking of her."

"What about my guys?" His voice cracked. "Where we gonna go now? Can't... can't let them..." His breathing quickened.

Aileen placed her sack lunch on the table, unwrapping her sandwich. "Share this with me? I always pack too much."

The familiar routine seemed to help. Scruffy carefully set the kitten down and accepted half the sandwich, eating methodically.

"I don't have answers right now," Aileen said, watching the kitten explore. "But I promise I'll help however I can. You and your men matter to this community."

"Something ain't right there, Ms. B." Scruffy's eyes cleared slightly. "That land... it's got secrets. Bad ones." He touched his chest, where Aileen knew he carried shrapnel. "I feel it, like before an ambush."

"I believe you." She meant it. "Will you trust me to look into it?"

Scruffy watched the kitten discover Bosco's box, the orange tabby surprisingly gentle with the newcomer. "You're good people, Ms. B. Like my old lieutenant. Never let us down."

"I'll do my best." She refilled his coffee. "Want to watch the kittens play while you finish that sandwich?"

He raised his chin, some of the tension leaving his shoulders. His eyes kept drifting to the window, toward the distant sound of heavy machinery that only he could hear from Bloomers, and Aileen knew his warning couldn't be ignored.

Discovery

The earth mover's blade bit deep into sun-baked soil, and Raymond Patton's nerve finally broke.

"Stop! STOP!" He sprinted toward the machine, arms windmilling. "Cut the engine! NOW!"

The operator backed his big Holt Cat crawler back a few feet and killed the power, more startled by Patton's wild-eyed panic than his words. Other workers ran toward the commotion.

"Everyone back!" Patton's voice cracked. "Get away from there!"

Where the blade had scraped, earth crumbled inward. A dark depression formed, widening as loose soil trickled into an unseen void. One worker stepped closer, peering down.

"Jesus Christ," the man whispered, stumbling backward. "There's something..."

Patton grabbed the man's vest, yanking him away. "Don't look! Nobody look!" His face had gone chalk-white, sweat pouring down his temples. "Police. We need... I have to..."

He spun in place twice, like a broken compass. The cell phone in his jacket pocket bounced against his chest, forgotten. With a strangled sound, he bolted toward the office trailer, feet tangling as he ran. He crashed into the trailer's metal steps, scrambled up, and disappeared inside.

The site foreman stepped forward, phone already in hand. "I'm calling Chief Couch."

Workers gathered at a safe distance from the settling ground, muttering among themselves. Nobody wanted to be the first to say what they'd glimpsed in that dark hollow: shapes that had no business being buried in an abandoned grocery store lot.

The morning breeze carried diesel fumes and darker scents across the field. In the trailer, they could hear Patton's voice rising and falling, high-pitched and hysterical, as he tried to explain the inexplicable to Silvergrove's emergency dispatcher.

First Response

Chief Roland Couch's cruiser screamed onto the construction site, lights flashing against the weathered Piggly Wiggly walls. He barely remembered to set the parking brake before lurching out, Delilah right behind him with the department's camera.

The depression had grown, dark earth still trickling inward. Couch approached carefully, boots crunching on loose soil. His face went slack when he saw what lay partially exposed.

"Everyone back!" He raised both arms. "Clear the area! This is now a crime scene." He turned to the site foreman. "Need some stakes or posts. Something sturdy."

Two workers ran for the supply pile. Delilah was already photographing, her phone recording quiet observations: "Initial discovery, approximately 0915 hours. Subsidence reveals... possible remains..."

"Like this, Chief?" The workers returned with t-posts.

Couch reached for the offering, taking four posts. He positioned them wide around the area, muttering as he worked. "Not Aileen again. Lord help me, I don't want her involved." He glanced at Delilah. "But we're gonna need her."

"Yes, sir." Delilah snapped another photo. "I'll call her once I've documented the initial scene."

Couch strung yellow tape between the posts, creating a barrier that seemed fragile against the weight of what they'd found. The construction crew huddled near their machines, sharing cigarettes and whispered speculations. In the office trailer, they could still hear Patton's broken voice, now talking to someone from the County Medical Examiner's office.

"Delilah?" Couch's voice cracked slightly.

"Already texted Levenson, sir." She lowered her camera. "And I'll call Aileen as soon as I finish this series."

Couch smiled, tugging his cap lower to shade his eyes. Or maybe to hide them. "Good girl. You're learning."

Breaking News

The bell over Brannigan's door jangled like a fire alarm as Manville Beadle barreled in, his security guard badge glinting on his pressed khaki shirt. "Aileen! You won't believe —" He caught his breath, eyes bright with excitement. "They found bodies! Multiple bodies! Could be a mass grave!"

"Manville, slow down." Aileen set aside her inventory clipboard. "What bodies? Where?"

"Over at the Piggly Wiggly site!" He gripped his Billy club like a conductor's baton, gesturing dramatically. "I heard it from Terilynn at the post office, who got it from her nephew Tommy. He's on the construction crew!" Manville leaned forward, lowering his voice. "They say it could be gang-related. Or maybe those carnival workers who disappeared in '85. Or —"

"How long ago did they find whatever they found?" Aileen interrupted, already moving toward the teens working out back.

"Just now! Police are there, and someone said the ME's coming, and —"

Aileen pushed through the back door. "Darwin! I need you on register. Rick, you're in charge." She turned to Manville. "Thank you for letting me know."

Her phone rang: Delilah's number.

"I've got to take this." She grabbed her purse, hurrying to her car. "Manville, please don't share those carnival worker theories around town."

Manville was already waddling out, Billy club swinging, eager to spread his news to a fresh audience. Behind her, she could hear him calling to someone on the street, "Did you hear about the bodies?"

Aileen slid into her car, answering the phone. "Delilah? What's happening?"

"We need you," Delilah's voice was steady but tight. "Chief says... he says to tell you it's bad. Really bad."

"On my way." Aileen started her engine, then paused. "Delilah? How many bodies?"

"Two, we think. And Aileen? They've been here a while."

Grave Truths

Heat mirages shimmered above the disturbed earth in the distance as Aileen ducked under the crime scene tape. Chief Couch handed her a paper mask. "Smell's getting worse as they dig."

Levenson knelt in the exposed depression, his white coveralls already stained with red clay. Sweat darkened his graying hair despite the portable canopy erected over the site. His movements remained precise, each brush stroke and gesture carefully considered.

"Female subject," he spoke into his lapel mic. "Textile degradation suggests three to six years exposure. Delilah, note the soil composition. Clay content may have accelerated certain decomposition processes while preserving others."

"Got it." Delilah's camera clicked steadily. "Chief, should I document the surrounding area again? The depression's grown since my first series."

"Good thinking," Couch agreed. "Aileen, see how the ground's settled? Like something bigger was here originally."

"A room?" Aileen stepped carefully around the perimeter. "Maybe part of the old store's foundation?"

"Storm cellar," Levenson interjected. "See these fragments? Typical storm cellar construction from near the turn of the last century, probably collapsed when they filled it in. I bet deeds will show some old farm house stood here." He brushed more soil away. "Delilah, close-up, please. Possible cranial trauma, though we'll need lab work to distinguish perimortem from postmortem damage."

"Storm cellar?" Couch frowned. "The Piggly Wiggly didn't have —"

A commotion at the perimeter cut him off. "Let me through!" Tamryn Mitchell's high-pitched shout rang across the site. "I need to know!"

Raymond Patton gripped her arm, trying to guide her toward Officer Martinez at the tape line. Tamryn wrenched free.

"Aileen!" She pressed forward. "Please! What have they found?"

"Mayor Mitchell, please stay back," Martinez called, but Tamryn ignored him.

"Significant find," Levenson announced. "Chain and pendant, religious iconography." He lifted it carefully. "Delilah, multiple angles please. Note the clasp configuration and —"

The silver cross shone in the late morning sun, tarnished silver glinting with its dull patina. Tamryn's scream shattered the quiet. Her knees buckled.

"Tam love, Tam love," Patton repeated softly, catching her. His own tears fell freely. "I'm here, Tam."

"Get those EMTs over here!" Couch barked.

While the medical team worked on Tamryn, Levenson continued his methodical processing of the burial site. "Second subject, adult male. Similar decomposition timeline. Multiple personal effects." He brushed dirt from a leather wallet. "Driver's license intact. Remarkable preservation in this soil matrix."

"James," Aileen said, using his first name, "who is it?"

Levenson held up the license. Camden Matheson's photo was still clear behind the yellowed plastic.

"Dear God," Couch muttered.

"Chief," Delilah called from her new position. "I've got what looks like shell casings. I'm not ballistics, but I think maybe .32 or .38 caliber."

"Tag them carefully," Levenson instructed. "Aileen, you recognize these victims, don't you?"

"Dana Mitchell and Camden Matheson." Aileen stood frozen, her gaze fixed on the ambulance doors as the closed on her friend. "Missing four years and three months."

"The teacher who was seeing her?" Couch's face hardened. "You think maybe he was grooming her?" Aileen shrugged.

"And the student who disappeared with him," Levenson added. "Though this scene suggests a different narrative. Delilah, document this stain pattern in the concrete. Could be important."

"Chief," Aileen said, her voice tight. "I need to go to the hospital."

Couch rubbed his eyes, smearing dirt on his face. "Go. This is going to take time. A lot of it."

"James?" Aileen paused. "How long for preliminary findings?"

"For you?" Levenson looked up, eyes sharp behind his protective glasses. "Stop by my office tomorrow morning. I'll have the initial report ready."

As Aileen walked to her car, she heard their voices fade:

Levenson: "Multiple gunshot wounds, both victims..."

Delilah: "Chief, look at the position of these bodies..."

Couch: "Like they fell. Or were placed..."

Aileen started her engine, the weight of the discoveries pressing down on her. Two bodies, four years of questions, and her friend Tamryn's dramatic collapse. Something darker than a simple disappearance lay buried here, and Aileen feared uncovering the truth might destroy more than just old mysteries.

Hospital Vigil

Gleason Memorial's emergency wing smelled of antiseptic and stale coffee. Aileen found Tamryn's room easily; Raymond Patton's nervous pacing outside the door marked it clearly. When he saw Aileen, he mumbled something unintelligible and fled down the corridor.

Inside, Tamryn lay against starched white pillows, her skin nearly as pale as the linens. An IV dripped clear fluid into her arm. Her eyes, usually sharp and focused, wandered the ceiling tiles.

"Tam?" Aileen kept her voice gentle. "How are you feeling?"

“The cross was tarnished.” Tamryn’s words slurred slightly. “I kept telling her to clean it. Every Sunday. ‘Dana, polish your cross.’ But she never did.”

Aileen pulled a chair closer. “Tam, I need to ask —”

“We were going to paint her room.” Tamryn’s fingers plucked at the blanket. “She wanted purple. Stephen said it was too dark, but I said...” She blinked rapidly. “Where’s Stephen? He should be here.”

“Stephen passed away, Tam. Remember?”

“Of course he did. Silly me.” A tear rolled down Tamryn’s cheek. “Cancer’s such a cruel thing. Unlike bullets. Bullets are quick.”

Aileen’s breath caught. “What do you mean?”

But Tamryn had shifted topics again. “Raymond brings me flowers. Every Thursday. I never wanted his flowers, not since high school. Why can’t he understand that?”

A soft knock interrupted. Dr. George Chambless stood in the doorway, his round face creased with concern. He gestured for Aileen to join him outside.

In the hallway, greenish fluorescent lights made everyone look sickly. “She’s severely dehydrated,” Chambless said. “And malnourished. When’s the last time anyone saw her eat a real meal?”

“I don’t know.” Aileen realized she couldn’t remember. “She’s been working such long hours...”

“This collapse wasn’t just emotional shock.” Chambless glanced at his charts. “Her blood work shows long-term stress markers. Sleep deprivation. Possible signs of prescription abuse, though we’ll need more tests.”

“Will she be okay?”

“Physically? Yes, with rest and proper care.” He hesitated. “But her mental state concerns me. Her responses are dissociative, moving between past and present. Could be medication, could be shock, or...”

“Or?”

“Or guilt.” He met Aileen’s eyes. “I’ve seen it before. When someone’s carried a heavy secret too long.”

"Guilt? Could it be delayed grief? Tam's daughter disappeared four years ago."

Dr. Chambless frowned. "Possible. I see what you're thinking. Unprocessed grief."

Through the door, they could hear Tamryn humming softly – a lullaby Aileen recognized from her own childhood.

"How long will you keep her?"

"At least overnight. Maybe longer, depending on psych evaluation."

Aileen nodded, her notebook feeling heavy in her purse. She needed to document this conversation, but her hand trembled slightly at the thought. This was her friend, after all. Her mentor in Silvergrove.

"One more thing," Chambless added. "Mr. Patton tried to get into her room earlier, before you arrived. She became quite agitated, screaming about promises and betrayal. We had to sedate her."

Aileen watched a nurse enter Tamryn's room with fresh IV bags. Through the door, she saw her friend's face: calm now, almost peaceful, but with something lurking behind hooded eyes. Something that looked too much like fear.

Or was it guilt, as Dr. Chambless suggested? And if so, guilt over what?

Closing Time

Aileen's hands trembled slightly as she unlocked Brannigan's front door. The teens turned to look at Aileen, tools in their hands. The afternoon light cast long shadows through the greenhouse glass.

"They found Dana Mitchell," Aileen said. "And Camden Matheson."

Jessie's clipboard clattered to the floor. Without a word, she turned and ran to the break room. The sound of her muffled sobs filtered through the closed door.

"I think we're done for today." Aileen's voice was gentle but firm. "Darwin, call your mother. Rick, please call an Uber for Verona."

"I'll stay," Rick said, already moving to lock the greenhouse doors. The others gathered their things, exchanging worried glances. A somber pall settled over the shop, contrasting with the bright colors of blooms and painted ceramics.

After the last customer receipts were filed and buildings secured, Rick and Aileen found Jessie curled in the break room's corner, her arms wrapped around her knees. The setting sun painted the room in amber and shadow.

"She used to braid my hair," Jessie whispered. "Every Sunday after church. Said I was the sister she never had." Fresh tears spilled, but her voice grew stronger. "I need... I need to know what happened to her, Mrs. B."

Aileen knelt beside her. "I know, honey. We'll find out. I promise."

"But not tonight," Rick added. "Tonight we remember her."

Jessie wiped her eyes. Her natural strength began to surface through the grief. "Mom and Dad are probably worried."

"I'll take you home," Aileen said, helping her up. "Rick?"

"I'll call Mr. Lendon. Tell him you'll need a few days." He squeezed Jessie's shoulder. "Take care of yourself, Hustle."

They walked out together into the purple dusk, crickets beginning their evening symphony. Jessie paused at Aileen's car, looking back at Brannigan's darkened windows.

"Dana would have loved this place," she said. "All the flowers. All the pretty life."

Aileen held her close for a moment before they got in the car. As they drove away, the garden center disappeared into gathering shadows, like a memory fading into night.

Chapter Six — Morning After

Processing Together

The bells on the door at Brannigan's Bloomers jingled as Rick pulled it open, his lean frame silhouetted against the bright morning sunshine. He was the last to arrive for their daily briefing. Aileen glanced at the wall clock: 7:58, still technically on time. She appreciated Rick's reliability, especially today when everything felt off balance.

"Morning," Rick mumbled, sliding into the last empty chair at the break room table.

Aileen studied the faces of her teens. The news had hit them all in different ways. Rick's usual quiet confidence remained, but he kept glancing toward Jessie. Verona fidgeted with her frizzy espresso-colored hair, unable to stay still. Garrett touched the strings of the guitar propped against his chair. Darwin sat ramrod straight, watching his laptop screen, his expression neutral as he arranged papers into precise stacks.

And Jessie, dear Jessie, sat with hands folded, her blue eyes rimmed red but composed. She'd refused Aileen's offer to take the day off.

"I've reassigned today's tasks," Aileen said, sliding the printed schedule across the worn wooden table. Sunlight filtered through the greenhouse glass, creating dappled patterns that seemed inappropriately cheerful. "Jessie, I've kept you on transplanting duty since you mentioned it helps clear your mind."

Jessie nodded. "Thanks, Mrs. B. I'd rather stay busy."

"I'll put some new bags of potting soil by the station," Rick volunteered.

Darwin cleared his throat. "I could work outside today if you'd prefer indoor tasks, Jessie." A sincere offer, though Darwin's fair skin burned with even minimal sun exposure.

"I appreciate that," Jessie managed a small smile. "But I need the fresh air. Honestly."

Relief flickered across Darwin's face as he smiled. "In that case, I can continue cataloging inventory and updating the customer database. I can do that and watch the sales desk."

"Perfect," Aileen said. "After our last adventure, I've learned we each deal with things in own way." She glanced around the table, meeting each teen's eyes. "This is going to be harder in some ways. The bodies discovered yesterday weren't ancient history."

The Boucheron investigations, including the Red Jade Cat burglary, had brought them together as a team last spring. This was different — personal for Jessie, unsettling for them all.

"The preliminary identification seems conclusive," Darwin offered, retreating to facts. "Dental records are being processed, but physical characteristics and personal effects match Dana Mitchell and Camden Matheson."

Verona reached for Jessie's hand. "I'm so sorry about your cousin."

Jessie squeezed back. "Thank you." She reached for a fresh tissue.

"Dana was what, almost seventeen when she disappeared?" Garrett asked, his voice soft.

"Three months from graduation," Jessie confirmed, voice steady despite the pain in her eyes. "Four years ago last March."

Rick placed a gentle hand on her shoulder. "We're here for you, whatever you need."

"The newspapers will be full of speculation," Darwin warned, checking something on his tablet. "Social media already is."

Aileen waved in agreement. "Which is why we focus on facts and supporting each other." She assigned the remaining tasks, balancing work needs with emotional support. "Customers may ask questions. You're welcome to say you don't know, or direct them to me."

As the teens gathered their things, Aileen caught Jessie's arm. "Are you sure you're okay to work today?"

Jessie straightened her shoulders. "Dana deserves justice, Mrs. B. And I need to be doing something, not sitting at home thinking about..." She trailed off, then continued in firm tones. "Besides, the lupines won't transplant themselves."

Aileen watched her walk toward the greenhouse, admiring Jessie's strength while worrying about the pain beneath it. Finding Dana's body had answered one question that had haunted Silvergrove for years, but it raised dozens more.

And Aileen Brannigan had never been able to leave a puzzle unsolved.

Lunch with Jessie

Rick wiped condensation from his water bottle, watching as his friends filtered into the break room for lunch. Through the doorway, he could see Aileen deep in conversation with the Hendersons about their anniversary garden. She'd told him to start without her.

"I brought extra sandwiches," he announced, spreading containers across the worn table. He'd been watching Jessie all morning, admiring how she'd channeled her grief into meticulous work with the seedlings.

Verona breezed in, her petite frame somehow managing to carry three containers. "Mom sent tamales," she said, placing them at the center of the table and sliding into the chair beside Jessie. "She always makes too many."

Darwin followed with his predictable peanut butter sandwich and precisely sliced apple, notebook tucked under his arm even at lunch. Garrett set his guitar case against the wall before joining them, his tall frame folding into a chair that seemed too small.

"Thanks, everyone," Jessie said, looking at the spread. Her hands trembled as she reached for a tamale. "I'm not really hungry, but..."

"But you need to eat anyway," Rick finished, passing her a napkin. The circles under her eyes showed she hadn't slept much.

An awkward silence fell as they began eating. Rick searched for something to say that wouldn't sound hollow. Darwin broke the silence with characteristic bluntness.

"Did Dana have any particular interests or activities?"

Rick winced, but Jessie responded, to his surprise.

"She loved sailing," she said, putting down her fork. "Uncle Stephen taught her when she was eight. After he died, she kept it up. Said it made her feel close to him."

"I didn't know that," Verona said, her silver-blue eyes curious. "Was she any good?"

A ghost of a smile touched Jessie's lips. "Won junior regatta three years running. Made some of the boys absolutely furious. Even her sailing friend, Goldie – Marigold, was jealous."

Rick watched Jessie relax a bit as memories flowed. Dana's competitive streak, her terrible singing voice that didn't stop her from belting out songs in the car.

"She collected superhero comics," Jessie added. "Kept them hidden because she thought it wasn't cool enough."

"Seriously?" Garrett asked. "What kind?"

"Wonder Woman. She had every issue since 1987."

Darwin perked up. "The George Pérez run? Those have appreciated significantly in value."

Verona rolled her eyes. "Not everything is about value, Darwin."

For a few precious minutes, Dana existed as more than a victim. Rick saw color return to Jessie's cheeks as she shared stories.

When Jessie checked her watch and stood to leave for her shift at Lendon's, Rick rose too.

"I've got to get going," she said. "Thanks for... this."

"We'll keep working," he promised, meeting her eyes. "Both on the back lot and... you know."

"I know." Jessie tossed her head, her blonde hair catching the afternoon light. "Thank you."

After she left, Rick started clearing the table, his mind already spinning with how they could help. The police would run their investigation, but Aileen's team had solved mysteries before. They would help solve this one too, for Jessie's sake.

Suspects and Kittens

Darwin adjusted his laptop screen, struggling to find an angle where sunlight didn't create glare. Aileen insisted on keeping the blinds partway open — "Plants need light, Darwin, and so do people" — but the afternoon rays threatened to obscure his carefully constructed database.

"Raymond Patton is our primary person of interest," he stated, creating a new entry in his suspect spreadsheet. The office smelled of potting soil and the lavender candle Aileen had lit, trying to improve concentration. "His connection to Mayor Mitchell spans approximately thirty years, with evidence suggesting romantic fixation."

"A thirty-year infatuation?" Aileen wondered.

"More like an obsessive disorder," Darwin offered. "Google calls it 'limerence,' whatever that is."

A small orange blur streaked across the floor, followed by a chocolate-point flash. Lotus, the tiny Siamese kitten with large ears, was chasing her older "brother" Bosco around the office. Darwin had objected to bringing Scruffy's latest rescue find to work, but Aileen overruled him, claiming they needed socialization before adoption.

"What specifically do we know about Patton's history with Tamryn?" Aileen asked, scratching notes on her legal pad. She sat cross-legged in her chair, gardening boots discarded under the desk.

Darwin pulled up county records, thankful for the municipal Wi-Fi upgrade last year. "They attended Keating High School together, graduating in 1996. Patton family wealth was substantial until about 2005, when a series of poor investments —"

Lotus launched herself onto the desk, racing across his keyboard. He opened his mouth to react.

skjhtREWAY78ijsoIXa:2387ujdksmn

"Feline contribution noted," Darwin said dryly, deleting the cat typing from his spreadsheet while Aileen laughed. He moved Lotus to the floor with care, where she pounced on Bosco's tail.

"I never expected to be running a garden center and cat orphanage," Aileen said, reaching down to separate the wrestling kittens.

Darwin returned to his analysis, pulling up Raymond's LinkedIn profile. "Patton Development hasn't completed a major project since 2008, yet maintains an office, vehicle fleet, and equipment. Financial records show minimal revenue with continued operational expenses."

"So where's the money coming from?" Aileen mused.

"Family reserves, perhaps. The Patton family once controlled significant timber operations in east Texas." Darwin opened another window. "Or recent influx of capital from unknown sources."

The office door opened as Rick, Garrett and Verona entered, sweaty from clearing brush at the back of the property.

"Making progress?" Rick asked, handing Garrett a bottle of cold water. Even after physical labor, Rick maintained his composed demeanor, a trait Darwin found commendable if perplexing.

Darwin updated them on their findings while Verona scooped up both kittens, cooing nonsense words.

"I've seen Raymond at the Rusty Nail," Garrett offered, leaning his tall frame against the door jamb. "About three weeks ago, he got pretty close to hammered." He strummed air guitar without thinking as he spoke, a habit Darwin had catalogued as occurring 73.4% of the time Garrett told stories.

Darwin's attention sharpened. "Elaborate, please."

"He started asking me to play some old song," Garrett continued. "Kept calling it 'Tammy.' Insisted it was 'their song' or something. I didn't know it, and he got kind of upset."

"Upset how?" Aileen pressed.

"Not violent," Garrett clarified. "More... desperate? He offered me fifty bucks to learn it for next time. Said when I played it, Tamryn would finally remember everything."

"Remember what?" Verona asked, Bosco purring in her arms.

"He didn't say. Just kept mumbling about 'what they had' and 'before everything went wrong.'" Garrett shrugged. "I figured it was just drunk talk."

Darwin added this to his notes, recognizing the psychological significance of Patton's musical preoccupation. "Classic nostalgic anchoring behavior. The song represents a happier period he seeks to recreate."

"In English?" Rick requested.

"He's trying to restore the past," Darwin translated. "Statistical analysis of similar behavior patterns suggests unhealthy attachment combined with reality rejection."

Lotus escaped Verona's grasp and leaped back onto Darwin's keyboard, sending his carefully arranged windows cascading across the screen.

"That's it," Darwin huffed, moving the kitten to Aileen's desk. "I'm implementing feline security protocols."

Verona giggled. "What, are you going to password-protect your keyboard against cat paws?"

"If necessary," Darwin muttered, restoring his work. He pulled up the county assessor's database. "Property records also show interesting patterns. Patton Development maintains ownership of multiple undeveloped parcels."

"Any near where the bodies were found?" Rick asked.

Darwin's fingers flew over the keyboard. "Affirmative. The Patton family owned adjacent land until recently."

As the others exchanged meaningful glances, Darwin added Raymond Patton to the top of his suspect database, assigning him a preliminary probability rating of 72.8%. Lotus meowed as if in agreement.

Evening Reflection

Aileen gave her chicken soup a distracted stir, watching steam curl into the quiet air of her apartment. The cheerful paneled kitchenette usually felt cozy, but tonight the silence pressed in after the day's discoveries. She'd left the kittens at Bloomers with plenty of food and bedding. She couldn't face their energy tonight.

Her spoon clinked against the ceramic bowl, a louder sound than any other in the room. Her appetite had vanished somewhere between Raymond's property records and Dana Mitchell's yearbook photo.

The phone's sharp ring startled her. Chief Couch's number flashed on the screen.

"Evening, Chief," she answered, setting aside her untouched dinner.

"Mrs. Brannigan." Roland's staccato voice came through, each word clipped and precise. In the background, Aileen heard the police station's distinctive fan squeak. "Coroner's preliminary report is in. Thought you'd want to know."

"I appreciate that." She reached for her puzzle magazine, a habit from years of solving crosswords. She pushed aside the games and opened her notebook.

"Both victims shot with .38 caliber." Roland paused, and Aileen imagined him glancing around to ensure privacy. "Mitchell once, clean through the heart. Matheson five times, three to chest, two to head. Two of those bullets added injuries to Mitchell."

"So Dana and Camden were next to each other." Aileen's pen moved across the page. "Different patterns suggest different killers?"

"Or one killer with very different feelings about each victim." The chair at the station creaked as Roland shifted. "DNA analysis ongoing. I'll keep you posted."

After hanging up, Aileen immediately dialed Darwin.

"Already got it," he answered without preamble.

"Got what?"

"Coroner's report. Also ballistics. Also Raymond Patton's financial records for the past decade."

Aileen pinched the bridge of her nose. "Darwin, we've talked about this."

"Hypothetically, if someone were to access certain secured databases, that someone might discover Patton hasn't had a legitimate development project in fourteen years and eight months." Darwin's voice maintained its usual analytical detachment. "Also hypothetically, that person might have found records of Patton visiting the shooting range monthly until four years ago, when he abruptly stopped."

Aileen sighed, a smile tugging at the corners of her mouth. Only Darwin. "Send me everything. And if I end up cellmates with Judge Canton, I'm blaming you."

"Technically impossible. Different incarceration facilities for members of the judiciary," Darwin replied with complete seriousness.

Aileen closed down her phone, shaking her head.

After reviewing Darwin's data, Aileen checked the weather app on her phone: rain forecast for tomorrow. Perfect for indoor investigation work.

She tried calling Tamryn, but the call went straight to voicemail; unusual for the always-available mayor. The knot in Aileen's stomach tightened.

The phone rang twenty minutes later. Tamryn's number on the display.

Aileen straightened, a small relief moving through her. "Tam. I was starting to worry."

"Just a council thing." Tamryn's voice came through clear and even. "The water management committee ran long. Then I saw your missed call. Is there something you needed?"

Aileen hesitated. She hadn't entirely worked out what she wanted to say ; just that Tamryn's silence had felt wrong against the backdrop of everything else. always asked about the kittens first, a running joke since Scruffy's rescue operation began, and tonight she didn't.

"I've been going over the cemetery records. Some things aren't adding up."

A beat of quiet. "What kind of things?"

"Transfer records, mostly. Some dates that don't line up the way you'd expect." She kept it vague. No point in showing all her cards through a phone screen. "I'd like to sit down and go through it with you when you have a minute."

"Of course." No hesitation. "Tomorrow morning? I can be at the shop by nine if that works."

"Nine works." Aileen exhaled a breath she hadn't realized she'd been holding. "Are you all right?" she asked, keeping her voice gentle.

"Fine." The word came a half-second too fast. "Tired. It's going to be difficult for the community these next few weeks." Another pause, just a breath too long. "I should let you eat. We'll talk soon."

Aileen heard the words that weren't said: *Difficult for me.*

"Drive safe, Tam."

She set the phone on the counter and looked at the notes spread across the kitchen table. The knot in her stomach had loosened, but it hadn't gone. Tamryn had sounded perfectly fine. Composed. In control.

That was the problem.

Plenty of new facts from today's research and talks to add to the growing collection of maybe-evidence. There's more going on in Silvergrove than she could imagine, Aileen mused, and she couldn't shake the feeling that today's discoveries were just the beginning.

Rainy Day Inquiry

Rain drummed against the greenhouse glass, creating a soothing rhythm that belied the intensity inside Brannigan's Bloomers. Droplets chased each other down the windows while puddles formed in the garden center's parking lot. Aileen watched a customer dash to their car, purple petunias protected by a plastic bag.

"Forecast says this will continue all day, off and on," Rick reported, glancing up from his phone. He'd moved a display of shade-loving ferns to accommodate their makeshift review center near the register.

Darwin had claimed the wooden potting table as command central, his laptop linked to Verona's and Rick's tablets. Garrett manned the phone, his charm and tenor voice perfect for extracting information from reluctant sources.

"Raymond Patton graduated with a Bachelor's in Business Administration from Texas A&M," Darwin announced, glasses reflecting his screen. "A C+ student, enough to graduate." He toggled screens. "Inherited family fortune primarily in timber and real estate, depleted by 87% since 2000."

"I've got the county property records pulled up," Rick added. "Patton Development still owns twelve parcels, including a warehouse near the old mill."

Verona looked up from her tablet. "His secretary thinks he's the greatest thing since sliced bread. When I called pretending I wanted to write a profile of Patton, she gushed about how he 'supports local charities' and 'never forgets her birthday.'"

The bell above the door chimed, bringing in a gust of damp air and Michael Selwyn's tall form. The insurance investigator shook raindrops from his dark jacket, his salt-and-pepper hair slicked by the rain.

"Mike!" Aileen called, signaling the teens to minimize their screens. "What brings you to Silvergrove?"

"Just passing through and thought I'd check on my favorite client," he said, approaching the counter. His eyes crinkled with genuine warmth as he scanned the sales room with a practiced eye. "How's everything since the repairs?"

"Fully recovered," Aileen replied, leading him away from the teens' investigation materials. "No more late day visitors with clubs and machetes, thankfully."

"Looking for something special today?" she prompted.

"Anniversary next week," Mike smiled. "Thinking orchids. Diane loves them, though I can't keep them alive."

As Aileen helped him select an arrangement, Mike glanced at the teens huddled around the computers. "Working on something special?"

"I'm testing them on inventory and scheduling for the new greenhouses," Aileen deflected, noting how Darwin stiffened at the lie. "Mike, you went to Keating High, right? Few years after Tamryn Mitchell?"

"Three years behind her and that shadow she could never shake. Raymond Patton." Mike chuckled, examining a deep purple orchid. "Poor guy followed her like a lost puppy all through school."

"They dated?" Aileen kept her tone casual.

"Briefly sophomore year, I think. After they broke up, he kept writing her these awful poems." Mike shook his head. "My older sister was one of Tamryn's friends. She said Raymond would wait outside classes, offer to carry books, the whole nine yards. Total cliché."

"Did it ever get... troubling?" Aileen arranged tissue paper around the orchid pot.

Mike raised an eyebrow. "This about those bodies they found? Terrible business."

"Just curious," Aileen said, ringing up the purchase. "Small towns and old stories."

"Well," Mike lowered his voice, "there was one incident their senior year. Raymond showed up at prom even though Tamryn went with Sam Hender. Caused quite a scene, demanding a dance. Principal had to escort him out."

Lost in thought, Aileen's head bobbed ever so slightly. "Sounds memorable."

"That's over twenty-five years ago and people still mention it," Mike confirmed, handing over his credit card. "Some folks just can't let go of the past."

After Mike left, the teens reconvened at the register.

"Patton Development has an office on Acacia Street," Darwin announced. "Open Tuesday through Thursday."

"Guess I know where I'm going tomorrow," Aileen said, watching rain stream down the windows.

"Want backup?" Rick asked.

Aileen shook her head. "Better for me to go alone. Less suspicious."

As a rumble of thunder shook the building's glass panes, Aileen wondered what other storms were brewing in Silvergrove's quiet streets. Raymond Patton's decades-long obsession with Tamryn Mitchell now seemed much more significant than small-town gossip.

Chapter Seven — Digging Deeper

Raymond's Office

Patton Development occupied a small storefront on Acacia Street, its facade desperately trying to project prosperity. Oversized gold lettering spelled out the company name above window displays showing architectural renderings of projects Aileen suspected existed only on paper. The morning light reflected off rain-slicked pavement as she approached the door, mentally rehearsing her cover story.

A brass bell jingled a cheery notice as she entered. The reception area featured leather furniture showing subtle wear, potted plants that needed attention, and framed awards from the early 2000s. Raymond looked up from a drafting table at the back, surprise flashing across his face before he masked it with a professional smile.

"Aileen! What brings Silvergrove's garden guru to my humble office?" He hurried forward, hand extended. At 48, Raymond still maintained his athletic build, though his salt-and-pepper hair was suspiciously even-toned, suggesting assistance from a bottle.

"The expansion at Bloomers has me thinking about landscape design," Aileen explained, shaking his hand. "I remembered you mentioning your background in landscape architecture."

"Happy to help," Raymond gestured to a client chair beside the drafting table. "Coffee? Tea? Water?"

"Coffee would be wonderful," Aileen accepted, using the moment he stepped away to study his workspace.

The office was organized to a fault: drafting tools aligned by size, magazines fanned in perfect chronological order, business cards arranged in precise rows. Trophy plants sat in identical ceramic pots, each exactly the same distance apart on the windowsill. A credenza behind his desk held framed photographs; business achievements and civic awards, but tucked among them stood a faded image of a young Tamryn in what appeared to be prom attire, Raymond beaming beside her. It was easy to see the frame was more expensive than any of the others.

"Sugar?" Raymond called from the small kitchenette.

"Black is fine," Aileen responded, shifting her gaze to a stack of blueprints.

As Raymond returned with two mugs, Aileen noticed his hand trembling a little, coffee sloshing dangerously close to the rim.

"So, Tamryn must be devastated by the discovery," he said, setting down the mugs. His expression remained composed, but his eyes watched her with unsettling intensity. "Have you spoken with her?"

Aileen noted how he brought up Tamryn first, not the victims. "Briefly. She's handling the press and coordinating with authorities."

"She's always been strong," Raymond's voice softened with unmistakable admiration. "Even back in school." He caught himself, returning to professional mode. "About your landscaping. What style were you thinking?"

Their conversation weaved between garden designs and subtle probing questions. Raymond mentioned attending most town council meetings "to support Tamryn" and seemed to know details about the mayor's schedule that struck Aileen as too specific.

"I saw her at Beaumont's Department Store on Saturday," he commented in a casual way. "She was buying a blue blouse. Her color, always has been."

Aileen weighed his words with a gentle incline of her head, wondering if Tamryn knew how closely Raymond monitored her movements.

"Let me show you our facilities," Raymond offered after they'd discussed designs. "We handle everything in-house."

The tour revealed a small warehouse attached to the office, containing equipment that raised questions in Aileen's mind: industrial tarps, various tools, a small backhoe "for foundation work," and an area that appeared to have been cleaned with strong chemicals in recent days.

"Business must be challenging with the economy," Aileen observed, noting the thin layer of dust on much of the equipment.

A flash of emotion crossed Raymond's face. Pride? Defensiveness? "Things are about to turn around. The supermarket project will revitalize the whole area."

"I'm sure you're right," Aileen agreed. "You've been in development a long time. Any projects you're particularly proud of?"

Raymond's smile tightened. "Too many to count. But the best is yet to come."

As Aileen left with promises to consider his proposals, she noticed Raymond watching her departure through the blinds, phone already at his ear. In the reflection of her car window, she saw him pacing back and forth, gesturing with emphasis as he spoke.

She slid behind the wheel, jotting quick notes before starting the engine. Raymond Patton was either the most detail-oriented businessman she'd ever met, or someone with deeply concerning control issues. Possibly both. And that warehouse had all the equipment needed to move and bury bodies.

Scruffy Suspected

The afternoon rush at Bloomers kept Aileen busy with customers seeking shelter from the rain as much as flowering plants. She carefully wrapped a peace lily for Mrs. Thornberry, explaining proper watering techniques while part of her mind sorted through the troubling details of Raymond's office. The bell above the door chimed again, and Aileen looked up to see Chief Roland Couch's imposing figure, raindrops dotting his summer khaki uniform despite the umbrella clutched in his hand.

"Afternoon, Mrs. Brannigan," he said, voice pitched low. His aqua-blue eyes darted around the shop, cataloging exits and customers in the reflexive habit of a career officer.

"Chief Couch," Aileen handed Mrs. Thornberry her receipt. "What brings you out in this weather?"

“Got a moment?” Roland tilted his head toward the fern display, away from curious ears. A slight tremor ran through his left hand, a lingering effect of his PTSD, which Aileen knew often worsened in rainy weather.

“Of course.” Aileen led him to a quiet corner. “News about the investigation?”

Roland shifted from foot to foot, rainwater dripping from his thinning hair onto his collar. “We’ve identified a person of interest. Thought you should know, given your... connection.”

Something in his tone raised Aileen’s defenses. “Connection to whom?”

“Scruffy Scruggs.” Roland’s eyes fixed on a point above her shoulder, avoiding direct contact. “He’s been living in that area for years. Knows it better than anyone.”

“Scruffy?” Aileen’s voice rose before she contained it. “That’s absurd.”

“Is it?” Roland countered, spine stiffening. “Homeless veteran with documented PTSD, history of paranoid behavior, territory near the burial site. Plus, he disappears regularly. No one can account for his whereabouts four years ago.”

From across the store, Rick and Verona listened in to the conversation, their concerned expressions telling Aileen they were overhearing.

“Chief, with respect,” Aileen kept her tone level, “Scruffy protected this community during the Boucheron situation. He’s troubled, yes, but he’s not violent toward innocents.”

“People said the same thing about lots of killers,” Roland said in flat tones. “We’re bringing him in for questioning when we locate him.”

“And how hard are you looking at other suspects?” Aileen challenged, thinking of Raymond’s warehouse.

“This is an official investigation, Mrs. Brannigan,” Roland’s voice hardened as his fingers tapped rhythmically against his holster. “Not another of your puzzles.”

Verona approached, as if to restock nearby potting soil. "Mrs. B, I forgot to tell you. Scruffy brought another kitten yesterday. Asked if we could help find it a home. Poor thing was half-starved."

The deliberate intervention made Roland uncomfortable. He tugged at his collar, revealing a glimpse of the scar where his left earlobe should have been.

"Just doing my job," he muttered. "Thought you should know."

After he left, Rick joined them, running a hand through his blond crew-cut. "Scruffy? Seriously?"

"It's the easy answer," Aileen sighed, watching rain streak the windows. "But it doesn't explain motive. Why would Scruffy harm Dana Mitchell or her teacher?"

Rick gave a quick, hot response. "Dana? Never. Camden? Depends on what Scruffy saw him doing."

"He wouldn't hurt Dana," Verona added, silver-blue eyes flashing. "He saves kittens."

"Exactly," Aileen nodded. "Which means we need to work faster to find who would."

"Did you learn anything from Patton?" Rick asked.

"Nothing solid," Aileen admitted. "But his warehouse has equipment that could have helped move and bury bodies, and he's certainly obsessed with Tamryn Mitchell."

"So what's our next step?" Verona asked.

Aileen glanced at her watch. "Research. I need to check the property records connected to that burial site. The history might tell us old reasons for present motives."

Outside, the rain intensified, drumming against the roof like impatient fingers. Somewhere in Silvergrove, a killer was hoping old secrets would stay buried. Aileen was determined they wouldn't.

Complicated Connections

The county records department smelled of dust and forgotten paper, a scent Aileen found comforting as she maneuvered past metal filing cabinets toward the digital terminal. Rain continued its steady patter against the high windows of the county building, casting watery light ripples on the linoleum floor. Three other researchers hunched over workstations, the tap of keyboards punctuating the quiet.

Mrs. Halloway, the elderly clerk who'd managed these archives for decades, looked up from her romance novel as Aileen approached. Her silver hair was arranged in a perfect bun, and half-moon glasses perched on her nose.

"Well, if it isn't our resident garden detective," she whispered with a conspiratorial smile. "Didn't expect you'd stay away long after yesterday's discoveries."

"Am I that predictable?" Aileen asked, returning the smile.

"Only to someone who's watched three generations of Silvergrove residents try to be subtle." Mrs. Halloway chuckled, rising with surprising agility. "Come on, I'll set you up on terminal four. It has the best screen."

As they walked, Mrs. Halloway lowered her voice further. "Searching for the old Piggly Wiggly site's history, I imagine?"

"For the garden center expansion planning," Aileen offered the prepared excuse.

Mrs. Halloway's eyes twinkled with understanding. "Of course, dear. Though most folks investigating those bodies aren't quite so forthcoming about their intentions."

"That transparent, am I?" Aileen sighed.

"Only to me." The clerk patted her arm. "Start with parcel number SG-432-B. And don't worry, my computer will show you accessed agricultural zoning records for your 'expansion.'"

Aileen squeezed the older woman's hand in silent thanks.

An hour of research revealed a complicated ownership history that made Aileen's gardening notebook fill with hastily scrawled dates and names. The Patton family once owned significant portions of northwestern Silvergrove, including both the Piggly Wiggly site and adjacent field where the bodies were found.

"Look at this," Aileen murmured, pulling up a 1946 deed transfer. Harold Wiggins had purchased the store site directly from Patton Land Holdings shortly after World War II.

The adjacent fields remained in Patton hands, eventually passing to Raymond after his uncle Edward's death in 1987. More surprisingly, property records showed Raymond sold the field to Excelsior Developments two years after Dana and Camden disappeared.

"Excelsior Developments," Aileen whispered, tapping her pen against her chin. The transaction price seemed quite low for prime development land. Barely sixty percent of market value.

Aileen searched for information on Excelsior, finding only a limited liability company registration with a Dallas address. Three more searches connected Excelsior to another shell company, Lone Star Holdings, which in turn connected to Cedar Grove Properties; Kenyon Vanstone's primary business entity.

"Well, that's interesting," Aileen muttered, copying the chain of ownership into her notebook.

A shadow fell across her screen. "Mrs. Brannigan."

Aileen looked up to find Warren Fletcher standing over her terminal, his sailing club windbreaker still damp from the rain. His thin face wore a polite smile that didn't reach his eyes.

"Mr. Fletcher," she acknowledged, resisting the urge to minimize her screen. "Doing research yourself today?"

"Marina ownership records," he replied, his gaze flicking to her monitor. "Property records? Interesting choice for gardening plans."

"History matters in planting decisions," Aileen replied. "Soil contamination, previous structures. They all affects what will grow."

"Indeed," Warren said, his tone suggesting he didn't believe her. "I'm researching the old sailing club property myself. Did you know Stephen Mitchell owned a beautiful sailboat? 'Dana's Dream,' he called it."

Aileen felt weight behind Warren's mention of Dana, and her eyes began picking apart his every gesture. "I didn't."

"Shame about what happened," Warren continued, voice dropping. "To Dana, I mean. My daughter sailed with her occasionally."

"News to me," Aileen murmured with false innocence, her mind racing to decode his unexpected sharing.

Warren's smile remained fixed. "Small town. We're all connected somehow." He tapped the edge of her terminal. "You might want to look into who owned the property where those poor souls were buried. History matters, as you said."

"I'll keep that in mind."

He moved to another terminal, leaving Aileen to wonder about his purpose in sharing that information.

A final search confirmed her suspicions: Excelsior Developments had purchased the burial site from Raymond Patton for a fraction of its value, then held it dormant until Kenyon Vanstone's supermarket project emerged.

Aileen closed her session, gathering her notes with a troubling question burning in her mind: Why would Raymond Patton practically give away land where bodies were buried? Unless he desperately needed someone else to own it before they were found?

Team Updates

Bloomers' closing ritual felt comforting after a day of disturbing discoveries. Aileen locked the front door, flipping the "Open" sign to "Closed" as sunset painted the sky in watercolor hues. The rain had stopped within the hour, leaving puddles reflecting pink and gold across the parking lot. Inside, routine prevailed: Rick counting the register, Verona sweeping, Garrett checking greenhouse temperatures.

The scent of coffee wafted from the break room where Darwin had established his command center. Aileen found him sitting cross-legged on the floor, three laptops arranged before him in a semicircle. Multicolored sticky notes formed a constellation on the wall behind him.

"I've compiled the data from everyone's research," Darwin announced without looking up, fingers dancing across keys with dizzying speed. "The patterns are... concerning."

"Let me grab coffee first," Aileen said, pouring herself a cup from the fresh pot. "Who made this?"

"Rick," Darwin replied. "Garrett's last attempt was 37% below acceptable caffeine levels and 42% above optimum bitterness."

Aileen smiled despite herself. "Good to know someone's tracking coffee metrics." Only Darwin.

The other teens wandered in as Aileen settled into a chair. Rick balanced the day's receipts on his knee, Verona clutched a kitten in each arm, and Garrett leaned his lanky build against the doorway, strumming air guitar chords with his fingers.

"What've we got?" Aileen asked, blowing steam from her mug.

"Raymond Patton's fixation on Mayor Mitchell extends beyond normal parameters," Darwin began, turning one screen toward Aileen. Charts and graphs filled the display. "Financial records show he's donated to every campaign she's run, always exactly 9.7% more than the next highest donor."

"That's... specific," Rick observed, raising an eyebrow.

"Also found he's attended most public events where she's spoken in the past decade, something like 94.3% of them," Darwin continued, wrinkling his nose to move his glasses up. "Statistical analysis suggests —"

"Real people terms, please," Verona interrupted, nuzzling Lotus's tiny head.

Darwin sighed with the patience of a genius surrounded by mere mortals. "He's obsessed with her. Has been since high school. The data indicates his interest has increased approximately 9% annually since her husband's death."

"His business troubles align with interesting timing," Verona added, setting Bosco down to explore the floor. "I called pretending to be a journalism student. His secretary mentioned they haven't had a major project in years, but he's paying all his bills and buying new equipment."

"Starting about when Dana disappeared?" Aileen asked, leaning forward.

"No," Verona frowned, twisting a strand of frizzy hair. "More recently. Last six months."

“Coinciding with the supermarket development plans,” Aileen mused.

Rick laid down the receipt book. “Something else weird. He’s the one who reported finding the bodies, right? But according to the construction crew I talked to, he wasn’t supposed to be on site that day. The foreman was surprised to see him there at all.”

Bosco pounced on a pencil that rolled across the floor while Aileen processed this information. She opened her mouth to respond. The bell over the front door jingled.

“We’re closed,” Garrett called, pushing off from the doorframe.

“It’s me,” Jessie’s voice replied. “I brought reinforcements.”

She appeared in the doorway, her blonde hair pulled back in a ponytail, eyes tired but determined. She carried a stack of yearbooks in her arms.

“Found these at home,” she said, placing them on the break room table. “Thought they might help.”

“How was work?” Rick asked.

“Busy. Good distraction.” Jessie’s smile didn’t reach her eyes. “Mom found these in the attic. Dana’s high school years.”

The team gathered as Jessie opened to a page showing Dana’s junior year activities. Among the photos, a tall young man with an athletic build appeared near Dana in several —Sailing Club pictures, homecoming parade, even a candid shot in the cafeteria.

“Travis Holcomb,” Jessie identified him, tapping the image. “He had the biggest crush on Dana. Used to leave notes in her locker, write her these tiny love stories.”

“Where is he now?” Aileen asked.

“Works at his dad’s garage in Milam,” Jessie said. “Mom said he took it really hard when Dana disappeared. Dropped out of college, came back to work for his dad.”

Darwin added Travis to his growing suspect database as Aileen shared her discoveries about Raymond’s property ownership and connection to Vanstone.

"So Raymond owned the burial site, sold it for a fraction of its value to Vanstone through shell companies, then 'discovered' the bodies himself?" Rick summarized, disbelief coloring his tone.

"That's what the records show," Aileen confirmed.

"Finding gold artifacts has approximately 2.4% probability in the back lot," Darwin announced, studying calculations on his third laptop.

The others groaned and threw crumpled paper at him.

"What? It's statistically relevant to our excavation project," he protested, dodging the paper missiles.

The door chimed again, and an elderly woman with immaculate silver hair peered in. "Excuse me, are you still open? I was hoping to ask about that famous cat statue from the news last year. My sister collects jade, you see, and I wondered if any of those stolen Boucheron pieces ever turned up."

Aileen smiled apologetically. "I'm afraid no other pieces were recovered. Not even the Red Jade Cat."

As she helped the woman with a small purchase despite the closed sign, Aileen glanced back at her team, already diving into yearbooks and databases, expanding their exploration another layer deeper. The list of suspects was growing, but so were the connections between them. Raymond Patton, Travis Holcomb, Warren Fletcher, and now potential links to Kenyon Vanstone.

The puzzle was taking shape, but the picture it revealed was darker and more tangled than Aileen had anticipated.

Chapter Eight — Confrontations

Morning Strategy

The morning sun filtered through Bloomers' front windows, splashing golden light across the whiteboard Aileen propped on an easel. She uncapped a dry-erase marker and drew a firm line down the center, writing 'DANA & CAMDEN' on one half and 'SUPERMARKET PROJECT' on the other. The sharp acetone scent of the marker mingled with the earthy aroma of potting soil and fresh coffee.

Morning mist pressed against the greenhouse glass while the teens clustered around the potting table, their hands wrapped around mugs like lifelines to consciousness. Jessie commanded the center, a general with a yearbook for a battle plan. Her eyes betrayed her sleepless nights, but her fingers moved through the pages, cataloging every trace of Dana's presence, each photo and posed smile part of a puzzle she refused to leave unsolved.

"We need to connect all the pieces," Aileen began, writing "Raymond Patton" at the top of both columns. "What we know so far: Raymond owned the burial site, sold it to Vanstone through shell companies, then 'discovered' the bodies himself."

"His obsession with Mayor Mitchell spans decades," Darwin added, tablet in hand. His silver-blue eyes scanned data only he could see. "I've compiled a timeline of his behaviors that suggests escalating fixation, with an increase in contact attempts following her husband's death."

"And Travis Holcomb had feelings for Dana," Jessie said in a near-whisper, tapping a photo in the yearbook. "He threatened Camden once at school when he saw them together. Everyone knew about it."

Aileen considered, adding Travis to the first column. "I'm going to interview him today. His garage is in Milam."

"Want company?" Rick offered, leaning against the counter with his characteristic calm. "Extra set of ears?"

"Better alone. Less intimidating," Aileen replied. "Meanwhile, Masters is returning to continue our expansion work today."

"Got it," Rick volunteered. "Garrett and Verona can help with the clearing."

"What about Vanstone?" Verona interjected, her silver-blue eyes flashing. "He shows up in town, suddenly gets this supermarket approved, and then bodies appear? Bizarre coincidence."

Aileen considered this, adding "Kenyon Vanstone" to the second column.

"Timing presents a problem with that hypothesis," Darwin countered, touching an earpiece. "Vanstone arrived in Silvergrove approximately eight months ago. The murders occurred four years prior."

"Could still be connected," Verona insisted. "Maybe he knew about the bodies somehow."

Garrett spoke up with a slight nod. "Maybe that's why he wanted that specific site."

"Why is Chief Couch so hooked on Scruffy?" Verona asked, scratching Bosco's ears as the kitten purred in contentment. "It makes no sense."

"Easy target," Aileen sighed, capping her marker. "Homeless veteran with PTSD. Many people in town don't want him or his friends in town."

"Right, Mrs. Charleton from church said people are actually pleased," Rick added with disgust. "Said she heard folks at the grocery store talking about how Couch is 'finally addressing the homeless problem.'"

"That's just plain mean," Jessie protested. "Scruffy never hurt anyone."

"I've been feeding his kittens when he's not around," Verona admitted. "He has a new litter hidden near the old warehouse on Dogwood. He's gentle with them, talks to them like they're his kids."

Aileen added this to her mental notes. "Let's focus on finding the truth. For Dana and Camden. And for Jessie," she said, meeting each teen's eyes in turn. "But also for Scruffy and others who can't defend themselves. Sometimes justice isn't just about solving a murder. Tt's about protecting the living, too."

The team agreed, their determination palpable in the morning light. On the whiteboard, the list of suspects grew: Raymond Patton, Travis Holcomb, Kenyon Vanstone. And a conspicuous blank space where Aileen hesitated to write another name.

Masters Returns

Rick squinted against the mid-morning sun as Masters' trucks rumbled into the back lot of Bloomers. Fewer vehicles than expected; just a backhoe, dump truck, and three workers including owner Roy Masters. The scent of diesel fuel and freshly disturbed earth filled the air as equipment positioned near the flagged expansion area.

"Thought you'd have more crew," Rick commented as Roy climbed down from his truck. The supervisor's weathered face bore the permanent tan of a man who'd spent decades outdoors.

"Half my team got pulled to another job," Roy explained, adjusting his hard hat with a resigned gesture. "County inspector's causing delays at the supermarket site, so Vanstone's scrambling. We're spread thin."

Rick grinned, watching Darwin reluctantly exchange his tablet for work gloves, his expression suggesting he'd rather be analyzing data than moving dirt. Verona and Garrett were already positioning stakes where the new greenhouse foundation would go, measuring tape stretched between them.

"So what's the plan today?" Rick asked, studying the survey markers.

Roy unfolded a set of blueprints across his truck hood, weighing the corners with stones. "Original plan was to excavate the entire footprint today, but with the reduced crew..." He traced a line with his calloused finger. "We'll focus on the drainage section first, then the main foundation tomorrow."

Rick considered the layout. "What if we start at the north corner instead? The soil's looser there from our earlier clearing. Might save time."

Roy looked surprised, then studied the area Rick indicated. "Not bad, kid. You've got an eye for this." He waved to his bucket operator. "Let's start at the north corner, Miguel."

As the backhoe roared to life, Rick organized the teens into teams: Garrett and Verona clearing additional brush while he and Darwin marked utility lines with surprising precision despite Darwin's complaints about dirt under his fingernails.

"Heard you were at the Piggly Wiggly when they found the bodies," Rick said to Roy as they watched the excavation begin.

Roy grimaced, removing his hard hat to wipe sweat from his brow. "Nasty business. Not what you expect first day on site."

"I heard Raymond Patton found them?"

"Yeah, which was weird since he wasn't supposed to be there," Roy mentioned, checking something on his clipboard. "Just showed up around eight, started walking the perimeter like he owned the place, then suddenly he's yelling about finding something."

Rick processed this, remembering Aileen's notes about Raymond selling the property years earlier. "He seemed surprised?"

"Hard to tell with that guy," Roy shrugged. "Always struck me as... off somehow. Too perfect, you know? Pressed slacks at a construction site, every hair in place."

"You worked with him before?"

"Few projects about five, six years back." Roy lowered his voice. "Between us, he's all show. His designs look pretty but have practical problems. Had to fix his mistakes on the fly at a couple of jobs. I quit bidding on his work. I had to have that supermarket job, though."

The backhoe operator called out, and Roy strode over to examine the first trench. Rick returned to checking Verona and Garrett's progress, his mind cataloging the new information about Patton.

"Rick!" Garrett called after another hour of steady work. "Check this out."

In the turned soil lay several tarnished coins. Rick crouched down, carefully lifting one. The date was barely visible: 1937.

"Whoa," Verona breathed, peering over his shoulder. "Buried treasure?"

"Probably just someone's lost pocket change," Rick replied, though he placed the coins in his palm. "But Mrs. B will want to see these."

Darwin appeared beside them, squinting at the find. "Providence Mint marks. Means it's 83.5% silver content. Approximately $4.27 current value each."

"No wonder you flunked poetry," Garrett muttered, but his eyes sparkled with excitement. "What else might be buried back here?"

"Let's keep working," Rick said, pocketing the coins. "And keep your eyes open."

Travis Interview

The twenty-minute drive to Milam gave Aileen time to organize her thoughts. Forests of East Texas pines flashed by her window, their evergreen scent seeping through the car's ventilation on occasion. She mentally reviewed what they knew about Camden Matheson: thirty-one years old, history teacher with a troubling pattern of inappropriate relationships with students, forced to relocate several times.

What puzzled Aileen most was the connection between Matheson and Raymond Patton. What reason would a property developer have to confront a teacher? Unless the connection wasn't about Matheson at all, but about Dana Mitchell. Perhaps Raymond's fixation on Tamryn extended to her daughter?

The GPS directed her to exit the highway. Milam was smaller than Silvergrove, a town that seemed permanently fastened to the 1980s. Holcomb's Garage occupied a corner lot, its faded red and white sign promising "Honest Work at Honest Prices Since 1962."

The bell jingled as Aileen pushed open the glass door, stepping into a cramped waiting area with ancient magazines scattered across a Formica table. A radio played classic country somewhere in the back. Merle Haggard lamenting lost love.

"Be right with you," a voice called.

Travis Holcomb emerged from the service bay, wiping grease from his hands with a red shop rag. At 23, he retained the athletic build from high school, but his eyes held a weariness beyond his years. Dark crescents beneath them suggested chronic sleeplessness. He froze for a moment when he saw Aileen.

"You're not here about car trouble," he stated in suspicion.

Aileen didn't bother with pretense. "I'm helping investigate Dana Mitchell's case."

Travis's jaw tightened. "Police already talked to me yesterday."

"I'm not police," Aileen replied. "I'm helping Dana's cousin, Jessie Mae Burnsides."

Something in Travis's expression shifted. "How's Jessie taking it?"

"Hard. But she wants answers."

Travis gestured toward a small office. "Dad's at lunch. We can talk in here."

The office was cluttered but organized, with framed certificates on the wall and the unmistakable smell of old paperwork and coffee. A photo of a younger Travis in a sailing competition sat on the desk. He sat heavily in the creaking chair, pointing Aileen to the visitor seat.

"What do you want to know?" he asked, his voice controlled.

"Jessie mentioned you had feelings for Dana," Aileen began.

"Half the guys at Keating did," Travis shrugged, but his knuckles whitened. "Dana was... special."

"You saw her with Camden Matheson before she disappeared?"

Travis's eyes darkened. "Week before. Behind the school. He had his hand on her arm, and she pulled away. I confronted him later."

"What happened?"

"Told him I'd break his jaw if he touched her again." Travis stared at his hands. "He laughed, said I didn't understand their 'special relationship.' I wanted to hit him, but..."

"But?" Aileen prompted.

"School security came by. Then next day, I saw Raymond Patton looking for Camden in the parking lot. They argued too."

This caught Aileen's attention. "Raymond Patton? The developer?"

"Yeah. Camden looked scared afterward." Travis's voice dropped. "Two days later, Dana was gone."

"Did you tell police about Raymond?"

"Sure, but they didn't seem interested. Said he was 'a respected businessman with no connection to the school.'"

Aileen made note of this confusing detail. "Is there anything else you remember? Anything unusual about Dana's behavior those last days?"

Travis hesitated. "She was scared of something. Wouldn't tell me what. But she was carrying her sailing compass everywhere. Her dad's old one. Said she might need to 'find her way home' soon."

On the drive back to Silvergrove, Aileen's mind raced faster than her sedan on the country highway. So much for Raymond Patton's polished public image. There he was, getting in Camden Matheson's face like a common street brawler. More significant, it suggested prior knowledge of Dana's situation; knowledge that a man with no connection to the school shouldn't have possessed.

She slowed as a tractor pulled onto the road ahead, giving her more time to process. The compass detail nagged at her. A girl who knew she might need to "find her way home." Had Dana planned to run away? Or had she discovered something that made her fear for her safety?

As Aileen passed the "Welcome to Silvergrove" sign, its cheerful flowers at odds with the town's secrets, she made a decision. She needed to speak with Tamryn as soon as she could. The pieces were fitting together in a pattern that implicated people she cared about, but the truth couldn't remain buried any longer.

Warehouse Standoff

Aileen's phone buzzed against the passenger seat as she crossed the Silver Creek Bridge, heading back toward Bloomers. Chief Couch's name flashed on the screen, unusual for mid-afternoon unless something was wrong. She pressed the speaker button.

"Chief? Everything alright?"

"Mrs. Brannigan —" His voice came through choppy and tense. The distinct sound of a police radio squawked in the background. "Need your assistance. Urgent situation."

"What's happened?" Aileen slowed the car, pulling onto the gravel shoulder.

"Scruffy." Couch's breathing sounded labored, his words clipped. "Barricaded. Abandoned warehouse. Dogwood Lane." Each phrase punctuated like individual sentences. "Claims armed veterans with him. Won't surrender."

"Have you called for negotiators?" Aileen asked, already checking her GPS for Dogwood Lane.

"County team en route. Forty minutes out. From Nacogdoches." A burst of static interrupted him. "He's asking for you specifically. Says won't talk to anyone else."

Aileen made a quick U-turn, tires skidding on gravel. "I'm on my way. Don't do anything until I get there."

"Not standard procedure —" Couch began.

"Roland." Aileen rarely used his first name. "We both know what might happen if this escalates. Just wait for me."

After hanging up, she called Rick.

"Everything okay with Travis?" he answered.

"Change of plans," Aileen explained, accelerating toward the southwest edge of town. "Chief Couch has Scruffy cornered at some abandoned warehouse. I'm heading there now."

"Want help?" Rick's voice held immediate concern.

"No. Too many people might make things worse." Aileen navigated around a slow-moving pickup. "Can you handle closing if I'm not back?"

"Of course." Rick paused. "Be careful, Mrs. B."

"Always am," she replied, though they both knew that wasn't true.

Ten minutes later, Aileen turned onto Dogwood Lane, a rutted dirt road that hadn't seen maintenance in years. The warehouse appeared around a bend: a hulking metal structure with broken windows and rust streaks down its sides like dried tears. Three police cruisers blocked the access road, their lights silently flashing against the metal walls.

Afternoon shadows stretched across the cracked pavement as Aileen parked behind Chief Couch's cruiser. The abandoned warehouse loomed against the darkening sky, its broken windows like jagged teeth. Two more police vehicles blocked the dirt access road.

Couch paced in small, rapid steps, his hand hovering near his holster. When he saw Aileen, relief washed over his face.

"Shouldn't be here," he said, his words staccato bursts. "Dangerous situation."

"What happened?" Aileen asked, noting the sheen of sweat on his forehead.

"Got tip about Scruffy. Found him here." Couch gestured toward the warehouse. "Claims he has three armed veterans with him. Won't come out."

"Let me try talking to him," Aileen suggested.

"Absolutely not," Couch snapped. "He's armed."

"Roland," Aileen said, using his first name with measured deliberation. "How many shots have been fired?"

"None yet, but —"

"Then there's still time to resolve this peacefully. Just keep your guns holstered." She stepped toward the warehouse entrance.

"Mrs. Brannigan!" Couch called after her, panic edging his voice. "You're violating direct orders!"

Aileen ignored him, approaching the corroded door. "Scruffy? It's Aileen Brannigan. I'm coming in to talk."

"No MPs!" Scruffy's voice echoed from inside. "Just you!"

"Just me," she confirmed, pushing the door open.

Inside, dust motes swirled in shafts of late afternoon light. The air smelled of mildew and fear. Aileen followed the faint sounds of mewling to a back corner where Scruffy crouched beside a cardboard box, a pellet rifle clutched in his trembling hands. Beside him sat another man, unarmed, silent and motionless.

"You shouldn't be here, ma'am," Scruffy said, eyes wild and unfocused. "Not safe. Enemy might return."

Aileen approached with care, hands showing. "There's no enemy here, Scruffy. Just friends."

"Can't abandon my platoon," he insisted, gesturing toward the box where tiny kittens cried. "Won't leave them behind again."

Understanding washed over Aileen. "Why are you trying to die today, Sergeant?"

The question seemed to pierce his delusion. Tears welled in his weathered face. "Failed them once. Not again."

Aileen knelt beside him, ignoring the grime on her knees. "The platoon needs you alive, not a hero."

She wrapped her arms around his thin shoulders, whispering into his matted beard. "Let me help you and your squad."

Slowly, the pellet rifle lowered. Aileen took it, setting it aside. Scruffy reached into the box, cradling a tiny black kitten against his chest. "Dang recruits, don't know how to salute properly."

"I called Judge Canton," Aileen said, putting her phone in a pocket. "She's bringing Dr. Laetner. They'll help us all walk out of here safely."

Fifteen minutes later, Judge Canton's authoritative presence filled the dusty warehouse. Dr. Valentine Laetner, in a white coat despite the setting, examined both veterans while speaking in calm, measured tones.

"We'll need to evaluate you properly," Dr. Laetner explained to Scruffy. "But I promise, no restraints."

"No VA!" Scruffy yelled, alarmed.

Dr. Laetner agreed with a calm voice. "Right, sir. No VA. Friends instead."

Scruffy relaxed, then said. "Not sir. Never an officer. Worked for a living."

Judge Canton approached Aileen, voice low. "You did well. This could have ended in a tragedy."

"He needs help, not jail," Aileen insisted.

"I'll ensure he gets proper care," Canton promised. "The justice system can show mercy when necessary. I've already talked to Delilah, she understands."

As they emerged into the bright daylight, Aileen carried the box of kittens while Scruffy clutched one tiny tabby in his jacket pocket. Chief Couch approached, handcuffs ready.

"The kitten stays with him," Aileen stated, her warning clear.

"Police protocol doesn't —" Couch began.

"Make an exception," Judge Canton interrupted. "Doctor's orders."

Couch gave one sharp nod, turning to deal with his charges.

Delilah January helped Scruffy into the back of her cruiser, her young face compassionate. "I'll make sure he keeps his little friend," she assured Aileen.

"I'll be there soon," Aileen promised Scruffy through the window. "As soon as you're settled."

As the cruisers pulled away, Judge Canton touched Aileen's arm. "How did you know?"

"Know what?"

"That the kittens were his anchor to reality."

Aileen chuckled. "I've got two of his 'platoon' at Bloomers right now." She looked down at the box in her arms. "Sometimes the smallest creatures give us the most important reasons to live."

Late Night Revelations

The Silvergrove Police Station hummed with fluorescent lighting as Aileen signed the visitor log. The building was quiet this late, with only the occasional crackle of the dispatch radio breaking the silence. Delilah led her down the corridor to the holding cells, her keys jingling with each step.

"How's he doing?" Aileen asked, clutching a paper bag from Cathy's Classy Cook Café.

"Calmer now," Delilah replied, her youthful face serious but not unkind. "Dr. Laetner gave him something mild. The kitten helps too. He won't let it out of his sight." She lowered her voice. "Between us, I left the cell door unlocked while I did paperwork. He could've walked right out, but he just sat there talking to the kitten."

Aileen tilted her head. "He's no flight risk. His honor is strong."

"Not with his 'corporal' and the kitten here," Delilah agreed. "Chief doesn't get it, but I've watched him with those cats. Different person when he's with them."

As they approached the cells, Scruffy's voice drifted down the hall. "...and that's when we took that hill, little sergeant. Lost Private Wilson that day, but we held the position."

Scruffy sat on the edge of the narrow cot, gently stroking the tabby kitten curled on his lap. His PTSD episode had passed, leaving behind a clearer-eyed man whose shoulders still hunched with perpetual wariness. The silent veteran from the warehouse occupied the adjacent cell, staring at the wall.

"Ma'am," Scruffy acknowledged Aileen with a respectful nod. "Didn't expect visitors this late."

"Brought reinforcements," Aileen said, offering the paper bag through the bars. "Cathy Mueller's apple pie."

Scruffy accepted it with visible gratitude. "Thank you, ma'am. Me and the corporal are mighty hungry. Any chance of a sandwich? No MREs though. Had enough of those to last ten lifetimes."

"I can order something from the diner," Delilah offered. "They deliver until eleven."

"Shoot, I was just there," Aileen said. "Didn't think."

"Don't trouble yourself," Scruffy said, though his eyes betrayed his hunger.

"I'll make a call," Delilah decided, heading back toward the front desk.

"Sorry 'bout today," Scruffy said once she'd left, breaking off a small piece of pie for the kitten. "Mind gets foggy sometimes. Think I'm back there..." His voice trailed off, lost in memories.

"No apologies, Sergeant." Aileen pulled up a chair. "The kittens are safe at Bloomers. Verona's watching them."

"Good young lady, that one." Scruffy responded with the barest of nods. "Comes by sometimes, brings tuna for the little troopers."

Delilah returned, carrying a plate with two stale-looking pastries. "Best I could do on short notice. Found these in the break room."

She passed them around, then hesitated. "I'll be at the desk if you need anything. Take your time, Mrs. Brannigan."

Once they were alone, Scruffy shared a Danish with his silent companion. "Guess they'll charge me now."

"Judge Canton is working on diversion to treatment instead of prosecution," Aileen assured him. "But Scruffy, I need to ask you something important."

He met her eyes, a new clarity in his gaze. "About the bodies."

"Yes. Did you see anything, four years ago?"

Scruffy was silent so long Aileen thought he wouldn't answer. After staring at the ceiling, he sighed. "Truck. White pickup with 'Patton Development' on the door. Middle of the night, by the old grocery."

Aileen kept her expression neutral despite her racing heart. "What time?"

"Middle of the night. Couldn't see clear what was happening." Scruffy petted the kitten in slow, even strokes. "Stayed back. Learned in Iraq. You don't go poking around when people do things at night."

"Anything else you remember from that time?"

Scruffy's brow furrowed with the effort of separating memory from his often-confused mind. "Dark car. Sedan. Came by several mornings in a row, before dawn. Always stayed on the road, nobody never got out. Then after it rained one day, never came back." His voice softened. "But there were flowers on the dirt the next morning."

"Flowers?" Aileen asked.

"White ones. Like at funerals." Scruffy looked down at the kitten. "Figured someone was saying goodbye."

Aileen thanked him, promised to return with more substantial food tomorrow, and walked to her car while thinking. The pieces were shifting in her mind. A white truck at night, a dark sedan in the mornings, flowers left in secret. Someone involved in the deaths, and someone else mourning from afar.

As she drove home through the quiet streets of Silvergrove, Aileen wondered how many layers of secrets she would need to peel away before finding the truth at the center.

Chapter Nine — Closing In

Morning Briefing

Sunlight streamed through the blinds in Bloomers' office, painting stripes across the expanded investigation board. Aileen stepped back, uncapping a fresh marker to add "Scruffy's Testimony" to the growing web of connections. The scent of French vanilla coffee mingled with potting soil and the cinnamon rolls Rick had picked up from the Classy Cook.

"Patton's truck at the site at night," she explained, writing the detail on the board. "And a dark sedan that came by several mornings in a row before dawn, always staying on the road."

"Who would visit but not get out?" Verona asked, feeding Bosco tiny bits of cinnamon roll.

""""Someone who couldn't risk being seen," he said, letting the words settle like dust. "Someone whose grief masked other motives."

"Scruffy said flowers appeared on the disturbed earth after a rainy day," Aileen added. "White ones, like at a funeral. After that, the car never returned."

A contemplative silence settled over the room. Jessie twisted a strand of blonde hair around her finger, her eyes fixed on Dana's yearbook photo pinned to the corner of the board.

"Could be anyone connected to Dana or Camden," she said.

"Or someone knowing what happened there," Garrett added.

"Statistical likelihood favors someone with emotional investment," Darwin noted, tablet balanced on his crossed legs as he sat lotus-style on the office floor. "Family member or close acquaintance of one victim."

"What's the connection between Raymond and Tamryn?" Rick asked, studying the board.

"High school sweethearts, briefly," Aileen explained. "According to multiple sources, Raymond never got over her."

"Obsession extending approximately thirty years," Darwin added, scrolling through data. "Fascinating psychological case study."

"Not the time, Darwin," Jessie said, frowning at her genius friend.

"Right. Apologies." He wiggled in his chair. "Financial records show Raymond's company was near bankruptcy four years ago, then mysteriously stabilized. No new projects, yet bills paid. Then six months ago, substantial cash infusion coinciding with supermarket development announcement."

"Where'd the money come from?" Garrett asked.

"Still tracing. Complex shell corporations." Darwin's fingers flew across his tablet. "But preliminary findings suggest Kenyon Vanstone could be the source."

"What about the property records?" Aileen prompted.

"Raymond sold the burial site to Vanstone's shell company two months after Dana disappeared," Darwin replied. "Significantly below market value."

Jessie stood without warning, moving to the window. "Dana knew something was wrong those last days." Her voice was quiet but steady. "She told me she had to make a difficult decision, but wouldn't explain what."

"What exactly did she say?" Aileen asked.

Jessie turned, eyes glistening. "That sometimes people aren't who you think they are. That even family can surprise you." She drew a deep breath. "I thought she meant boys, typical teenage drama. Now I wonder..."

"If she discovered some dark detail about someone close to her," Aileen finished.

The office fell silent again, broken only by the soft purring of Bosco in Verona's lap.

"We need more concrete evidence," Rick said in definitive tones. "Suspicions aren't enough."

"Agreed," Aileen said. "I'll talk to Tamryn today, feel her out. Meanwhile, we need to investigate Raymond more thoroughly."

"I'll search through more of his financial records," Darwin volunteered.

"Do you need Felicity to help with that? She was so helpful before."

Darwin tilted his head. "Let's wait. I learned a lot from her, and Patton's records aren't nearly as convoluted as the Boucherons accounts were."

"Garrett and I can watch his office," Verona suggested.

"No," Aileen said, her voice filled with resolve. "If Raymond is dangerous enough to commit murder, I don't want any of you taking unnecessary risks."

"But —" Verona began.

"This isn't negotiable," Aileen cut her off. "We gather information in safe ways or not at all. Understand?"

One by one, the teenagers gave in with sighs and half-hearted shrugs.

"Good," Aileen capped her marker. "Let's focus on what we know, not what we suspect. The truth is in the details. And we're getting closer."

As the teens filed out to open the shop, Aileen studied the complex web of relationships and events on the board. After years of solving puzzles in magazines, she was now untangling the most challenging mystery of her life. One that might cost her oldest friendship in Silvergrove.

Patton's Paranoia

Raymond Patton straightened the framed photograph of Tamryn Mitchell on his credenza for the third time that morning. The glass scattered the sunlight, highlighting her smile; the same smile he'd first fallen for in Mrs. Sutterfield's English class thirty years ago. His office was immaculate as always: drafting tools aligned by size, architectural magazines arranged by publication date, plants evenly spaced on the windowsill.

Order was essential. Control was everything.

His hands trembled as he adjusted his tie in the reflection of his computer monitor. Sleep had eluded him for the fourth night in a row. Every time he closed his eyes, he saw Dana Mitchell's face in that final moment of recognition before —

The phone's shrill ring interrupted his thoughts.

"Patton Development," he answered, his voice professionally modulated despite the chaos in his mind.

"Mr. Patton, it's Officer Newsome." The police officer's voice was low, almost conspiratorial. "Thought you'd want to know about a visitor to the county records office yesterday."

Raymond's grip tightened on the receiver. "Who?"

"Aileen Brannigan. Spent almost two hours looking at property records. Specifically, the old Piggly Wiggly site and surrounding parcels."

Cold sweat beaded on Raymond's forehead. "Did she access the transaction records?"

"Everything. Including the sale to Excelsior four years ago."

Raymond thanked the officer, promising the usual arrangement, and hung up. His reflection in the window showed a composed businessman in a tailored suit, but inside, panic threatened to crack his brittle facade.

First that garden woman visiting his office with transparent excuses, now digging through property records. How much did she know? How close was she getting to the truth?

The intercom buzzed. "Mr. Patton, your ten o'clock is here," his secretary announced.

"Reschedule," he snapped, then caught himself. "Please, Margaret. Something urgent has come up."

He needed to think, to plan. Everything had been perfect. Four years of careful silence. The bodies were never supposed to be found. That was the agreement. Then Vanstone had changed the building plans without telling him, and now everything was unraveling.

Raymond opened his desk drawer, extracting a worn leather address book. He flipped to a section marked with a red tab, finding the number he'd hoped never to use again. His finger hesitated over the keypad before dialing.

"It's Patton," he said when a gruff voice answered. "I need that service we discussed. Nothing permanent, just a warning."

The voice asked a question.

"Brannigan. Aileen Brannigan. The garden center owner here in Silvergrove," Raymond replied. "She needs to understand that some questions are dangerous to ask."

After hanging up, Raymond moved to the window, staring at the Silvergrove streets below. Everything he'd done had been for Tamryn. She might not understand now, but someday she would see that he'd only ever tried to protect her, to preserve the future they were meant to share.

His secretary knocked. "Mr. Patton? Are you alright?"

Raymond composed his features into a pleasant mask before turning. "Perfectly fine, Margaret. Just planning our next big project."

As she left, Raymond returned to the photograph of Tamryn, touching the glass gently. "I won't let anyone come between us again," he whispered. "Not now. Not after everything I've done for you."

Garden Confrontation

The afternoon sun warmed Aileen's back as she worked behind the greenhouse, preparing new planting beds for the expansion. She found peace in the repetitive motions of turning soil and removing stones. The teens were front of house, handling customers while she took advantage of the quiet to process everything they'd learned.

The scuff of boots on gravel was her only warning before a shadow fell across her work. Aileen turned, trowel still in hand, to find a tall man in a denim jacket watching her. His face was unfamiliar; angular, weathered, with a thin scar bisecting his left eyebrow.

"Help you with something?" she asked, maintaining her friendly shopkeeper tone while calculating the distance to the greenhouse door.

"Hear you're asking questions about the old Piggly Wiggly site," the man said, his voice eerily casual. "About some of the business people involved."

Aileen straightened, brushing dirt from her gardening gloves. "I'm expanding my business. Property research is normal due diligence."

The man smiled, but it didn't reach his eyes. "Sure it is. Just like visiting Travis Holcomb was all about your car troubles."

A chill ran through Aileen that had nothing to do with the spring breeze. "Who exactly are you?"

"Merely a concerned citizen," he replied, taking a step closer. "Concerned that a nice lady like yourself might get hurt sticking her nose where it doesn't belong."

Aileen held her ground. "Are you threatening me?"

"Advising," he corrected, glancing around the empty garden area. "Some secrets stay buried for good reasons. People who dig them up tend to find themselves in holes of their own."

"Is Raymond Patton paying you well to deliver that message?" Aileen asked, her voice steadier than she felt.

The man's expression hardened. "You're not hearing me clearly, Mrs. Brannigan. This isn't about money. It's about staying healthy. For you and those kids you've got helping you."

At the mention of the teens, Aileen's hand squeezed the trowel as her protective anger surged. "You should leave. Now."

"After you agree to drop this investigation," he countered, stepping close enough that Aileen could smell tobacco and mint on his breath. "Otherwise, accidents happen. Even in nice towns like Silvergrove."

The greenhouse door banged open. "Mrs. B?" Rick called, stepping outside with a watering can. He froze when he saw the scene, assessing the tension in an instant. "Everything okay out here?"

The man stepped back, his threatening demeanor morphing into casual politeness. "Just asking about some landscaping service. Think I've got my answer." He waved to Rick, then turned back to Aileen. "Remember what I said about accidents. They're so unpredictable."

Aileen and Rick watched in silence as the man strolled around the corner of the building. Only when his car engine revved in the distance did Aileen release her white-knuckled grip on the trowel.

"Who was that?" Rick asked, setting down the watering can.

"Raymond Patton's messenger, I think," Aileen replied, her voice unsteady. "We must be getting close to the truth if he's resorting to threats."

"We should call Chief Couch," Rick said, pulling out his phone.

Aileen shook her head. "No evidence, only veiled threats. And if Couch is still focused on Scruffy as his prime suspect, he won't take this seriously."

"Did he threaten the team? Us?" Rick pointed out, his typical calm demeanor shaken. "That crosses a line."

"It does," Aileen agreed. "Which is why I want you all to step back from the investigation. This just became too dangerous."

Rick's blue-gray eyes met hers. "With respect, Mrs. B, that's not happening. We started this together, and we'll finish it the same way."

Aileen recognized the stubborn set of his jaw: the same expression he wore when defending a classmate from bullies or working through a difficult task at the garden center. She sighed.

"At least promise me you'll all be extra careful. No one goes anywhere alone, and report anything suspicious immediately."

Rick tapped on his phone. "Already texting the others now. Buddies at all times."

Aileen's skin prickled despite the afternoon heat. Raymond Patton's carefully constructed front had cracked just enough. Not in what his hired runner said, but in the calculated way he'd said nothing at all. They'd pushed, and he'd pushed back with the precision of someone who knew exactly how far was too far. Now it was a race against whatever clock he'd started, and Aileen couldn't shake the feeling that time was running short.

Mayor's Office

Town Hall's stately brick façade gleamed in the late afternoon sun as Aileen climbed the steps to the main entrance. Inside, the hushed atmosphere of government efficiency surrounded her: phones ringing in the distance, the soft click of computer keys, the occasional burst of a copy machine.

"Mrs. Brannigan," the receptionist greeted her. "Mayor Mitchell is expecting you. Go right in."

Aileen had visited this office dozens of times over the past three years, but today felt different. The familiar route down the carpeted hallway seemed longer, heavier with the weight of what she now suspected.

She knocked with a light touch on the door marked Mayor Tamryn Mitchell.

"Come in, Aileen," Tamryn called.

The mayor sat behind her desk, elegant as always in a navy suit, her reddish-silver hair styled to perfection. Aileen noticed the subtle signs of strain; the tightness around her friend's blue eyes, the slight tremor in her hand as she set down her pen.

"Thanks for making time," Aileen said, taking a seat across from her.

"Always time for my favorite garden guru," Tamryn replied with a tired smile. "How's the expansion going?"

"Moving along," Aileen answered, studying her friend's face. "We've had some interesting finds in the back lot."

"Nothing like what they found at the Piggly Wiggly site, I hope," Tamryn said, her tone deliberately light though her fingers tightened on her pen.

"Just some old coins so far," Aileen assured her. "But speaking of the bigger discovery, I wanted to update you on some community concerns."

"Oh?" Tamryn's expression remained neutral.

"People are worried about Scruffy being held as a suspect," Aileen explained. "Particularly since there seem to be other leads worth exploring."

"Such as?" Tamryn asked, reaching for her water glass with an unsteady hand.

"Raymond Patton's connection to the property, for one," Aileen said, watching closely. "Did you know he sold that land to Vanstone's company shortly after Dana disappeared?"

A flicker of reaction crossed Tamryn's face. Fear? Recognition? "I wasn't aware. Raymond and I don't discuss business."

"But you do talk?" Aileen pressed.

"Occasionally," Tamryn conceded. "He's been supportive of various city initiatives. A dedicated citizen."

"He seems very dedicated to you personally," Aileen observed. "Has been since high school, from what I hear."

Tamryn set down her water glass with deliberate care. "Ancient history. We dated briefly as teenagers. Nothing more."

"He was at the construction site when the bodies were found," Aileen continued. "Even though he had no official construction role in the project."

"Aileen," Tamryn interrupted, her voice carrying an unexpected sharpness. "What exactly are you suggesting?"

"I'm not suggesting anything," Aileen replied with care. "I'm investigating a double homicide that happened to include your daughter, and following the evidence where it leads."

Tamryn's professional composure faltered. "Dana was everything to me. You know that."

"I do," Aileen said. "Which is why I believe you'd want the truth, regardless of where it might lead. Or who it might implicate."

Tamryn's expression broke; a moment of naked vulnerability that vanished almost before it could be noticed. She opened her mouth as if to confess something, then stopped as her phone buzzed.

"I have to take this," she said, relief and regret mingling in her voice. "The county commissioner about the project to widen Highway 21."

Aileen responded with a slight nod, rising from her chair. "We'll finish this conversation another time."

At the door, Aileen paused. "Tam, whatever happened four years ago, you know you can talk to me, right? As your friend, not as an investigator."

Tamryn's blue eyes met hers, filled with an emotion Aileen couldn't quite decipher. "Some secrets can't be shared, Leena. Even with friends. Especially with friends."

The use of Aileen's childhood nickname, something Tamryn had never done before, lingered in the air as Aileen left the office, more certain than ever that her friend knew far more about Dana's death than she'd ever admitted.

✧ ⌑ ✧ ⌑ ✧

Nightfall Plans

The soft ticking of the kitchen clock and the occasional distant rumble of traffic didn't disturb the quiet in Aileen's home. She sat at her small dining table, case notes spread before her under the warm glow of a hanging lamp. The pieces were forming a troubling pattern, but critical connections remained elusive.

Her phone buzzed with an incoming call from Judge Canton.

"Aileen," the judge's distinctive voice came through. "Thought you'd want an update on Mr. Scruggs."

"How is he?" Aileen asked, setting down her pen.

"Responding well to Dr. Laetner's initial treatment. The VA hospital in Houston has a bed for him tomorrow. The charges have been reduced to a misdemeanor, disturbing the peace."

"Scruffy's agreed to go to VA?"

"Yes," Judge Canton continued, "reluctantly. Valentine can be quite persuasive."

"And his friend?"

"Already transferred to the VA this afternoon. The kitten is proving surprisingly therapeutic," Canton added with a hint of amusement. "Laetner's considering recommending formal animal therapy for both men."

"That's good news," Aileen said with sincerity. "Thank you for intervening."

"Thank you for preventing what could have been a tragedy," Canton replied. "Now, what's this I hear about threatening visitors at your garden center?"

Aileen straightened. "News travels fast."

"Small towns," Canton said. "Should I be concerned?"

"I'm handling it," Aileen assured her, though her gaze drifted to the deadbolt she'd double-checked earlier.

"The Pattons were once powerful in this county," Canton said with obvious care. "Raymond is the last of the line, but he still has... connections."

"I'm learning that," Aileen acknowledged.

After promising to be careful, Aileen hung up and returned to her notes. The timeline was taking shape: Dana learns upsetting details about Camden, possibly involving her mother. Raymond confronts Camden. Both Dana and Camden disappear the same night.

But what connected these pieces into a coherent story? And where did Tamryn fit in?

Her phone buzzed again with a text from Darwin: *Financial analysis complete. Raymond Patton received $50,000 cash deposit four days after Dana disappeared. Source uncertain, routed through offshore anonymous account. Initial transaction origin concealed.*

Aileen stared at the message, considering the implications. Who would pay Raymond that kind of money, and why? Blackmail seemed likely. But who was being blackmailed, and over what?

Another piece of Scruffy's testimony came back to her: his mention of the dark sedan that visited the old Piggly Wiggly site several mornings in a row before dawn, always staying on the road, never approaching the disturbed earth. Then after a rainy morning, the car never returned, though flowers appeared on the site.

Someone mourning. Someone who couldn't approach openly.

Another text arrived, this time from Rick: **Strange activity at Patton Development. Lights on after hours, Raymond loading something into his truck. Looked heavy.**

Aileen's fingers flew across the keys of her phone, her pulse pounding in her ears. **Where are you? Don't approach him.**

Rick's response came in seconds: **Safe at home now. Just drove past on my way from Garrett's. Should we alert Chief Couch?**

After a moment's consideration, Aileen responded: **Not yet. Need definitive evidence first. Meeting tomorrow morning to plan next steps. STAY SAFE.**

She set down her phone and moved to the window, gazing out at the darkened streets of Silvergrove. Tomorrow, she would confront Raymond Patton. With or without concrete evidence, it was time to force the truth into the open, regardless of the consequences.

As she turned back to her notes, Aileen didn't notice the black sedan that cruised slowly past her house, its driver watching her silhouette against the window before continuing into the night.

Chapter Ten — Mounting Pressure

Breakfast Conference

The Mission Dolores Lodge's presidential suite boasted a panoramic view of the town square, though Kenyon Vanstone paid it no attention. His focus remained fixed on the elaborate breakfast spread before him: Belgian waffles, Kobe beef sausages, fresh berries, and a silver carafe of single-origin coffee. The fine china plate balanced on his silk pajama-clad knee as he reviewed contract amendments on his tablet.

A sharp knock interrupted his routine. Vanstone checked his Rolex. Just gone 7:35 a.m. Too early for housekeeping.

"Who is it?" he called, irritation evident.

"Raymond Patton. We need to talk."

Vanstone sighed, setting aside his breakfast. "One moment."

When he opened the door, the contrast between the two men couldn't have been more striking. While Vanstone exuded polished confidence in his monogrammed pajamas, Raymond Patton stood in the hallway looking like he hadn't slept in days. His usually immaculate suit was rumpled, hair wild, and a light sheen of sweat glistened on his forehead despite the morning's moderate temperature.

"You look terrible," Vanstone observed, stepping aside to let Raymond enter. "Coffee?"

"Something stronger," Raymond muttered, pacing the suite's living area.

Vanstone snorted. "It's not even eight. Pull yourself together."

Raymond stopped, hands trembling as he straightened his tie. "We have a problem. That garden shop woman. Brannigan. She's investigating. And she's connected."

"Everyone in this backwater town is 'connected,'" Vanstone dismissed, returning to his breakfast. "Small-town gossip hardly concerns me."

"You misunderstand. I mean connecting us," Raymond insisted. "She's been to the county records office examining our property transactions. She's interviewed Travis about the Dana. And she's got a direct line to Judge Canton and Chief Couch."

This caught Vanstone's attention. "The judge? Are you certain?"

"Positive. My source at the courthouse confirmed it yesterday," Raymond lowered his voice. "She knows something's wrong with the timing of the land sale."

Vanstone set his plate down with exaggerated care, appetite gone. "How much does she know about our arrangement?"

"I don't know," Raymond admitted, running a hand through his thinning hair. "I sent someone to warn her off, but apparently it didn't take."

"You did what?" Vanstone's voice turned glacial. "Without consulting me?"

"I handled it discreetly —"

"Like you've handled everything else?" Vanstone cut him off. "You didn't tell me about the bodies. I had no idea you were mixed up in that."

Raymond's face flushed. "You changed the excavation plans without telling me. We agreed to build on the existing foundation, not dig new footings!"

Vanstone waved, dismissing the objection. "Engineering necessity. The point is, your amateur intimidation tactics have likely made things worse."

He stood, moving to the window to survey the town below. His town, or it would be once the development was complete. After a moment of contemplation, he turned back to Raymond.

"We need to discourage Ms. Brannigan more effectively. Create distractions, apply pressure from multiple directions." His eyes narrowed. "Doesn't that councilman, Morales, owe me a favor? The one whose brother-in-law I kept out of ICE custody?"

Raymond weighed Vanstone's words, eyes focused in the distance. "Abel Morales. Yes, he's in your debt."

"Good. Sometimes the best attack comes from an unexpected direction." Vanstone reached for his phone. "Leave this to me. Just keep your mouth shut and stay away from the Brannigan woman."

After Raymond departed, looking no less anxious than when he arrived, Vanstone made a series of calls. First to Abel Morales about organizing a protest. Then to a private security contractor about surveillance. Last, he dialed an associate with connections to local online review sites.

As he hung up from the last call, Vanstone smiled at his reflection in the window. Aileen Brannigan would soon learn that curiosity carried consequences in Silvergrove. Especially when it threatened his investments.

Raining Trouble

The rain hammered against the greenhouse glass in rhythmic sheets, creating a percussive backdrop to Aileen's conversation with Rick. Water pooled in the garden center's rear lot, turning the expansion area into a miniature lake. Lightning struck close enough that the following thunder rattled the door chimes.

"Masters called," Rick reported, glancing at the deluge outside. "Crew's canceled until the rain stops. Forecast says at least two days."

Aileen marked the calendar. "Probably for the best. Gives us time to focus on the investigation."

The phone rang, interrupting their planning. Rick answered with Brannigan's standard greeting, then frowned.

"Hello?" he repeated. "Anyone there?"

After a moment, he hung up. "Just breathing, then they hung up."

"Third one this morning," Aileen observed, turning back to the investigation board they'd hidden behind a rolling shelf of seed packets.

Darwin bustled in, rain dripping from his slicker. Despite the weather, his eyes sparkled with the thrill of discovery.

"The financial trail paid dividends," he announced, pulling a tablet from his waterproof bag. "Raymond Patton's company was functionally insolvent four years ago, just when Dana Mitchell disappeared. Then ," he paused for effect, " a mysterious stabilization occurred. No new projects, yet all creditors paid."

"Source of funds?" Aileen asked.

"Obscured through multiple shell corporations," Darwin replied, "but the original transfer appears to have come through a Cayman Islands account linked to —"

The phone rang again, cutting him off. This time Aileen answered, hearing only silence before the line went dead.

"Another hang-up?" Rick asked.

Aileen thought about the calls with growing unease. "Someone's trying to rattle us."

"Mrs. B!" Jessie called from the front counter, laptop in hand. "You might want to see this."

They gathered around the screen, where Jessie had pulled up Brannigan's Bloomers' online review page. Where yesterday there had been mostly five-star ratings, now a flood of one-star reviews dominated the feed.

"'Worst plants I ever purchased,'" Jessie read. "'All died within days.' This one says, 'Rude service and overpriced products.' These are all fake. They're not even customers!"

"Coordinated attack," Darwin observed. "Statistically improbable to receive seventeen negative reviews in under three hours naturally."

The crash of breaking glass interrupted them. Aileen sprinted toward the sound, finding a jagged hole in one of the greenhouse panels. On the floor beneath, surrounded by glittering shards, lay a rock wrapped in paper.

Rick unwrapped it to reveal a crudely written note: "MIND YOUR OWN BUSINESS."

Aileen surveyed her shaken team, rain now spitting through the broken panel onto tender seedlings below.

"Well," she said with forced calm, "I think we've struck a nerve."

"This isn't just Raymond," Rick observed, examining the rock. "This is organized. Multiple approaches."

"Logical conclusion: Vanstone's involved," Darwin added. "Corporate methods consistent with documented intimidation strategies."

Jessie looked up from her phone. "I've reported the fake reviews and contacted Chief Couch about the vandalism."

Aileen gathered paper towels to blot water from endangered plants. "They're escalating because we're getting close. The question is, what is it we're close to? What exactly are they so desperate to hide?"

As they worked to cover the broken panel with plastic sheeting, the phone rang again. This time, no one bothered to answer.

Unexpected Protest

The midday break in the rain allowed watery sunlight to illuminate the parking lot, where Rick was repositioning the "Spring Specials" sign that had collapsed in the downpour. The rumble of approaching engines drew his attention to the street, where three pickup trucks pulled alongside Bloomers' lot.

The lead vehicle, a red Ford with decals for "Morales Construction," parked at the entrance. Six men climbed out, most holding hand-made signs. Rick recognized Abel Morales, a stocky man with streaked gray hair who occasionally handled smaller construction projects around town.

"UNFAIR TO LATINO WORKERS," declared the largest sign. Others proclaimed "NO JUSTICE, NO PEACE" and "BRANNIGAN DISCRIMINATES."

Rick's stomach clenched into a knot as he approached the gathering group. Inside, Jessie was helping a customer, while Aileen dealt with the insurance adjuster assessing the broken greenhouse panel. He'd have to handle this alone.

"Mr. Morales," Rick called as the men arranged themselves in a loose picket line. "What's going on?"

Abel stepped forward, his expression stern though his eyes wouldn't quite meet Rick's. "Your boss has been unfair to Latino workers. We're here to make a statement."

"Unfair how, exactly?" Rick asked. "I'm the only employee here, and Mrs. B treats me more than fair."

Abel hesitated, glancing at his companions. "The expansion project. She's not hiring Latino contractors."

"Roy Masters handles the contracting," Rick pointed out. "And his crew is at least half Hispanic. Ernesto Diaz is the foreman."

"Well, there are other issues," Abel insisted. "Pay discrimination."

Rick crossed his arms. "Sir, with respect, I think someone's been feeding you bad information. Would it be Mr. Vanstone, by chance?"

A flicker of uncertainty crossed Abel's face.

Rick pulled out his phone. "Let me call someone who can clear this up." He dialed Gloriano's number, explaining the situation.

Ten minutes later, Gloriano's distinctive lowrider pulled into the lot, followed by his cousin Diego's truck. The teen approached the protesters with confident swagger, nodding respectfully to Abel.

"*¿Quién dice que Doña Brannigan es injusta con nosotros?*" Gloriano demanded. "Who says Mrs. Brannigan treats us unfairly?"

Abel shifted back and forth. "We heard —"

"From who? Vanstone?" Gloriano interrupted. "The man who promised construction jobs for the supermarket but hired outside contractors from Dallas instead?"

Diego stepped forward. "Mrs. Brannigan gave my sister her first job when no one else would hire her. She pays fair and treats everyone with respect."

The protesters exchanged uncomfortable glances as more of Gloriano's friends arrived, all voicing support for Aileen. The demonstration's energy visibly deflated.

Abel's phone buzzed. He checked it, frowning at whatever message he received, then sighed.

"I think we may have been misinformed," he conceded.

The gray clouds chose that moment to open again, rain beginning to pelt down. Aileen appeared at the garden center door, surveying the scene.

"Everyone come inside," she called over the strengthening downpour. "No sense getting soaked."

Twenty minutes later, an unlikely gathering filled Bloomers' break room. Aileen poured tea while Verona distributed cookies. The protesters, now sheepish, sat alongside Gloriano's friends as Abel explained how Vanstone had convinced him Brannigan's discriminated against Latino workers.

"He said you were trying to shut down the supermarket project to keep jobs away from our community," Abel admitted. "He showed me a letter with your signature."

"Forgery," Darwin declared with confidence from the corner. "Mrs. Brannigan's distinctive loop on her 'B' is inimitable without significant practice."

"I'm not against the supermarket," Aileen clarified. "I'm against building on a site where two bodies were buried without a proper investigation."

Abel's measured nod punctuated his new understanding. "Vanstone never mentioned that part."

As the impromptu gathering continued, Rick observed the transformation from conflict to community. Aileen's talent for connecting people was working its magic once again. Even Abel was laughing at one of Gloriano's jokes, protest signs forgotten in the corner.

Outside, the rain intensified, drumming against the roof. Nature's percussion accompanying this unexpected melody of unity.

Vandal in the Night

The security system alert jarred Aileen from fitful sleep. Her phone screen blazed 2:18 AM as the Bloomers' alarm notification pulsed with urgency. She tapped to view the camera feed, breath catching at the sight of shattered glass and a hooded figure moving through the darkened garden center.

Not again, she sighed to herself. Why do they always have to break Bloomers?

Within minutes, she was dressed and driving through sheets of rain toward her shop, wipers struggling against the deluge. She called Chief Couch en route, his sleepy voice sharpening as she explained the situation.

By the time Aileen pulled into the parking lot, two police cruisers were already there, light bars painting the rainfall in alternating red and blue. She ducked through the downpour to where Couch stood in the shelter of the entrance overhang.

"Perpetrator gone," he reported, voice clipped with tension. "Delilah checking perimeter."

"How bad?" Aileen asked, peering through the glass doors.

"See for yourself," Couch replied, pushing the door open.

Inside, chaos reigned. Plant displays had been overturned, pottery smashed, and soil dumped across the floors. But the destruction wasn't random: it centered on the office and break room. Filing cabinets stood open, their contents scattered.

"Business records targeted," Couch observed, unusually perceptive for once. "Not typical vandalism."

Aileen rushed to the hidden investigation board behind the seed rack, finding it torn down, photos of Dana and Camden ripped to pieces. The timeline, witness statements, and property records lay scattered and muddied with potting soil.

"Camera footage?" she asked, trying to maintain composure.

Couch gestured to where Delilah stood reviewing security monitors. "Got something, but the perpetrator wore a mask. Generic build, height. Impossible to say in the gloom."

Aileen made a mental note to get some security lights attached to the system.

"What about the recent threats?" Aileen pressed. "The hang-up calls, broken window, fake reviews?"

Couch shifted in discomfort. "Need evidence connecting incidents. Could be unrelated."

"Unrelated?" Aileen echoed, incredulous. "This is clearly targeted intimidation because we're investigating the bodies found at the development site."

"Speculation," Couch replied, though his eyes showed doubt. "Can't accuse prominent businessmen without proof."

"Like Raymond Patton?" Aileen challenged.

Couch avoided her gaze. "We'll process the scene properly. Delilah's taking photographs now."

As they spoke, Rick arrived, having received Aileen's text. He rolled up from the deep dark looking like a damp specter under a hooded gray slicker. His face darkened as he surveyed the destruction.

Rick sighed. "Just like before. I'll start cleaning up," he said, reaching for the broom.

"Evidence first," Couch corrected, but with less authority than usual.

Over the next hour, the rest of Aileen's team trickled in despite the time. Jessie, carrying coffee for everyone. Darwin with a backup of their research data. Garrett and Verona ready to help clean.

While police finished their documentation, Aileen led her team in salvaging what they could. The physical destruction was disheartening, but as Darwin pointed out, their most important asset, their collective knowledge of the case, remained intact. His daily photos of the evidence board and documents meant they'd lost no evidence.

"They wouldn't risk this if we weren't close to something important," Jessie observed, carefully retrieving photo fragments from the wreckage.

By dawn, the immediate chaos had been contained. Couch and Delilah departed with promises to "investigate thoroughly." Words Aileen found little comfort in.

As moonlight filtered through the rain-streaked windows, Aileen surveyed her team. Despite their exhaustion, determination shone in their eyes.

"They think they've set us back," she said, "but they've just confirmed we're on the right track."

She was rinsing her hands at the utility sink when headlights swept across the parking lot.

Tamryn. Still dressed from the night before, a strand of hair escaping her pin. Dark circles that suggested she hadn't slept any better than the rest of them.

Aileen dried her hands and pushed open the door. The mayor was already crossing the gravel, coat buttoned against the night air, expression unreadable in the amber glow of the security light.

"I heard." Tamryn looked past her into the shop's shadowed interior. "The scanner. The files. Did they get to your files?"

"Darwin backs everything up." Aileen stepped aside to let her in. "Nothing permanent."

"Good." A nod, quick and businesslike. Then, as if remembering: "Are you hurt?"

"No. Just the shop." Aileen leaned against the door frame. "We got lucky."

Tamryn's gaze moved around the broken shelving, the scattered inventory, the glass still crunching underfoot. "I'll make some calls in the morning. There are people who need to know this has escalated."

She didn't say who. Aileen didn't ask. "Thank you, Tam."

Aileen stood in the doorway long after Tamryn's taillights disappeared down Pine Street.

Darwin's voice came from the break room.

"She asked about the files before she asked if you were hurt."

Aileen didn't turn around. "I noticed."

Midnight Strategy

The Bloomers break room had never felt so crowded, or so energized, at five in the morning. Despite their exhaustion from hours of cleaning, Aileen's team huddled around the small table, determined to reclaim momentum after the vandalism.

Rick distributed fresh coffee as Darwin connected his tablet to the portable projector they often used for garden seminars.

"I've reconstructed our timeline," Darwin announced, displaying a complex chart on the wall. "And added a secondary track correlating our discoveries with threat escalation."

The pattern was unmistakable. Each significant breakthrough in their case had been followed by increasingly aggressive attempts to derail them.

"They're watching us," Garrett observed, leaning against the counter. "Somehow they know what we're finding almost as soon as we find it."

"But which 'they'?" Aileen questioned. "Raymond Patton or Kenyon Vanstone? Or both together?"

"Behavioral patterns suggest different actors," Darwin responded. "The online reviews and protest bear hallmarks of corporate maneuvers, Vanstone's style. The direct physical intimidation aligns more with Patton's approach."

"We need direct evidence," Verona suggested, stroking Bosco who had emerged from hiding after the police left. "Something concrete from Patton Development."

A meaningful glance passed between the teens; brief, but not brief enough to escape Aileen's notice.

"Whatever you're thinking, stop it," she warned. "Breaking and entering isn't on our evidence-gathering menu."

"Just contemplating legal means of information research," Darwin replied, adjusting his glasses using a slow gesture.

Aileen sighed. "My concern is that we might be targeting the wrong people. Yes, Raymond and Vanstone are involved in something shady, but what if they're not the actual killers?"

"You still think Mayor Mitchell might be involved," Rick stated. It wasn't a question.

Aileen stared into her coffee. "I don't want to believe it. But we can't ignore her connection to Dana, or the timing of certain financial transactions."

"Or the fact that someone in a dark sedan visited the burial site for several mornings after the deaths," Jessie added.

Silence fell as they contemplated the implications.

"I'm going to confront Patton directly," Aileen decided. "Draw him out, see how he responds under pressure."

"That's dangerous," Rick objected.

"Not in a public place," Aileen countered. "Sally's Sauerbraten Cellar. He's a regular there, and I'll make sure we're visible to other diners."

The teens' shared look of suspicion dissolved into unwilling acceptance.

"Meanwhile," Aileen continued, "I need you all to consolidate what we know about the financial connections. Darwin, focus on those offshore accounts. Jessie, compile everything we have on Dana's last days. Garrett, check with your lab contact about soil comparison."

She fixed them with a stern look. "No unauthorized field trips, understood? We do this carefully and legally."

Their agreements came perhaps too fast, too earnestly, but Aileen was so exhausted she couldn't press further. As they gathered their belongings to depart, she noticed Rick hanging back.

"You don't believe they'll actually stay put, do you?" he asked once the others had left.

"About as much as I believe Bosco will ignore an open bag of catnip," Aileen admitted. "But I'm hoping they'll at least be careful."

Rick raised his eyebrows, concern evident in his tired eyes. "You be careful too. With Patton."

"Always am," Aileen replied, the familiar lie settling between them like an old, worn blanket, comfortable in its dishonesty.

Outside, the rain had stopped. The first hints of dawn in the eastern sky promised a new day, and perhaps, new answers in their increasingly dangerous pursuit of truth.

Chapter Eleven — Breaking Points

Dinner Deception

Sally's Sauerbraten Cellar occupied a stone-walled basement on Silvergrove's north side, its low ceilings and amber lighting creating an atmosphere of old-world intimacy. Sally Stimson, a retired cabaret dancer from Europe who changed her name when she reached Silvergrove, had the finest German rathskeller for over a hundred miles in any direction. She took great pride in authenticity, and it showed: hand-dressed stone walls, painted bier steins from various German cities, and an original Munich Oktoberfest banner and barrel. Even the tables and chairs had an Old World feel.

Aileen arrived twenty minutes early, requesting a corner table with good sightlines to both entrances. The hostess, a plump woman with a German accent as thick as her braids, seated Aileen with a smile and a wink.

"First date jitters?" she asked, lighting the table's candle.

"Business meeting," Aileen corrected, though her nerves mimicked pre-date anxiety. She wouldn't enjoy this dinner nearly as much as she would with Andy.

Once alone, she discreetly checked Darwin's microphone, disguised as an ordinary brooch pinned to her blouse. The teen had spent hours ensuring it would capture conversation despite background noise. The matching recorder nestled in her purse, no larger than a lipstick tube.

At precisely seven o'clock, Raymond Patton entered, pausing to exchange greetings with the staff. Unlike their previous encounters, he appeared composed: suit crisp, silver hair immaculately styled, his trademark confident smile firmly in place. No sign remained of the disheveled man who had found a forgotten grave a few days earlier.

"Mrs. Brannigan," he greeted, sliding into the opposite chair. "A pleasant surprise to receive your invitation. I've always believed gardening and development could find common ground."

"That's one way of putting it," Aileen replied, forcing a polite smile. "I thought a neutral setting might help us clear the air."

A server appeared with menus, reciting the evening's specials. Raymond ordered without consulting the options, clearly a regular. Aileen requested the house specialty and a glass of Riesling to steady her nerves.

Once they were alone again, Raymond leaned forward a bit. "I understand you've had some troubles at your shop. Vandalism, protests. Silvergrove used to be such a peaceful town."

The subtle emphasis on "used to be" sent a chill down Aileen's spine.

"Yes, strange coincidence," she replied, matching his tone. "These troubles began right after I started asking questions about the bodies at your former property."

Raymond's smile never wavered. "Well, coincidences do happen, as they say. Speaking of questions, I understand you've been quite the detective lately. County records, construction timelines, even my truck's whereabouts." He sipped his water. "Impressive initiative."

Aileen maintained her composure despite the revelation that he knew what she'd been researching. "The bodies were found on property you sold to Vanstone shortly after Dana Mitchell disappeared."

"Ah, another coincidence," Raymond replied, waving away the observation. "That parcel had been in my family for generations. Simply the right time to liquidate underperforming assets."

Their food arrived, pausing the verbal sparring for a moment. Aileen took the opportunity to recalibrate, deciding on direct questions while the microphone captured his responses.

"Your truck was seen at the burial site the night Dana and Camden disappeared," she stated once the server departed.

Raymond cut his schnitzel with surgical precision. "Fascinating claim. May I ask who made this observation?"

"A reliable witness," Aileen evaded.

"The mysterious homeless veteran, I assume," Raymond said. "The same one who believes cats are his fellow warriors? I'm afraid his testimony wouldn't hold up well. Especially given that my truck was reported stolen that very week."

Aileen faltered. "Stolen?"

"Indeed. Filed a police report, insurance claim, the works. Records are public." Raymond dabbed his lips with his napkin. "In fact, it was recovered three days later, abandoned near the county line. Quite muddy, as I recall."

As Raymond excused himself to wash his hands, Aileen quickly checked the recorder. The small green light confirmed it was functioning. She took a fortifying sip of wine, preparing for his return.

When Raymond reappeared, something had shifted in his demeanor. His smile remained, but his eyes had hardened.

"You know, Mrs. Brannigan," he said conversationally, "I admire your dedication to this investigation. But I wonder..." He reached into his jacket pocket and placed an object on the table between them.

Aileen stared at the small microphone brooch; identical to the one she was wearing.

"Technology these days," Raymond continued in pleasant fashion. "So sophisticated, yet so easily detected with the right equipment." He gestured to his own tie pin. "Signal detector. Vibrates when it encounters unauthorized recording devices."

The blood drained from Aileen's face as Raymond continued eating as if nothing had happened.

"Your timeline has other flaws," he noted. "The night before Dana disappeared, I was in Houston at a developer's conference. Twenty witnesses, hotel records, receipts. All verifiable."

Each point he made dismantled another piece of Aileen's case against him. For every connection she raised, Raymond had a reasonable explanation backed by documentation.

"You seem very prepared for these questions," Aileen observed.

"When one reaches a certain position in the community, one learns to maintain impeccable records." Raymond signaled for the check. "Especially when one has enemies."

As the server processed his credit card, Raymond leaned closer. "A word of advice, Mrs. Brannigan. True culprits often hide behind the most respectable facades. The person who killed Dana Mitchell knew her intimately. Knew her patterns, her secrets."

"You sound very certain about who killed her," Aileen noted.

"Merely speculation," Raymond replied, signing the receipt with a flourish. "But if I were investigating, I'd look closer to the victim's inner circle. Sometimes the person we protect the most is the one who hides the darkest truth."

He stood to leave, then paused. "Good luck with your investigation, Mrs. Brannigan." His tone carried the false sweetness of antifreeze. "I do hope you find what you're looking for. But remember, not everyone who searches for answers lives to share them."

As Raymond departed, Aileen remained at the table, staring at the disabled microphone. The dinner had been a complete failure on her part. Raymond's parting words burrowed under her skin like splinters, menacing, impossible to brush away. Was he implying what she thought? Pointing her toward Tamryn without explicitly saying so? Would continuing to search risk her life? More frightening, the lives of her teens?

Threats to her own safety she could stomach. She'd made her choice. But every time she looked at her teens' determined faces, her courage crumbled like sand. They hadn't signed up to be casualties in this war.

She gathered her belongings, leaving her wine untouched. Outside, the summer night air felt heavy in her lungs after the restaurant's air-conditioned chill. Raymond's car was gone.

Aileen couldn't shake the feeling that rather than interrogating him, she had been the one questioned. And found wanting.

Warehouse Break-In

Rick cut the headlights as they approached the industrial park on Silvergrove's outskirts, allowing momentum to carry his Honda Civic into an empty lot behind an abandoned tractor supply store. The warehouse district lay in midnight silence; a far cry from Dallas or Houston, where such areas would buzz with activity around the clock.

"You know this is a really bad idea, right?" Garrett asked from the back seat.

"Consider it payback for the damage to Bloomers," Rick said, heat and menace coloring his low tone.

"Patton Development is the third building from the end," Darwin whispered, consulting the satellite image on his tablet. "Minimal security. One night watchman who makes rounds every hour, eight surveillance cameras."

"Which you're sure you can handle?" Garrett prompted.

Darwin sniffed with mild indignation. "The system runs on LexGuard 5.0. Essentially prehistoric. I've already mapped the blind spots."

Verona fidgeted with her dark hoodie. "We should have told Mrs. B."

"And she would have stopped us," Rick countered, though guilt shadowed his face. "Sometimes it's better to ask forgiveness than permission."

They waited until Darwin confirmed the guard had begun his hourly circuit before exiting the car. Moving in single file, they crossed two empty lots, keeping to the shadows. The spring night carried a silken-damp chill, a remnant of the recent rains.

Patton Development's warehouse loomed ahead, a utilitarian metal structure distinguished only by its signage. Darwin led them to a side entrance partially obscured by dumpsters.

"Stay behind me," he instructed, extracting a small device from his backpack. "The camera above this door operates on a rotating circuit. When I disable it, we'll have forty seconds before the system registers the disruption."

Rick glanced at his teammates' nervous faces. "Last chance to back out."

No one moved. With a nod to Darwin, the operation began.

The teen genius aimed his device at the camera, tapped several commands into his tablet, and gave a thumbs-up when the camera's indicator light blinked out. Rick went to work on the door lock, a skill learned during his troubled early teens that occasionally proved useful in more legitimate contexts.

The lock yielded with surprising ease. Inside, emergency lights cast blue-tinged gloom on the walls and construction materials. The teens moved like ghosts through the warehouse's main storage area, where tarps covered pallets of supplies and equipment.

"Office should be in the back," Darwin whispered, consulting his building schematic.

They found it easily enough: a glass-walled room overlooking the warehouse floor, containing a desk, filing cabinets, and a small conference table. The door was unlocked, to their great surprise.

"Too simple," Rick muttered, unease growing. Nevertheless, they entered.

While Darwin attempted to crack the digital lock on a lateral file cabinet, the others searched the office. Rick examined a stack of tarps in a storage closet, noting dark stains on several.

"Guys," he called in a stage-whisper, pulling one out. "Look at this."

Garrett shined his penlight on the material. "Could be blood."

"Or paint," Verona countered, though she took photos with her phone.

"Check the dates on these supply orders," Garrett prompted, pointing to documents on the desk. "Three new tarps ordered the week Dana disappeared."

As they continued searching, Verona drifted toward a storage area containing more construction supplies. The beam of her flashlight caught on something metallic behind a stack of painter's buckets.

"I'll check it out," she breathed, but Rick's only response was to lean closer to the drawings spread before him.

Verona squeezed past shelving into the narrow space, her flashlight revealing a small safe hidden behind the supplies. As she turned to call the others, a piercing alarm shattered the silence.

"Security breach! Motion detector!" Darwin shouted.

"Get out!" Rick commanded. "Rendezvous at the car!"

In the chaos that followed, Verona glimpsed the night guard's flashlight beam sweeping across the main floor. She ducked further into the storage area as her teammates fled toward the exit they'd entered through.

"Verona!" Rick yelled.

"Go!" she hissed. "I'll find another way out!"

Heart pounding, she watched through a crack as Rick hesitated, then disappeared into the shadows, the guard's footsteps approaching rapidly.

Verona pressed herself against the wall, holding her breath as the guard passed only a few feet away. Once he'd moved toward the office, she crept along the perimeter wall, searching for another exit.

Her flashlight caught on the damaged, stained tarp they'd been examining. On impulse, she grabbed a section, tearing it free before continuing her escape.

At the rear of the warehouse, she found a loading dock door with an emergency release. Triggering it, she slipped outside just as police sirens wailed in the distance.

The rain had started again, light but persistent. Verona oriented herself, realizing she was on the opposite side of the industrial park from their meeting point. With no choice but to circle around, she began running, clutching the tarp fragment to her chest.

Headlights appeared on the access road. Panicking, Verona dove into a drainage ditch beside the parking lot, landing hard in muddy water. She curled into the smallest possible shape as the police cruiser swept the area with its spotlight.

"Come out with your hands up!" an officer called through a loudspeaker.

Verona remained motionless, shivering in the cold water as rain pattered on her back. The tarp sample was now soaked, but she maintained her grip on what might be crucial evidence.

After what felt like hours, the police presence diminished. Verona waited, teeth chattering, until she was certain it was safe to move. Far across the complex, she could see flashlights searching the main warehouse.

Rising from the ditch like a submarine snorkel, she oriented herself. The tractor supply store lay almost a half a mile away. With no phone, dropped somewhere between the warehouse and the ditch, she would have to make her way there on foot, avoiding roads and staying in the shadows.

Tucking the tarp sample inside her jacket, Verona set out, wondering if the others had escaped. The evidence had better be worth it, she thought grimly, or Aileen might never forgive any of them for this night's work.

Bench Conference

Davita Canton stirred her coffee with precision, three clockwise turns, no more. The Classy Cook Café had cleared out after the breakfast rush, leaving only the occasional clatter from the kitchen to disturb her thoughts. She'd requested this corner booth on purpose: secluded enough for privacy, with clear views of the entrance and the kitchen.

When Roland Couch pushed through the door, his uniform creased but expression rumpled, Davita suppressed a sigh. After fifteen years on the bench, she recognized that particular look of reluctance.

"Chief," she greeted, gesturing to the seat opposite. "Thank you for making time."

Roland frowned, sliding into the booth. His aqua-blue eyes darted around the café before settling on her face. "Judge Canton. Not often you request unofficial meetings."

Cathy Mueller appeared with coffee for Couch, who accepted it with a grateful nod. Davita waited until they were alone again before speaking.

"I've been hearing concerning reports relayed from our friend Scruffy." She kept her voice level and even-paced. Judge's voice, her clerks called it. "He mentioned seeing multiple vehicles at the old Piggly Wiggly site the night Dana Mitchell disappeared. Vehicles that weren't included in your original report."

Roland's coffee cup paused halfway to his lips. "Scruffy Scruggs isn't exactly a credible witness, Davita."

"He was a decorated staff sergeant before his troubles." Davita held his gaze. "And he has no reason to lie about what he saw four years ago."

"What exactly are you suggesting?" A defensive edge sharpened Roland's tone.

"I'm suggesting that this community has connections that sometimes interfere with proper investigations." She tapped one manicured nail against the ceramic mug. "Personal considerations can cloud professional judgment."

Roland set his cup down hard, sloshing coffee on the table. "My department conducted a thorough inquiry. The fact that we didn't interview every homeless person —"

"The fact that Stephen Mitchell, Warren Fletcher and Camden Matheson were all members of your sailing club might have influenced the direction of your efforts," Davita interrupted.

A flush crept up Roland's neck. "That's unfair."

"Is it?" Davita leaned forward. "Warren has a documented temper. He confronted Camden at school days before the disappearance, according to three separate faculty reports. Yet your department never followed up."

Roland's jaw worked without noise. The PTSD that shadowed him since the truck stop incident manifested in a slight tremor of his left hand, which he quickly hid beneath the table.

The door chimed. Davita glanced up to see Aileen Brannigan entering the café, carrying a stack of garden magazines. Their eyes met for an instant before Aileen took a seat at the counter, acknowledging them with a slight nod.

"Mrs. Brannigan seems quite invested in local matters these days," Davita observed.

"She's looking into things that are better left alone," Roland muttered.

"Are they? Or are they things that should have been examined more thoroughly from the beginning?"

Roland's posture stiffened. "You're overstepping, Davita."

"Perhaps." She gathered her belongings, preparing to leave. "Or perhaps I'm finally stepping up where others haven't."

As she rose, she placed a hand on Roland's shoulder. "Sometimes justice requires uncomfortable truths, Roland. Are you prepared for that?"

She crossed to the counter, exchanged a few pleasant words with Aileen about summer flower planting, then headed toward the door. She paused, looking back at Roland sitting motionless in the booth, his coffee cooling, untouched.

The weight of twenty-one years on the bench had taught Davita to recognize when a case was about to break open. Silvergrove's long-buried secrets were beginning to work their way to the surface.

A False Lead

Sunshine painted Brannigan's Bloomers in soft bronze as Aileen paced the office, phone pressed to her ear. The night had been sleepless, her calls to Verona going straight to voicemail since Rick's frantic message about the warehouse break-in.

"Still nothing," she reported to Rick, who sat slumped in the office chair, exhaustion etched on his young face. Darwin and Garrett occupied the small sofa, equally haggard.

"We shouldn't have left her," Rick said for perhaps the twentieth time.

"You had no choice," Aileen reminded him, though her tone lacked conviction. "If you'd all been caught, we'd be arranging bail money instead of just worrying."

"At least we don't think Patton will press charges. Darwin managed to blank all the video footage."

The bell above the shop door jingled. Aileen rushed out to find Verona standing in the entryway, mud-streaked, damp, but triumphantly alive. Her silver-blue eyes sparkled despite obvious exhaustion.

"Where have you been?" Aileen demanded, relief and anger competing in her voice. "We've been calling all night!"

"Lost my phone in the weeds," Verona explained, accepting Aileen's fierce hug before being enveloped by her fellow investigators. "Had to hide in a ditch for hours until the police left, then walk to the highway and hitch a ride with a truck."

"You hitchhiked?" Aileen shouted.

"With Mrs. Dominguez from the tortilla factory," Verona clarified. "She recognized me from church."

Aileen closed her eyes for a moment. "Everyone in the break room. Now."

Once the door was shut, Aileen regarded the teens with a mixture of frustration and reluctant admiration. "I specifically told you not to do exactly what you did."

"We found something," Verona announced, reaching inside her filthy jacket to extract a soggy, wadded piece of material. "Evidence."

She spread the tarp fragment on the desk. Despite the mud and water damage, dark stains were visible on the blue vinyl.

"Blood?" Aileen asked, leaning closer.

"Possibly," Darwin replied, examining it. "The tarp matches those stored in Patton's warehouse. According to documents we observed, new tarps were ordered the week before Dana disappeared."

"We need to test it," Garrett said. "My music admirer friend still works at the lab in Milam. You remember, he analyzed the Boucheron evidence we got." He blanched, realizing he'd just focused Aileen's attention on their previous break-in.

Aileen frowned. "This was obtained illegally. We can't take it to authorities."

"But we can know for ourselves," Rick pointed out. "If it's blood, we at least know we're on the right track."

Aileen studied their determined faces, realizing the futility of further reprimands. "I should ground all of you from the investigation. Send you home to consider your sins the rest of the summer."

"With respect, Mrs. B," Rick said, "you can't solve this alone. And we're already involved, whether you want us in or not."

"We're careful," Verona added. "And we have each other's backs."

Darwin agreed in support. "Statistically speaking, our collective investigative capacity far exceeds individual capabilities."

Aileen sighed, recognizing defeat. "Get that to your contact immediately, Garrett. And from now on, every move gets cleared with me first. No exceptions." Tired nods showed all around.

After Garrett departed with the sample, Aileen instituted mandatory rest for the remaining teens while she opened the shop. The morning passed in a blur of routine tasks, her mind always returning to her failed dinner with Raymond and the teens' dangerous night.

By mid-afternoon, they had reassembled in the office, somewhat refreshed though still subdued. Garrett entered last, his expression telling the story before he spoke.

"Not blood," he announced. "Mixture of rust and leaf tannins, probably from where the tarp was used to cover building materials, then stored against metal shelving."

The disappointment was palpable. Another dead end.

"So we risked everything for nothing," Verona said, shoulders slumping.

"Not nothing," Aileen corrected. "We've eliminated a possibility. And learned a key detail about Patton. He's careful about evidence."

"Unless he's not involved," Darwin said. "Then there'd be no evidence."

"Oh, he's involved. But you're right too, Darwin."

She moved to the investigation board, adding notes about Raymond's alibis and the warehouse findings. "Dinner with Patton was also unproductive. He has documentation for everything, including his truck being stolen the week Dana disappeared."

"Convenient," Rick observed.

"Too convenient," Aileen agreed. "But we can't prove otherwise."

"Hand me the recording, Mrs. B," Darwin said, holding out his hand.

She shook her head. "He had a signal blocker. Nothing there."

Darwin kept his hand out. "My gear. I bet it still got something I can work with."

Aileen handed over the brooch and recorder.

"So where does this leave us?" Jessie asked, having joined them after her shift.

Aileen stared at the central photo on their board. Dana Mitchell's coming-out party portrait, her smile eerily similar to her mother's. Tamryn Mitchell: Aileen's friend, Dana's mother, and increasingly, the connection they'd been avoiding examining.

"I need to talk to Tamryn," Aileen said. "Not as the mayor, not as a witness. As Dana's mother. There might be details she's never shared, things that seemed unimportant at the time."

"You sure that's wise?" Rick asked, caution in his voice. "If she is involved..."

"She's my friend," Aileen replied, though uncertainty clouded her voice. "And she deserves a chance to help find the truth about her daughter."

As the teens departed to their varied responsibilities, Aileen remained before the investigation board. Raymond's parting words echoed in her mind: *Sometimes the person we protect the most is the one who hides the darkest truth.*

She reached for her phone, dialing Tamryn's number before she could reconsider.

"Tam? It's Aileen. I was wondering if I could stop by tonight. Just to check in, see how you're doing with everything."

As she arranged the visit, Aileen couldn't escape the feeling that she was crossing a threshold to another world. One from which their friendship might never recover.

Chapter Twelve — A New Direction

Social Media Insight

Rain pelted the greenhouse roof in a steady, soothing rhythm. Aileen wiped condensation from the glass, watching rivulets form intricate patterns that resembled miniature river deltas. After three days of relentless downpour, the storm was moving off, a metaphor for her investigation that felt too on-the-nose for comfort. The earthy perfume of damp soil and green growth filled the humid air, punctuated by the sharp tang of fertilizer from the bags stacked against the far wall.

"Another dead end," Rick sighed, slumping onto a wooden stool. His soccer jersey was splattered with mud from the morning deliveries, leaving smudges on the worn seat. "Patton's alibi checks out for all three nights surrounding the disappearance. The bartender at The Rusty Nail remembers him clearly."

Darwin's head bobbed, fingers tapping his tablet. The blue glow from the screen illuminated his face in the gray-green light of the rainy morning. "And the warehouse records were a complete bust. Those weren't body bags. Just standard agricultural tarps. The invoice matched what they claimed. Delivery timing's off as well."

Aileen turned from the window, brushing potting soil from her apron. A ceramic mug of cooling coffee sat untouched on the workbench, steam no longer rising from its surface. "We're missing something. Patton and Vanstone are connected somehow, but we can't seem to find the link."

The radio on the potting bench crackled with static before the hourly news update broke through: "City Council has called a special session to discuss the supermarket development project. Mayor Mitchell is expressing concerns over delays in the permitting process, while Councilwoman Bresslin questions whether the project will proceed as originally presented..."

“Sounds like trouble in paradise,” Rick commented, stretching his sore shoulders.

“I heard Vanstone missed two meetings with the planning commission last week,” Darwin added. “Someone at the bank mentioned permit applications haven’t been processed.”

“Could be nothing,” Aileen said, moving a tray of seedlings into better light. The tiny green shoots stretched upward, resilient despite the gloomy weather. “Bureaucratic delays happen all the time with projects this size.”

“Or it could be something,” Rick countered. “Vanstone seemed awfully confident at the council meeting. Now there are ‘concerns’ and ‘delays’?”

Darwin spread his evidence notes across the workbench, careful to avoid a puddle of water dripping from the ceiling. “Let’s review what we know. Two bodies buried at the development site. Patton conveniently ‘discovers’ them. The project stalls immediately afterward.”

“But no concrete evidence connecting either of them directly to the murders,” Aileen added, tapping her fingernail against her ceramic mug, the soft ping echoing in the humid greenhouse.

The greenhouse door burst open with a squeak of hinges, admitting a gust of damp air that rustled the hanging ferns and a breathless Jessie Burnsides. Her blonde hair was plastered to her face, blue eyes wide and troubled. Raindrops sparkled on her eyelashes and the shoulders of her yellow slicker.

“Sorry I’m late,” she gasped, rainwater pooling around her boots on the concrete floor. “I just saw —” She held up her phone, hand trembling. “Tina Markham posted this.”

Aileen took the phone, eyes scanning the social media post. A black-and-white photo showed Dana Mitchell smiling, arm slung around another girl’s shoulders. The caption read: “Remembering Dana on what would have been her 21st birthday. You protected your friends until the end. Wish you could have protected yourself too.”

“Protected her friends?” Darwin frowned, leaning over to see the screen. “From what? Or whom?”

Jessie wiped rain from her face, though Aileen suspected some droplets might be tears. “Dana never mentioned feeling threatened. But the week before she disappeared, she was gathering information about something. She kept saying someone needed to be stopped."

"Camden Matheson?" Rick suggested, the wooden stool creaking as he shifted forward.

"I always assumed so." Jessie took back her phone, her fingerprints leaving smudges on the screen. "But what if it wasn't just about her and Camden? What if she was protecting someone else?"

Aileen felt the familiar tingle at the base of her skull. The sensation that accompanied puzzle pieces on the verge of rearrangement. Outside, a patch of blue sky appeared between clouds, sending a shaft of sunlight through the greenhouse glass that created a rainbow prism on the concrete floor.

"We've been looking at this wrong. We've assumed Dana was a victim because of her relationship with Camden."

"What if she was a victim because of what she knew?" Darwin asked.

The final raindrops pattered against the glass as sunshine broke through in earnest, steam beginning to rise from the greenhouse roof. Aileen reached for her car keys, the metal cool in her palm.

"Darwin, Rick, I need you to visit town records. Look up everything connected to Camden Matheson's employment history."

"What are we looking for?" Rick asked, already reaching for his jacket, shaking moisture from the sleeves.

"I don't know yet," Aileen admitted. "But Dana was protecting someone. And that changes everything."

Hidden Connections

The Records Office smelled of dust and aging paper, a scent Darwin associated with discovery and possibility. Morning sunlight streamed through tall windows, illuminating dancing dust motes and the weathered spines of leather-bound record books.

"Property deeds are in the east wing," Mrs. Hatfield, the elderly clerk, instructed. "Employment records in the north cabinets." She squinted at them over wire-rimmed glasses. "This for a school project?"

Rick flashed his most charming smile. "Research for Mayor Mitchell. Historical context for the development project."

Not technically a lie, Darwin thought, following Rick toward the north cabinets.

They worked through Camden Matheson's employment files with care — standard contracts, performance reviews, nothing remarkable. Darwin moved to property records while Rick checked business registrations.

"Darwin," Rick called after twenty minutes. "Look at this."

A yellowed property transfer showed Warren Fletcher's signature beside Stephen Mitchell's — Tamryn's deceased husband — on a business venture called Lakeview Holdings, dissolved shortly before Stephen's death.

"There's a third signature," Darwin noted, pointing to an almost illegible scrawl. "Tamryn Mitchell as partner, not actively participating. On the board. Isn't that what they call a 'silent partner'?"

"And look at this," Rick slid another document forward. "Warren facilitated the high school's extracurricular arts program where Camden volunteered. It's how he had access to high school students even though he taught eighth grade."

Darwin's analytical mind began connecting dots. "Camden ran the theater program where both Dana and Marigold volunteered. Easy access to the girls."

Darwin saw Rick wandering down a different rack of record boxes. "What are you after?" he whispered.

"Patton's business filings. Must be a record of his vehicles. Maybe we'll find the police report on the stolen truck."

"Make it quick," Darwin urged.

A few minutes later, Rick pulled a hefty folder from a dusty box. "Here!" he said. "Come photograph these." He spread out tax records for Patton's firm. "There's the police report, all right. But look! He had two trucks at that time! He could have used the other one to move bodies."

Darwin snapped photos in a rush, and then the fellows put the records back in the box.

They continued digging, moving through dusty files with increasing urgency. In a misfiled folder marked "County Development," Rick discovered a manila envelope that didn't belong.

"This isn't property-related," he murmured, carefully emptying the contents.

Personal papers spilled out: insurance documents, a boat registration, and — most significant — a receipt for a .38 caliber Smith & Wesson revolver, purchased by Warren Fletcher three weeks before Dana's disappearance.

Darwin's pulse quickened. "The ballistics report mentioned a .38 caliber."

"Wait," Rick's voice dropped. "So Warren sponsored the program where Camden met the girls, including his own daughter?"

"Yes." Darwin's mind raced ahead. "If Warren discovered Camden was inappropriately involved with Marigold..."

Mrs. Hatfield's footsteps approached. Rick photographed the receipt with his phone before replacing the documents.

"Finding everything?" she asked, eyeing their huddled posture with suspicion.

"Yes, ma'am," Darwin replied, summoning his most innocent expression. "Just some fascinating historical connections."

After she retreated Rick whispered, "Warren Fletcher had means, motive, and opportunity."

"And a gun that matches the murder weapon," Darwin added, already texting Aileen. "We need to talk to Jessie about what happened in that theater program."

Painful Memories

The memorial garden behind Second Baptist Church bloomed with late spring flowers, a riot of colors against carefully tended grass. Jessie knelt before a small bronze plaque, fingertips tracing the engraved name: Dana B. Mitchell.

Aileen approached with slow steps, allowing Jessie her moment of reflection before speaking. "It's beautiful here."

Jessie spoke in hushed tones without turning. "We planted the yellow roses together for her sixteenth birthday. The day of her debutante party." Her exhausted whisper held the weight of memory. "She said yellow was the color of friendship."

Aileen settled beside her on the stone bench. The message from Darwin burned in her pocket like a hot coal. "Jessie, I need to ask you something difficult. About Marigold Fletcher."

Jessie wrinkled her nose. Recognition, then reluctance. "Goldie? What about her?"

"Was she close to Dana?"

"Yes, I think so." Jessie's hands twisted in her lap. "They were in the same history club, and they sailed together lots of weekends. Why?"

Aileen chose her words with care. "Darwin and Rick found a receipt. Warren Fletcher purchased a .38 caliber revolver three weeks before Dana disappeared."

Jessie's sharp intake of breath confirmed Aileen's suspicion that this meant something.

"The same caliber as the murder weapon," Jessie whispered.

Aileen waited, allowing Jessie to process. Church bells chimed in the distance, marking noon with resonant tones.

"Dana told me something." Jessie's voice had dropped so low Aileen had to lean forward to hear. "About three weeks before she disappeared. She said Camden was paying special attention to Goldie. Not appropriate attention."

"Did Dana report it?"

Jessie shook her head. "She wanted proof first. Said she was 'gathering evidence' to make sure it couldn't be dismissed." Her blue eyes clouded with memory. "Dana was like that. You know, methodical, protective. She wouldn't make accusations without being certain."

"Did Warren know?"

"I don't know, maybe. Dana mentioned Warren confronted Camden at school." Jessie plucked a blade of grass, twisting it between her fingers. "There was a huge scene in the faculty lounge. Principal Burrell had to intervene."

Aileen felt pieces clicking into place. "If Warren discovered Camden was inappropriate with his daughter..."

"And Dana was helping gather evidence..."

"But something went wrong," Aileen finished.

Jessie looked up, tears welling. "Warren's a good man, Aileen. Everyone respects him. His wife died of cancer when Goldie was ten. He's raised her alone."

"Good people sometimes make terrible mistakes, especially protecting their children." Aileen gentled her voice. "Did you ever tell the police about Camden's behavior toward Goldie?"

"No." Shame colored Jessie's admission. "After Dana disappeared, Goldie denied everything. Said Dana misunderstood. I didn't want to make things worse." Her shoulders slumped. "Did I make a mistake?"

Aileen placed a comforting hand on Jessie's shoulder. "You were fourteen, dealing with your cousin's disappearance. No one expects perfect judgment."

A robin landed nearby, cocking its head at them before pecking at the recently turned earth.

"What happens now?" Jessie asked, her voice a slight whisper.

"We follow the evidence, wherever it leads." Aileen stood, offering Jessie her hand. "Even if it points to people we respect."

The Gun Theory

Brannigan's Bloomers' office had transformed into a full-fledged investigation headquarters. Evidence photos and timeline printouts covered the walls. Five pizza boxes lay almost empty on the desk, testament to the team's lengthy strategy session.

"Let's make sure we have this straight," Aileen said, tapping the whiteboard where Darwin had constructed an intricate timeline. "Three weeks before the disappearance, Warren Fletcher purchases a .38 caliber revolver."

"Same caliber as the murder weapon," Chief Couch confirmed from his corner chair. His presence, unofficial but significant, lent additional gravity to their proceedings. Aileen had invited him, fully expecting him to decline since Warren was one of the Chief's good friends. Aileen was grateful for his counterbalancing presence.

"Two weeks before," Darwin continued, laser pointer tracking across the timeline, "Dana tells Jessie that Camden is showing inappropriate interest in Marigold Fletcher."

"And Dana begins gathering evidence," Rick added.

"One week before," Verona piped up from her perch on the filing cabinet, "Warren confronts Camden at school. Principal Burrell has to break it up."

Aileen smiled at the thought of Andy breaking up a fight. Maybe she had more to learn about her dear friend.

"Somewhere in here, a Patton Development pickup truck is stolen. But there were two at that time, both white."

Jessie hugged herself. "Dana disappears three days later, along with Camden."

Aileen stepped back, studying the evidence board. "The theory fits. Warren confronts Camden about inappropriate behavior toward Marigold. The confrontation escalates. Somehow Dana becomes involved —"

"Maybe trying to protect Camden," Verona suggested. "Or present her evidence."

"Or trying to protect Goldie," Jessie countered.

Darwin pushed his glasses up his nose. "The situation becomes violent. Warren uses his newly purchased gun. Two people dead, bodies to dispose of."

"That's where Patton comes in," Rick theorized. "Warren needed transportation and a disposal site. Patton's construction company had equipment, access to the abandoned Piggly Wiggly site."

"But why would Patton help?" Aileen wondered.

"Blackmail?" Veronica suggested. "Or maybe Warren paid him."

"Wait," Jessie interrupted. "Didn't you just say the Patton pickup was stolen about that time?"

Aileen nodded. "One was, yes. So we don't know for sure that Patton was involved."

Darwin agreed. "That aligns with Felicity's discovery of large cash withdrawals immediately after the disappearance."

Aileen turned to Chief Couch. "This is more than coincidence, Roland. We have motive, means, opportunity, and suspicious financial activity."

Couch sighed, the weight of twenty-six years in law enforcement evident in his slumped shoulders. "It's compelling circumstantial evidence, but not conclusive proof."

"It's enough for a warrant," Aileen pressed.

"Maybe." Couch rubbed his jaw. "I'll need to consult with the district attorney."

Jessie stepped forward, her voice steady despite the emotion in her eyes. "Dana deserves justice, Chief. Regardless of who's responsible."

A heavy silence settled over the room. Outside, the garden center sprinklers activated with a gentle hissing sound, watering newly planted beds under the setting sun.

"We need to approach this carefully," Aileen said after some reflection. "Warren Fletcher is respected in this community. We can't make accusations without absolute certainty."

"What about Goldie?" Rick asked. "If we interview her, she might confirm Dana's concerns about Camden."

"Or deny everything to protect her father," Verona countered.

"Either way, we might learn something important," Rick said.

Darwin closed his tablet with a decisive click. "We need more financial evidence. Bank records showing transactions between Warren and Patton would strengthen the connection."

"That requires a warrant," Couch reminded them.

Aileen took a deep breath, her decision clear. "Then let's get one. Tomorrow morning, we take everything to Judge Canton."

"You realize what you're suggesting?" Couch's gravel-filled voice contained a note of warning. "Accusing Warren Fletcher of double homicide will send shockwaves through Silvergrove."

"I realize exactly what I'm suggesting." Aileen met his gaze without flinching. "Two people died. Their families deserve truth, no matter how uncomfortable. I remind you, we're not accusing. Only if someone lets the cat out of the bag would anybody in town have reason to know."

Bosco chose that moment to chase Lotus across the big table, scattering papers like a small tornado. Aileen stood up. "I guess we've done all we can for now."

While gathering the scattered pages, one stopped her. Not evidence, just a printout Darwin had clipped to the corner of the board. A screengrab from the county assessor's site: the acreage boundary proposed for Vanstone's commercial development, overlaid on an old topographical survey.

Aileen smoothed it flat against the table. The project's eastern boundary ran directly along the edge of the unregistered cemetery section; the acres that appeared on no official plat, claimed by no estate, noticed by no one, because no one had thought to look.

Warren Fletcher had signed the original deed transfer on that adjacent parcel. She'd registered that fact an hour ago.

But Vanstone's name wasn't in Warren's files. And the development approval had moved through city planning the same month Dana Mitchell disappeared.

She folded the printout and tucked it into her own pocket, away from the board. No sense muddying the Warren theory now. They had enough for Judge Canton, and she wasn't ready to scatter their focus. But something in that overlap, the unregistered graves, old deeds, a tidy approval, twenty-six-year-old deaths, scratched at a corner of her mind she couldn't yet reach. She thought as she gathered up the scattered papers.

She'd sleep on it. She was wrong a lot less often when she did.

As the team gathered their belongings, preparing to disperse for the night, Rick paused at the door. "How do we approach questioning Goldie without tipping off Warren?"

The question hung in the air, unanswered. Through the window, Aileen watched shadows lengthen across her garden center, a reminder that even in places of growth and beauty, darkness still fell in its own time.

"Carefully," she said at last. "Very, very carefully."

Chapter Thirteen — Warranted Suspicions

Judicial Matters

Judge Davita Canton's courtroom stood empty save for the four figures seated in the front row. The afternoon sunlight filtered through blinds, casting . Court was not in session; the official docket had ended an hour earlier.

Aileen smoothed her skirt, the same navy pencil skirt she'd worn to her divorce proceedings, and glanced at her improbable delegation. Chief Couch tugged at his collar, uniform neatly pressed for the occasion. Darwin sat ramrod straight, tablet clutched to his chest, looking simultaneously terrified and fascinated. Felicity Quick maintained professional composure in her charcoal pantsuit, though her fingers tapped the leather portfolio in her lap with a steady rhythm.

The door to chambers opened. Judge Canton emerged in full judicial robes, her silver-streaked hair pulled back. Without preamble, she took her seat at the bench.

"This is highly irregular, Mrs. Brannigan," Judge Canton began, her voice carrying the practiced neutrality of decades on the bench. "I agreed to hear you because of your service to this community, but procedures exist for reasons."

Aileen rose. "Thank you, Your Honor. We understand the unconventional nature of our request."

"Do you?" The judge's eyebrow arched. "You're asking for judicial authorization to access private financial records without a formal criminal investigation. Chief Couch isn't even the requesting officer."

Chief Couch cleared his throat. "Judge Canton, I'm present as departmental representation. Given the sensitive nature —"

"Given your friendship with Mr. Fletcher," Judge Canton corrected sharply. "Let's not dress this up, Roland. I spoke to District Attorney Hughes. He won't oppose whatever action I take, so long as I report daily on progress."

The judge turned her attention to Felicity. "And you, Ms. Quick. I understand Northside Bank has prepared documentation?"

Felicity approached the bench, extending her portfolio. "Yes, Your Honor. Patrick Hamilton, our CFO, has authorized my temporary designation as financial counsel for the limited purpose of this specific investigation."

Judge Canton reviewed the documents, lips pursed. "Convenient arrangement." Her gaze shifted to Darwin. "And what exactly is Mr. Henslee's role in this extraordinary gathering?"

Darwin's Adam's apple bobbed twice. "Data analysis and pattern recognition, Your Honor."

"You're fourteen."

"Nearly thirteen, actually." Darwin's voice cracked. "But I've developed proprietary algorithms for transactional pattern recognition that exceed standard banking software by approximately 27% in accuracy."

A flicker of reaction, amusement or perhaps respect, crossed the judge's face. "Is that so?"

"I can demonstrate if—"

"That won't be necessary. Your educational record and special achievements have been brought to my attention." Darwin deflated with relief as Judge Canton set the papers aside, eyes sweeping over the group. "Mrs. Brannigan, you're asking me to authorize extraordinary access to private records based on circumstantial evidence against a prominent citizen. You realize the gravity of such a request?"

"I do, Your Honor," Aileen replied. "We've discovered Warren Fletcher purchased a .38 caliber handgun, matching the murder weapon in type, three weeks before Dana Mitchell disappeared. Combined with his confrontation with Camden Matheson days before the murders and suspicious financial activity afterward, we believe there's sufficient cause."

The judge's expression remained impassive. "Chief Couch, as the only law enforcement officer present, what's your position?"

Couch shifted, his discomfort plain to see. "The evidence warrants deeper investigation, Judge. Despite my... personal connections."

Judge Canton dipped her chin once. "I'll consider your request. Wait here."

She swept from the courtroom, the door to chambers closing with a solid thud that echoed in the silence.

The minutes stretched into pained waiting. Chief Couch paced by the windows. Darwin mumbled statistical probabilities under his breath. Felicity reviewed documents, making occasional notations. Aileen remained seated, watching the wall clock tick through sixty-three excruciating minutes. She thought she might now have sympathy for any criminal waiting for a jury verdict.

When Judge Canton returned, she carried a sealed document. Her expression remained serious as she resumed her seat.

"I've prepared a limited judicial warrant," she announced. "It authorizes Ms. Quick, under Northside Bank's legal umbrella, to access specified financial records pertaining to Warren Fletcher for the period three months before and six months after Dana Mitchell's disappearance."

She unsealed the document and read the specific limitations aloud. The scope of records, the confidentiality requirements, the prohibition against unauthorized sharing of information.

"Do each of you understand these limitations?"

Four voices answered in agreement.

"And do you swear to abide by these restrictions, under penalty of contempt of court?"

Again, four solemn affirmations.

Judge Canton passed the warrant to Felicity. "This expires in seventy-two hours. Whatever you find or don't find must be reported directly to me before any action is taken. I will expect daily updates."

She struck her gavel once. "This proceeding is adjourned."

As they gathered their materials, the judge's formal demeanor softened fractionally. The corner of her mouth curved upward as she tucked her reading glasses into her robe.

"Good hunting," she said, before disappearing once more into her chambers.

Financial Forensics

The conference room at Northside Bank & Credit gleamed with the blue glow of multiple monitors. Despite the "Closed" sign hanging in the front window, three figures hunched over financial records spread across the polished table.

Felicity Quick's fingers danced across her keyboard with practiced efficiency. Her straight black hair was pulled back in a practical ponytail, cornflower blue eyes narrowed in concentration as she navigated through financial databases.

"Judge Canton's authorization gives us limited access," Felicity explained, "but it's enough to see the basic framework of Warren's finances."

Darwin leaned forward, studying a transaction list with intensity. "Can you pull historical patterns for comparison?"

Focused on her screen, Felicity executed a command without looking. "Already running that algorithm."

Aileen watched their interaction with quiet appreciation. During the Boucheron case, Felicity had proven invaluable, and the young financial analyst seemed even more confident now.

"Here," Felicity said, highlighting a section on her screen. "Warren Fletcher's business struggled for two years before Dana's disappearance. Then, within three months after she vanished, his company stabilized significantly."

"Correlation doesn't imply causation."

"True," Felicity replied, "but this might." She pulled up another window. "Warren withdrew $8,500 cash three days before purchasing the gun. Then four separate withdrawals of exactly $4,000 each following Dana's disappearance."

"Structured to avoid reporting requirements," Darwin observed.

Felicity chuffed out a sigh. "Someone trained him well."

Aileen studied the patterns. "Are we looking at evidence of payoffs?"

"Possibly." Felicity opened another record. "More interesting are these transfers from accounts linked to Excelsior Development Group, Stephen Mitchell's former company, to Warren's business. They're disguised as consulting fees but follow an unusual schedule."

Darwin's excitement grew visible. "The timing aligns perfectly with our timeline of events!"

"There's more," Felicity continued, revealing another screen. "Warren established a secondary account two weeks after Dana disappeared, receiving funds from a shell company that appears connected to Patton Development."

"That's it!" Darwin exclaimed. "Financial connection between Warren and Patton!"

Aileen's lips tightened into a thin slash, a sense of hard-won satisfaction filling her chest. "If Warren killed Camden and Dana, and Patton helped dispose of the bodies..."

"These could be payment for services rendered," Felicity finished, though her expression remained neutral.

Darwin began furiously taking notes on his tablet. "The pattern is conclusive. Warren had motive, means, and now we have the financial aftermath."

Felicity's brow furrowed as she studied a different section of data. "Wait." Her voice slowed. "This doesn't align fully."

"What do you mean?" Aileen asked.

Felicity highlighted several transactions. "These offshore transfers... analyzing the routing patterns... they have characteristics of legitimate business investment rather than blackmail or payoff."

"But the cash withdrawals —" Darwin began.

"Remain suspicious," Felicity acknowledged. "But look here." She pulled up additional records. "The shell company was established before Dana disappeared, not after. And these transactions... their structure doesn't match typical silence payments."

Darwin frowned, reluctant to see cracks in their theory. "Could they be deliberately structured to appear legitimate?"

"Possibly." Felicity's voice held professional caution. "But in financial forensics, we look for patterns that disprove our theory as much as those that support it."

Aileen felt the certainty of moments ago wavering. "What's your professional assessment?"

Felicity leaned back, considering. "There's definitely something unusual in Warren's finances. The cash withdrawals and timing coincidence are concerning. But the overall pattern isn't exactly consistent with someone covering up murder."

"What would help clarify?" Aileen asked.

"We need Warren's banking activity from his Houston trip," Felicity replied. "And verification of what those consulting payments actually covered." She turned to Darwin. "Your algorithm for patterns is impressive, but financial truth is rarely straightforward. The same transaction tells different stories depending on context."

As they gathered their evidence, Aileen noticed Felicity's lingering glance at the screen, a hint of professional doubt in her expression.

"Thank you, Felicity," Aileen said. "This helps tremendously, even if it complicates our theory."

"I'll keep digging," Felicity promised. "Sometimes money reveals secrets even their owners have forgotten."

Confronting Doubt

Student artwork plastered the walls of Andy Burrell's office; colorful interpretations of literary characters Aileen couldn't quite identify. A ceramic mug on his desk proclaiming "Principals Make a Difference" stood half-full of cold coffee. Aileen checked her watch: 2:15. Andy was running late, as usual.

The door burst open, and Andy stumbled in, arms full of manila folders that threatened to spill. His bow tie, navy with yellow polka dots, clashed in spectacular fashion with his striped shirt.

"Aileen! Sorry I'm late. Teacher conference ran long." He deposited the folders on his already cluttered desk, sending several cascading to the floor. "Oh, shoot."

Aileen knelt to help collect the scattered papers. "No problem, Andy. I appreciate you making time."

Their hands brushed as they reached for the same folder, causing Andy to fumble and drop everything he'd just gathered. A flush crept up his neck.

"I've been meaning to organize these," he mumbled, stacking papers in a rush.

Once seated behind his desk, Andy transformed from flustered administrator to focused educator. He consulted his two wristwatches, one on each arm, before speaking.

"You wanted to discuss the confrontation between Warren Fletcher and Camden Matheson?"

"Yes." Aileen leaned forward. "I understand you broke it up?"

Andy agreed. "Four years ago, faculty lounge. Warren was... incensed. Shouting about Camden 'staying away from my daughter.'"

"What exactly happened?"

"Camden was running the after-school theater program. High schoolers, including Marigold Fletcher and Dana Mitchell, volunteered as mentors for middle school productions." Andy opened a drawer, extracting a thin file. "Warren supported the program financially. He and Camden were friendly until..."

"Until what?"

Andy's expression grew troubled. "Warren saw something at rehearsal one evening. I wasn't there, but Sheila Novotny, our art teacher, said Warren watched from the back for about fifteen minutes, then left without speaking to anyone."

"When was this?"

"Approximately one week before the confrontation." Andy consulted both watches, though Aileen noticed one showed 2:23 while the other read 2:29. "The interesting part is what Camden told me afterward."

"Which was?"

"He said Warren had misunderstood a directorial choice. That he was only showing Marigold correct positioning for a scene." Andy's posture gave away his doubts. "But Camden had been reported before."

Aileen's pulse raced. "For inappropriate behavior with students?"

"Nothing proven." Andy slid a document across the desk. "Three separate reports from teachers at his previous school in Oklahoma. All dismissed for 'insufficient evidence.'"

Aileen scanned the paper. "Why wasn't this in the police investigation?"

"It was." Andy looked uncomfortable. "At least, I gave it to Chief Couch. Whether it made it into the official record..." He shrugged.

"What happened after the confrontation?"

"Warren wanted Camden fired. I placed Camden on administrative leave pending investigation." Andy tapped a form. "Effective the day before Dana disappeared."

Aileen felt her timeline, constructed with meticulous care, wobble. "He wasn't even teaching that final day?"

"No. But he still had access to the building to collect personal items." Andy straightened papers to relieve his nerves. "Here's what troubles me, Aileen. Warren initially helped Camden get the theater position. There were... rumors they knew each other before."

"Knew each other how?"

"I don't know. But Warren's recommendation was emphatic." Andy removed his glasses, pinching the bridge of his nose. "Then suddenly, he wanted Camden gone."

Aileen's thoughts raced. If Camden was already on leave, the scenario they'd constructed around Warren confronting an actively teaching Camden didn't align.

"Here's a curious thing," Andy added. "The day Dana disappeared, Warren called asking if I'd seen her. This was hours before anyone reported her missing."

"Why would Warren be looking for Dana?"

"He said she was supposed to bring documents to him." Andy's expression was troubled. "About Camden."

Aileen made a mental note. This piece changed things a little. "Anything else?"

The school bell rang, signaling the end of a period. Andy glanced at his watches, frowning when they showed different times.

"Oh, not again." He tapped the left watch, which read 2:41. "This one's six minutes fast. That's why I wear two. I never know which is accurate."

Despite the gravity of their conversation, Aileen smiled. "Why not just set one correctly?"

"Well, I tried that," Andy began. "But the silver one was my father's, and it runs fast no matter how often it's serviced. The gold one was a gift from the PTA, and it loses exactly two minutes per day, which means every thirty days it's minute-hand is accurate, but then begins falling behind again, so I have to mentally calculate —"

The intercom buzzed. "Mr. Burrell, your three o'clock is here."

Andy looked at both watches, confused. "Is it three already?"

"It's 2:44," Aileen said, a small smile on her face.

Andy took a deep breath. "Then there's the letter," he said. "Came in the mail the day after the pair disappeared. Camden resigned his position, was leaving town."

Aileen opened her eyes wide in surprise. "Really? Do you still have that letter?"

Andy shook his head. "Not me. It was addressed to the Board. I never saw it, actually."

"I need that letter," Aileen mumbled. She hoped it was still with the school administration, somewhere.

"Right." Andy stood, straightening his mismatched ensemble. "Aileen, be careful with this investigation. Whatever happened between

Warren, Camden, and Dana... I sense it's more complicated than it appears."

As Aileen gathered her notes, Andy added, "For what it's worth, Warren always struck me as a devoted father. Protective to a fault, perhaps, but not violent."

Stepping into the hallway filled with students changing classes, Aileen felt certainty slipping away. The case against Warren remained strong, but fractures were appearing in their theory; tiny but significant.

Her phone buzzed with a text from Rick: "Fletcher just got call. Looking agitated. Going to follow if he leaves."

Aileen texted back: "Be careful. Meet me later with team."

She walked out into the afternoon sunlight, the neat pattern they'd constructed now showing troubling gaps.

Teen Detection Network

The afternoon rush at Classy Cook Café had dwindled to a few regulars nursing coffees and pastries. Verona claimed their usual corner booth, strategically positioned with sight lines to both entrances. Rick slid in opposite her, soccer cleats still muddied from practice.

"Any sign of Jessie?" Rick asked, scanning the diner.

"She's running late." Verona pushed an empty plate aside. "Cathy already hooked us up."

As if summoned, Cathy Mueller appeared with a tray of milkshakes. "On the house for my favorite amateur sleuths," she announced, distributing tall glasses topped with whipped cream. "Working on another case?"

Rick smiled. "Just comparing notes on a school project."

"Sure you are." Cathy winked before returning to the counter.

The bell above the door jingled as Jessie arrived, sliding into the booth beside Verona. "Sorry. Had to finish my shift at Lendon's."

"No Darwin?" Rick asked.

"Still with Felicity at the bank." Jessie pulled a folder from her backpack. "But I found something."

The door chimed again. Gloriano Jesus Saltillo entered, wearing sunglasses, and bizarrely, a mustache that was clearly fake, bushy and slightly askew.

"What in the world?" Verona whispered.

Gloriano slipped into the booth, glancing dramatically around the almost-empty diner. "Had to take precautions," he explained in a stage whisper. "Fletcher knows my face."

"Why are you wearing a disguise to a team meeting?" Rick asked, fighting a smile.

"It's tradecraft," Gloriano said defensively. "I watched Fletcher's house for three hours. Had to ensure I wasn't made."

"And the mustache helps... how?" Verona couldn't contain her laughter.

"Disguise 101," Gloriano insisted, adjusting the synthetic hair that was beginning to peel at one corner. "Change your most identifiable feature."

"Your most identifiable feature is being seventeen and Hispanic in a town where everybody knows everybody," Jessie pointed out. "The mustache makes you look suspicious."

"And like a 1970s adult film star," Verona added, dissolving into giggles.

Gloriano scowled but accepted the milkshake Rick slid toward him. "Whatever. I got results. Fletcher received two calls that made him agitated. First one at 1:15, second at 2:30."

"I saw him after the second call," Rick confirmed. "He was pacing in his office. Checked his watch a dozen times."

Jessie opened her folder. "This might explain why. Look what I found in Dana's yearbook."

She revealed a photograph of the middle school theater program. Camden stood center, surrounded by students. His arm rested on Marigold Fletcher's shoulder, casual but proprietary. Dana stood behind them, her expression concerned rather than smiling.

"Dana was worried about Marigold," Jessie said. "She told me she was gathering evidence, but I thought it was about her own relationship with Camden."

"What if she was actually documenting his behavior with Marigold?" Verona suggested.

Rick studied the photo. "If Warren found out —"

"Boom." Gloriano slapped the table. "Motive for murder."

"But who else was in that program?" Verona asked. "We need to talk to other students who might have observed Camden with Marigold."

"I can check the yearbooks for names," Jessie offered.

"The mustache and I will continue surveillance," Gloriano declared.

"The mustache stays home," Rick said. "We need subtlety, not fake facial hair."

"I could wear a different hat?" Gloriano suggested.

Verona rolled her eyes. "You could try being inconspicuous. Novel concept."

"Here's the plan," Rick said, taking charge. "Jessie, compile a list of theater program students. Verona, you and I will track Warren's movements. Gloriano..." he paused. "Maybe just lose the disguise?"

Cathy approached with refills, startling Gloriano who jerked backward. His fake mustache detached on one side, hanging precariously. Cathy froze, coffee pot mid-pour, wide-eyed.

"Is that... supposed to happen?" she asked.

"Tactical equipment malfunction," Gloriano muttered, attempting to reattach the mustache upside down in his confusion.

The entire table dissolved into laughter, even Jessie despite the seriousness of their investigation. Cathy shook her head, amused, as she finished passing out sodas.

"You kids are either the worst spies in Texas or the best entertainment in Silvergrove," she remarked.

As they dispersed into the late afternoon sunshine, Gloriano's mustache surrendered completely, floating to the pavement.

"Disguise 102," Verona called over her shoulder. "Make sure your fake facial hair uses better adhesive!"

Despite their laughter, a sense of purpose united them. Warren Fletcher was hiding a secret, and they were determined to discover what.

Night Watch

Aileen's kitchen table had disappeared beneath case notes, financial records, and photographs. Her favorite puzzle book lay open but untouched beside a cooling mug of chamomile tea. The clock above her refrigerator read 11:17 PM.

The air conditioner hummed in the background, counterpoint to the occasional crackle of her police scanner. She'd borrowed it from Roland — "unofficially" — to monitor any calls involving Warren Fletcher's neighborhood.

Her phone sat centered on the table, silent for the past forty minutes since Rick's last update: "Fletcher still home. Lights on in study."

Aileen rubbed her eyes, fatigue settling into her bones. The scatter of evidence told conflicting stories. Warren's purchase of a .38 caliber weapon. His confrontation with Camden. Financial transactions suggesting payoffs or blackmail. All pointed toward guilt.

Yet Andy's revelations complicated everything. Camden already on administrative leave. Warren supporting Camden's career at first. Warren looking for Dana before she was reported missing. Camden's resignation letter.

Aileen's gaze drifted to her windowsill where a potted African violet drooped, its once-vibrant purple flowers now brown and withered. A garden center owner who couldn't keep houseplants alive; the irony wasn't lost on her.

"Sorry, little one," she murmured, touching a crisp petal. "Solving murders is easier than remembering to water you."

Her phone rang, Tamryn's name lighting the screen.

"It's after eleven," Aileen answered. "Shouldn't mayors be getting their beauty sleep?"

"Said the garden center owner who's still awake," Tamryn countered. "I saw lights on at your place. Thought I'd check if you've made progress."

Aileen hesitated. How much should she share about Warren Fletcher? Tamryn knew him well; they'd served on committees together, attended the same community events.

"We're following several leads," she said, guarding her thoughts. "Judge Canton authorized limited financial investigation."

"Into Ray Patton's records?"

"Among others."

A weighted pause followed. "I heard Warren Fletcher's name mentioned."

Aileen tensed. "Where did you hear that?"

"Small town," Tamryn replied. "Are you seriously investigating Warren?"

"The evidence leads that direction."

Another pause, longer this time. "Warren's been in Silvergrove twenty years, Aileen. He's on the hospital board, sponsors the summer youth program. He's not a murderer."

"Good people sometimes make terrible mistakes," Aileen countered, "especially protecting those they love."

"What does that mean?"

"We have reason to believe Camden Matheson was behaving inappropriately toward Warren's daughter."

The silence stretched too long before Tamryn spoke again, her voice strained. "Be careful with accusations like that. Warren's respected. Dana was troubled. People will believe him over a ghost."

Something in Tamryn's tone sent a warning signal through Aileen's mind. "You sound concerned about more than just community perception."

"I'm concerned about my friend pursuing a potentially devastating path without sufficient evidence." Tamryn's voice hardened. "Warren Fletcher isn't your murderer, Aileen. Trust me on this."

Before Aileen could respond, her phone buzzed with an incoming text. "I need to go," she said. "Let's talk tomorrow."

After disconnecting, Aileen checked the message from Rick: "Fletcher just left home. Received phone call 10 mins ago. Driving toward county line. Following."

Aileen's heart rate accelerated. She typed in haste: "Maintain safe distance. Who's with you?"

"Solo. Everyone else unavailable."

Concern flooded Aileen. A seventeen-year-old following a potential murderer alone at night? "Return home now. Do not pursue alone. That's an order, Rick."

The response came after an anxiety-inducing delay: "Turning back now. But you should know, Fletcher met car with Houston plates at old lumber mill. Brief exchange, then both left in opposite directions."

Aileen added this information to her evidence board, mind racing. Why would Warren meet someone from Houston secretly at night? For that matter, why would Tamryn so declare Warren's innocence with such confidence?

Her gaze fell on the wilted African violet. Perhaps she wasn't the only one failing to tend to something in her care. What if Warren's actions, like her neglected plant, represented not malice but desperation?

Her phone pinged with a message from Felicity: **Found concerning discrepancy in Fletcher's finances. The pattern doesn't match our theory. Need to meet first thing tomorrow.**

Aileen stared at the message, uncertainty creeping through her carefully constructed case. The clock ticked past midnight as she sat surrounded by evidence pointing in conflicting directions. They'd built their case around Warren Fletcher brick by logical brick, but standing back now, the whole structure seemed to lean, threatening to collapse under the weight of awkward questions.

Outside her window, clouds obscured the moon, casting Silvergrove in darkness. Somewhere in that darkness, Warren Fletcher was keeping secrets. But whether they were the secrets of a murderer or something else, Aileen could no longer say.

Chapter Fourteen — Suited for Trouble

Greenhouse Foundations

Morning sun flowed across the cleared land behind Brannigan's Bloomers, transforming mud and machinery into something almost scenic. Aileen breathed in the distinctive scent of wet earth and diesel as the cement mixer rumbled, its drum rotating hypnotically. Yellow caution tape marked the outlines of what would soon become two new greenhouses. Physical manifestations of a dream taking shape.

Rick approached, clipboard in hand, mud caking his work boots. He moved through the space with the quiet triumph of an artist unveiling a masterpiece, each gesture infused with pride he failed to contain.

"Forms are set perfectly," he reported. "Inspection passed yesterday afternoon. We pour the first foundation this morning, second tomorrow if the weather holds."

Aileen took a moment, feeling a moment of satisfaction untainted by the investigation that had consumed so much of her energy. "Everyone's been working hard. Especially you, Rick."

A flush of pleasure colored his cheeks. "Just doing my job."

"You're doing much more than that." She surveyed the transformation of what had been overgrown wasteland just weeks earlier. "When I bought this place, I never imagined we'd expand so quickly."

"That reward money came at the perfect time," Rick said, checking measurements on his clipboard.

"Every penny accounted for." Aileen smiled. "And stretched thin. The plumbing alone cost more than I expected."

"Worth it for proper irrigation systems." Rick pointed to where PVC pipes emerged from new trenches. "No more dragging hoses around the new section."

Aileen watched as four construction workers maneuvered powered concrete finishing trowels into position, their movements synchronized from experience. The concrete truck driver gave a thumbs up. They were ready to begin pouring.

"We need to focus more on the business," Aileen said, half to herself. "I've been distracted with the investigation."

"The teens are handling inventory and sales today," Rick assured her. "Jessie's coordinating with the wholesale nursery delivery, and Verona's rearranging the front displays."

"Good." Aileen nodded. "It's important to find our balance. Build something positive while digging into secrets."

Rick looked at her curiously, perhaps catching the uncharacteristic note in her voice. As he started to comment, the rumble of another engine drew their attention to the delivery entrance. A flatbed truck laden with lumber and steel supports backed through the gate at turtle speed.

The driver hopped down, clipboard in hand. "Delivery for Brannigan's Bloomers? Greenhouse framing materials."

"You're early," Aileen said, surprised. "We weren't expecting this until next week."

The man shrugged. "Schedule opened up. Where d'you want it?"

"Over there," Rick pointed to the storage area they'd prepared. "We'll help unload."

"Appreciate it." The driver handed Aileen the invoice. "Passed something interesting on the way into town. A fancy white car, long as a boat. Like something from a gangster movie. Not what you expect on country roads."

Aileen shivered despite the warming day. "No, it's not."

As the driver returned to his truck, Aileen's phone vibrated in her pocket. The screen displayed "Unknown Caller." She hesitated, thumb hovering over the answer button, a sudden sense of foreboding washing over her.

"Everything okay?" Rick asked, watching her expression.

"Fine," Aileen said, accepting the call and raising the phone to her ear. "This is Aileen Brannigan."

The voice on the other end was smooth, cultured, and unfamiliar. "Mrs. Brannigan. How fortunate to reach you. My associates would very much like to meet with you this morning. Shall we say in thirty minutes? On Main Street, perhaps?"

"Who is this?" Aileen asked, moving away from Rick.

"A friend of friends with interests in Silvergrove's development." The voice remained pleasant, conversational. "It would be most convenient if you could accommodate our request."

Not a request, Aileen understood. A summons.

"I have appointments," she replied as if speaking to a child.

"Reschedule them." All pleasantness vanished. "Thirty minutes. Main Street. My colleagues will find you."

The line went dead. Aileen stared at her phone, the concrete pouring now beginning in the background, its gray mass flowing like destiny, taking shape in predetermined forms.

Unscheduled Appointment

Main Street gleamed in the mid-morning sun, storefronts welcoming with colorful awnings and window displays. Aileen walked toward Northside Bank & Credit at a brisk clip, checking her watch. Already ten minutes late for her meeting with Felicity about Warren Fletcher's financial discrepancies. Her sensible walking shoes clicked against the sidewalk in a rhythm that matched her racing heart.

"Morning, Mrs. B!" Manville Beadle called from his hardware store doorway. "Garden center's looking busy today!"

"Yes, pouring foundations," Aileen replied, not breaking stride.

"Those teens of yours sorted my fertilizer delivery. Fine young folks!" Manville's voice faded as Aileen continued past.

She constructed apologies for her tardiness when a man materialized beside her. Tall, broad-shouldered, in a dark linen suit that cost more than most Silvergrove residents earned in a month. His smile was practiced and empty. A small bulge near one armpit disrupted the bruiser's symmetry.

"Mrs. Brannigan, good morning," he said with a soft menace. "Let's take a walk."

"I have an appointment," Aileen responded, continuing toward the bank.

A second man appeared on her other side, his build similar to the first, his suit navy rather than charcoal. "Your appointment's been canceled," he said as if commenting on the warm weather.

"That's impossible. No one —"

"Miss Quick received an urgent call from her supervisor," the first man explained. "Something requiring her immediate attention. Unfortunate timing."

The implication was clear: they knew who she was meeting and had arranged Felicity's absence. Aileen felt a cold knot form in her stomach.

"What do you want?" she asked, maintaining her pace.

"Just a conversation," the second man said. His accent suggested Dallas or perhaps Fort Worth. "We can do this pleasantly, in private, or we can create a scene that might involve your young employees back at Brannigan's Bloomers."

Aileen faltered mid-step, earning a satisfied nod from the first man.

"Wise choice," he murmured. "Our employer values discretion."

"Your employer who conveniently remains nameless," Aileen observed.

"Names are overrated," the second man replied. "Particularly in our line of work."

They continued walking, the perfect tableau of casual acquaintances strolling down Main Street. Mrs. Novak waved from the bakery. Councilman Mossberger waved a greeting from his office doorway. None would suspect the veiled threats passing between Aileen and her companions.

"There's our transportation now," the first man said as a gleaming white limousine glided to the curb. It seemed impossibly long against the backdrop of Silvergrove's modest buildings, a shark among minnows.

The door opened without noise of any kind. Inside, leather seats and dark-tinted windows promised both luxury and isolation.

"After you," the second man gestured cordially.

Aileen's hand dove into her pocket, typing blindly on her phone. She managed to press send on "Delayed. Tell Couch" to Felicity just before the first man plucked the device from her fingers.

"You won't need this," he said, powering it off with practiced efficiency. "We won't be long."

Aileen took a deep breath and entered the limousine. The door closed with the soft finality of a crypt sealing shut.

Riding with the Suits

The limousine's interior smelled of leather, expensive cologne, and the peaty aroma of aged Scotch. The windows, tinted to opacity, revealed nothing of the outside world as they smoothed away from the curb. Aileen found herself seated facing backward, sandwiched between her two escorts from Main Street, their substantial frames preventing any thought of escape.

Across from her, separated by a generous expanse of carpeted floor, sat a single figure. A man of perhaps fifty-five, with silver hair visible beneath a slate-gray silk fedora. His suit was tailored, dark as a raven's wing against the cream leather upholstery. A heavy gold ring adorned his left pinky finger, catching light when he raised a cut-crystal tumbler to his lips.

"Mrs. Brannigan, so good of you to join us," the man said, voice smooth as the Scotch he sipped. "I apologize for the unorthodox introduction."

"Who are you?" Aileen asked, consciously keeping her tone neutral despite the hammering of her heart.

The man smiled, revealing teeth whitened to Hollywood standards. "A businessman with diverse interests. Some of which intersect with Silvergrove's future development."

Through the privacy partition, Aileen glimpsed the driver navigating onto the county highway, away from town. Fields of young corn stretched in emerald waves outside, incongruously peaceful.

"You've been very naughty, Mrs. Brannigan," the man continued, swirling his drink. Ice clinked against crystal. "Involving yourself in matters beyond your expertise. Investigating powerful people whose interests don't concern garden centers."

"I investigate murders," Aileen said, "not business interests."

"Yet here we are." The man gestured expansively around the limousine's interior. "My understanding is that a colleague from Dallas previously offered friendly advice regarding your... hobby."

Aileen recalled the man who'd approached her outside Bloomers earlier. "I consider justice more than a hobby."

"Semantics." The man dismissed her words with a flick of his bejeweled hand. "The point remains, you chose to ignore that good and reasonable advice. Your expanded meddling has now come to the attention of new interested parties, who would also like to advise you on future endeavors."

"Which parties?" Aileen asked.

The crime boss sipped his whiskey, regarding her over the rim with eyes the color of tarnished pennies.

"It doesn't really matter," he said. "What matters is that certain development plans for Silvergrove will proceed without amateur detective interference. Otherwise, the town might become rather perilous for you and your young associates."

The threat hung in the air between them, acrid as burning tires. Aileen thought of Rick pouring concrete foundations, of Jessie coordinating deliveries, of Darwin and his brilliant, vulnerable mind.

"I understand," she said, back as stiff as Texas cedar fence posts.

"Excellent." The man smiled without warmth. "You will be a good girl in the future then, Mrs. Brannigan. Yes?"

Something hardened in Aileen's heart at the condescension. "I'm always good," she replied, meeting his gaze without blinking. "And I will endeavor to be better."

The crime lord studied her for a long moment, perhaps sensing the steel beneath her composed exterior. After a long pause he pushed his chin out and waved to the men beside her. One tapped sharply on the glass partition.

The limousine slowed, then pulled onto the shoulder, gravel crunching beneath expensive tires. They had traveled perhaps eight miles from Silvergrove, surrounded by nothing but cornfields and distant farmhouses.

"Your phone," the boss said, nodding to the man on Aileen's right who returned the device, still powered off. "And your purse."

Items restored, the door opened. One of the suits gestured for her to exit. Standing in the dry roadside dust, Aileen watched the white limousine pull away, its license plate muddied beyond identification.

When the vehicle disappeared around a bend, she powered on her phone. No signal. Of course. She began walking toward Silvergrove, the Texas sun beating down on her back, the taste of dust and something like defiance in her mouth.

A mile later, her phone finally caught a signal. She dialed Roland Couch's number, continuing to walk as it rang.

"Couch here."

"Roland, it's Aileen. I need a ride."

Changing Tactics

Chief Couch's office smelled of gun oil, stale coffee, and uncontained fury. Roland paced behind his desk, uniform crisp despite the emotion distorting his features. With each turn, he passed the wall-mounted clock: 4:17 PM, hours after Aileen's roadside extraction.

"Organized crime," Roland muttered, running a hand over his thinning hair. "In my jurisdiction."

“We defeated organized criminals before, Roland,” she offered, remembering the recent takedown of the Boucheron crime family.

Roland stopped and peered through slitted eyes at Aileen. “That was local,” he said.

Aileen cradled a mug of coffee gone cold, her third since arriving. “Not technically in your jurisdiction. We crossed the county line.”

“Don’t split hairs, Aileen. They grabbed you on Main Street! MY Main Street, my town.” Roland’s voice rose before he reined himself in. “Did they specifically threaten the teens?”

“Not by name.” Aileen set down her mug. “But the implication was clear.”

Roland’s aqua eyes narrowed. “White limousine, maybe Houston plates, crime boss with a fedora. Sounds like Vincent Marchesi’s operation.”

“You know him?”

“By reputation only. His family controls shipping through Galveston, among other enterprises.” Roland resumed pacing. “The question is, what’s his interest in Silvergrove?”

A knock interrupted them. Felicity Quick entered, arms laden with folders, expression troubled beneath her professional composure.

“Chief Couch, Mrs. Brannigan,” she greeted them. “I came as soon as I could. Someone claiming to be my regional supervisor called me to The Woodlands for an emergency meeting. When I arrived, no one knew anything about it. I get back and Patrick said he was worried to see I was absent.”

“Convenient timing,” Aileen observed.

“Very.” Felicity laid her folders on Roland’s desk. “But it allowed me to access additional records while there. What I found changes everything about Warren Fletcher.”

Roland stopped pacing. “How so?”

Felicity opened the top folder, revealing spreadsheets and transaction records. “The financial pattern doesn’t match what we’d expect from someone paying to cover up murders. Instead, Warren’s accounts show regular withdrawals followed by deposits of slightly smaller amounts through circuitous routes.”

"Meaning what?" Roland asked.

"He's not paying someone off," Felicity explained. "He's being extorted. Large cash withdrawals, followed by deposits minus whatever percentage the blackmailer keeps."

Aileen leaned forward. "How long has this been happening?"

"Four years," Felicity confirmed. "Beginning one week after Dana and Camden disappeared."

The implications settled over them like dust after an explosion.

"If Warren is being blackmailed," Aileen said, "does that make him our killer?"

"Or he's being blackmailed by the actual killer who's keeping him from speaking out," Roland countered.

Felicity shook her head. "The financial pattern doesn't support that. This is classic extortion. Regular, systematic, increasing over time. If it were payment for a single crime, the pattern would be different."

"So someone is blackmailing Warren over something connected to Camden and Dana," Aileen reasoned, "but not because he killed them."

"That aligns with his late-night meetings," Roland added. "Rick reported Warren meeting someone with Houston plates at the lumber mill."

"Houston," Aileen repeated. "Like our friends in the white limousine. Maybe."

The three exchanged looks as connections formed.

"Wait," Roland interjected. "Why would organized crime be blackmailing Warren Fletcher over two local murders? And why threaten you for investigating?"

"Because it's not just about the murders," Aileen realized. "It's about the development project. The supermarket site just happens to be where the bodies were buried."

Felicity considered the implications. "If the development stalls because of a murder investigation..."

"Someone loses money," Roland finished. "A lot of money."

Aileen stood, moving to the window that overlooked Main Street. The afternoon was waning, shadows lengthening across Silvergrove's tidy sidewalks. Somewhere within this peaceful scene lurked answers to both murders and threats.

"We need to change directions," she said. "Redirect our investigation away from Warren, at least overtly."

"And focus on what?" Roland asked.

"The connection between organized crime and Silvergrove's development. Who benefits if that supermarket gets built? Who loses if it doesn't?"

Roland tilted his head back and forth. "I'll request that limo be traced, though I suspect it'll lead to a shell company."

"Meanwhile," Aileen continued, "we need to protect the teens. They've been too visible in their surveillance of Warren."

"You want to pull them off the investigation?" Roland sounded surprised.

"Just redirect them," Aileen clarified. "Safety first, but they're valuable assets."

"I'll continue analyzing the financial records," Felicity offered. "There may be connections we've missed. We're on the clock with Judge Canton's warrant."

As they finalized their adjusted approach, Aileen's phone buzzed with Darwin's specific ringtone: the theme from a popular science fiction show. She punched on the speaker.

"Darwin," she answered. "Everything alright?"

"Better than alright," came his excited voice. "I've been researching Camden Matheson's past. Employment records before Silvergrove. Aileen, you won't believe what I found. Before he was a teacher, he worked as an account exec for a real estate development company in Houston."

"Which company?" Aileen asked, heart rate accelerating.

"Marchesi Holdings," Darwin replied. "Is that significant?"

Aileen met Roland's gaze across the office, watching his expression shift from confusion to dawning comprehension.

"Very significant," Aileen told Darwin. "But I need you to stop researching immediately. Tell no one what you've found. We'll meet tomorrow at Bloomers."

After ending the call, Aileen turned to Roland and Felicity. "Camden worked for Marchesi before becoming a teacher."

"The connection we're missing isn't Warren," Felicity said. "It's Camden himself."

Roland sank into his chair. "This just got significantly more complicated."

Outside, the first streetlights flickered on along Main Street. Somewhere beyond Silvergrove's peaceful borders, a white limousine carried threats back to Houston, while in town, foundations for new greenhouses set and cured, taking permanent shape in the Texas soil.

The investigation was evolving, but one thing remained constant: Aileen's determination to uncover the truth, regardless of how dangerous the pursuit might become.

Chapter Fifteen — A Case Unravels

Green and Growing

Morning sunshine slanted through the metal framework of the new greenhouses, creating a geometric lattice of light and shadow across the new, uncured concrete floors. The air smelled of damp earth, plastic sheeting, and possibility. Aileen surveyed the progress with quiet satisfaction as Rick and Gloriano stretched a massive sheet of translucent polymer across the curved roof supports of the first structure.

"Pull it tight!" Rick called, muscles straining as he secured his corner. "We don't want any sagging when it rains."

Gloriano, serious and focused, adjusted his grip and pulled, the material snapping taut between them. Darwin stood below, calculator in hand, verifying measurements while Verona and Jessie arranged flats of seedlings along the temporary tables.

"The framework went up faster than I expected," Aileen remarked, running her hand along a metal support.

"Prefabricated sections," Darwin explained without looking up from his calculations. "Engineered for rapid assembly and optimal light penetration. The polycarbonate covering is rated for twenty years of UV exposure."

"In English: we got lucky with good weather and a great crew," Rick translated, securing the plastic with specialized clips.

Two days had passed since the limousine incident, and Aileen had gathered her team for greenhouse construction and for critical discussion. With the last section of covering in place, she called them together near the seedling tables.

"Before we continue," she began, "we need to talk about the investigation."

The teens exchanged glances, sensing her serious tone. They formed a loose circle, Rick wiping sweat from his forehead, Verona perching on a stack of empty pots.

"What's wrong?" Jessie asked. "Is this about Warren Fletcher?"

"Partially." Aileen chose her words with care. "The situation has become more complicated, and potentially more dangerous. I've received... warnings to stop investigating."

"Warnings?" Rick straightened, eyes narrowing. "What kind of warnings?"

"The kind delivered in white limousines by men who don't introduce themselves." Aileen kept her voice matter-of-fact despite the teens' widening eyes.

"You were threatened?" Verona's voice rose in pitch.

"Let's call it strongly encouraged to redirect my attention to gardening." Aileen smiled through thin lips. "Which is why we need to adjust our approach. Darwin, tell them what you discovered about Camden."

Darwin pushed his glasses up, excitement at his discovery overriding any concern. "Camden Matheson worked for Marchesi Holdings before becoming a teacher. He had an account manager position with a real estate development division."

"Marchesi?" Gloriano tensed his shoulders. "As in Vincent Marchesi? The Houston guy?"

Aileen noted his reaction with interest. "You know the name?"

"Everyone in Texas knows that name," Gloriano muttered. "My *tío* Lupe says never do business with Marchesi unless you're comfortable sleeping with *los peces*."

"Exactly why we're being careful," Aileen agreed. "Camden's connection to Marchesi may explain why powerful people are interested in keeping these murders buried. Literally and figuratively."

"What about Warren?" Jessie asked. "All the evidence points to him."

"We now believe Warren is being blackmailed," Aileen explained. "Regular payments starting immediately after the disappearances."

"So he's not the killer?" Jessie pressed.

"We're no longer considering him our primary suspect," Aileen confirmed. "But he's connected somehow.Possibly being extorted for knowledge of the crimes rather than committing them."

Darwin repositioned his tablet so everyone could see the screen. "I've been tracing Camden's work history. He was involved in preliminary proposals for Silvergrove development projects years before he became a teacher here."

"Including the supermarket site?" Rick asked.

"Exactly," Darwin said. "Camden wasn't just a random teacher. He had specific knowledge about development plans for that property."

As they discussed implications, Aileen moved to the first seedling tray. She lifted a tomato start in expert fingers, its leaves vibrant green against the rich potting soil, and transferred it to a larger container.

"Investigations are like transplanting," she said, gently tamping soil around the fragile stem. "You need a solid foundation, proper conditions, and patience. Pull too hard on a root, and you damage the whole plant."

The teens watched as she continued transplanting, her hands sure and gentle.

"We've been pulling at Warren Fletcher," she continued. "But he's not the root we need. We have to look deeper. To Vanstone, Patton, and whoever they're connected to in Houston."

"What do you need us to do?" Rick asked.

"Continue helping here at Bloomers. At least so long as anyone can see." Aileen emphasized the last word. "I want whoever's watching to see us focused on greenhouse construction. Meanwhile, Darwin continues research, but carefully. No more visiting courthouse records offices."

"Speaking of Warren..." Verona stood in a rush, pointing toward the road. "Isn't that him?"

They turned to see Warren Fletcher's silver sedan passing slowly by Brannigan's Bloomers. Even from a distance, Warren's tense posture was evident.

"He looks nervous," Jessie observed.

"He should be," Gloriano muttered. "If Marchesi's people are squeezing him, he's got plenty to be nervous about."

As Warren's car disappeared around the curve, Aileen returned to transplanting seedlings. Each plant represented growth and future harvest; tangible progress, unlike the murky investigation with its shifting suspects and shadowy threats.

"Back to work," she said. "Greenhouses don't build themselves."

As the teens returned to their tasks, she noted the irony. While constructing spaces designed to nurture life, they were simultaneously unraveling how and why two lives had ended. The contrast wasn't lost on her, nor was the fact that both endeavors required patience, precision, and the right foundation.

The Accountant's Trail

The microfilm reader hummed with a soft whir, its blue-white glow illuminating Darwin's concentrated face. Around him, the Silvergrove Public Library maintained its reverential quiet, broken only by a turning page or whispered request. The familiar scent of old books and furniture polish provided comfort as he navigated through digitized newspapers from five years earlier.

Darwin had constructed Camden Matheson's professional timeline, working backward from his Silvergrove teaching position through employment gaps and career shifts. Three hours of methodical research had yielded a pattern that fascinated him.

"There you are," he murmured, scribbling notes as another article appeared on screen.

The Houston Business Journal reported accounting irregularities at Marchesi Holdings' development subsidiary. No names were mentioned, but the timing aligned with Camden's departure from the company. Darwin cross-referenced with Camden's employment application to the school in Oklahoma. The dates matched. And a year later, Bradley Middle School.

Mrs. Hildebrand, the head librarian, approached with stealth born of thirty years' practice. "Finding what you need, Darwin?" she whispered.

"Almost," he replied, whispering as well. "Any chance the library has archived school board minutes from four to five years ago?"

"East wall, bottom shelves, blue binders." She smiled knowingly. "Researching local history?"

"Something like that," Darwin said.

When she moved away, Darwin gathered his notes and relocated to the east wall. The blue binders were arranged in chronological order, well maintained despite their minimal usage. He selected volumes covering the year before and after Camden's arrival in Silvergrove.

The pattern clarified with each document. Camden left Marchesi under a cloud of suspicion but faced no formal charges. His teaching certification review included character references, including one from Warren Fletcher, who described Camden as "a valued family friend with exceptional insight into educational finance."

"Family friend," Darwin muttered, the connection solidifying.

He found Warren's name again in school board meeting minutes, this time as committee chair for the after-school arts program that Camden later supervised. The program where high school students like Dana and Marigold volunteered.

Darwin's analytical mind assembled the relationship: Warren knew Camden as a colleague, helped him secure teaching certification after leaving Marchesi under suspicious circumstances, then sponsored the program where Camden had access to students beyond his regular classes.

But the most significant discovery came in the meeting minutes from March 12th, four years earlier; the night Dana and Camden disappeared. Warren Fletcher was documented as present during an emergency budget committee meeting that ran from 6:30 PM until 11:45 PM, with twenty witnesses.

"He couldn't have done it," Darwin whispered, scanning the attendance record again to confirm. "Warren couldn't have committed the murders."

He pulled out his phone to text Aileen, then hesitated, remembering her cautions about electronic communications. Instead, he photographed the relevant pages and continued searching.

A small article in the Silvergrove Sentinel caught his attention: "Local Businessman Sponsors Career Day." The photograph showed Camden and Warren together at Keating High, both smiling as Camden spoke to students about finance careers. Among the students visible in the background was Dana Mitchell, her expression troubled rather than engaged.

The final piece clicked into place when Darwin found records of a real estate holding company, Eastern Pine Investments, with Warren Fletcher listed as minority partner. The company had purchased three properties in Silvergrove. All parcels later sold to developers affiliated with Marchesi Holdings at substantial profit.

"He wasn't being blackmailed about murder," Darwin realized. "It was about insider trading and development kickbacks."

Warren's suspicious behavior, the late-night meetings, the financial transactions; everything pointed to a man caught in an extortion scheme related to real estate dealings, not homicide. The gun purchase was probably for protection as the situation escalated, not for murder.

"Closing in fifteen minutes," Mrs. Hildebrand announced, her voice carrying despite its softness.

Darwin gathered his research, photographing final documents before returning the binders to their shelves. His mind raced ahead, connecting the new information to their existing knowledge.

The revelation hit like a key turning in a lock: Warren Fletcher's guilt was real enough, just not the kind that left blood on his hands. It lived in ledgers and locked drawers, in the convenient timing of the development project's delays, in whatever Camden had discovered beneath the surface of legitimate business. Someone had killed to protect those secrets, but Warren's role was puppet master, not executioner. Equally damning, but far more difficult to prove.

As he left the library, Darwin texted the group: "Warren cleared. Definitive alibi for night of murders. His real connection to Camden involved business dealings, not personal grudge. Call when safe to talk."

The evening air felt cooler against his skin as he hurried toward Brannigan's Bloomers, the weight of discovery propelling him forward while the implications settled like stones in his mind.

✧ ⌑ ✧ ⌑ ✧

Blackmail Unveiled

Judge Davita Canton's chambers exuded quiet authority. Leather-bound law books lined mahogany shelves, diplomas and commendations hung in precise formation, and a large desk dominated the space without overwhelming it. Two scents told conflicting stories - the lemon polish all business, the coffee pure comfort.

Aileen sat beside Chief Couch, with Felicity Quick completing their small semi-circle before the judge's desk. Outside, late afternoon sun cast highlighted the old Civil War statues on the courthouse lawn as the town carried on, unaware of the dramatic shifts occurring in the investigation.

"Let me understand this in detail," Judge Canton said, reviewing the documents before her. "You're abandoning Warren Fletcher as a suspect based on these financial records?"

Felicity stood straight, her professional composure intact despite the tension in the room. "The pattern is unambiguous, Your Honor. Classic extortion. Regular withdrawals followed by deposits of smaller amounts through shell companies. The transactions accelerate over time as demands typically increase."

"And this has continued for four years?" Judge Canton's keen eyes surveyed the timeline Felicity had constructed.

"Without interruption," Felicity confirmed. "Beginning exactly one week after the disappearances."

Chief Couch shifted in his chair. "Plus, he has an alibi. Board meeting with twenty witnesses the entire evening."

"So Warren Fletcher isn't a murderer," Judge Canton concluded, "but a blackmail victim."

"Precisely," Aileen agreed. "Though we believe he's being blackmailed about something connected to the murders, if not the murders themselves."

Judge Canton steepled her fingers, consideration evident in her expression. "Have you considered confronting him directly?"

"I advised against it," Chief Couch interjected. "Blackmail victims rarely cooperate of their own free will. They're trapped between fear of their blackmailer and dread of legal consequences for whatever they're hiding."

"Besides," Aileen added, "after my... interaction with our limousine friends, I'm concerned about pushing too hard in any public way."

Judge Canton's eyebrows rose. "You believe the blackmail is connected to organized crime?"

"Camden Matheson worked for Marchesi Holdings before teaching," Aileen explained. "And Warren Fletcher has business connections to development projects associated with Marchesi subsidiaries."

"That's troubling," Judge Canton murmured, tapping her pen against the desk. "Marchesi's influence has historically stopped at county lines further south. Their interest in Silvergrove is... concerning."

"We believe it's related to the supermarket development," Felicity explained. "The financial projections suggest the project is worth much more than stated in public filings. Perhaps because of plans beyond just a supermarket."

"Such as?" the judge prompted.

"We're not certain," Aileen admitted. "But the urgency with which they've tried to shut down our investigation suggests something valuable is at stake."

Chief Couch's phone buzzed, drawing their attention. He checked the message, then passed his phone to Aileen. "From Darwin. Confirms everything and adds context."

Aileen scanned Darwin's text about Warren's business connections to Camden. "Warren and Camden weren't enemies, they were business associates. Warren helped Camden get his teaching job after he left Marchesi under suspicious circumstances."

"Suspicious how?" Judge Canton asked, her tone sharp.

"Accounting irregularities," Aileen read from the text. "Never formally charged. Warren wrote him a character reference for his teaching certification."

"So Camden may have known something compromising about Warren's business dealings," Felicity suggested. "Perhaps involving insider information about development sites."

"And Dana?" Judge Canton asked. "How does she fit into this scenario?"

A heavy silence fell over the room. That connection remained elusive despite their progress untangling other aspects of the case.

"We don't know yet," Aileen admitted. "But Camden supervised the arts program where Dana volunteered. She may have overheard something, or Camden might have confided in her."

Chief Couch ran a hand over his balding head. "If Camden was planning to reveal whatever they were hiding —"

"It would provide motive," Judge Canton finished. "But not for Warren, who apparently couldn't have committed the actual murders."

"Exactly," Aileen agreed. "Which redirects our focus to Vanstone and Patton. They discovered the bodies, they're pushing the development, and they both seem connected to interests beyond Silvergrove."

Judge Canton gathered the documents, arranging them into a neat stack. "I believe your judicial authorizations remain appropriate, but redirected toward these new suspects. Chief Couch, I suggest surveillance on both Vanstone and Patton, though discreetly given the potential connections."

"In progress," Roland confirmed.

"And Mrs. Brannigan," Judge Canton turned her penetrating gaze to Aileen, "I understand your commitment to justice, but please exercise extreme caution. If Marchesi is involved, the stakes are considerably higher than a local property developer's ambitions."

"I understand," Aileen assured her.

A knock at the door interrupted them. Judge Canton's clerk entered, looking apologetic.

"I'm sorry to disturb you, Your Honor, but I have an urgent message. Mayor Mitchell has called an emergency closed session of the town council regarding the development project. Seven o'clock tonight."

Judge Canton thanked her clerk, then turned back to the group after the door closed. "Interesting timing. I wonder what prompted this sudden meeting."

"Mayor Mitchell has supported the development from the beginning," Chief Couch noted. "Perhaps she's trying to salvage the project despite the complications."

"Or perhaps," Aileen suggested, "she knows more than she's been sharing."

The implication hung in the air, uncomfortable but impossible to ignore. Tamryn Mitchell had been deeply involved in town development projects for years, had known Camden as a teacher at the local school, and had lost her niece in the disappearance.

"That's speculative," Judge Canton cautioned, though her expression suggested she wasn't dismissing the possibility. "Focus on evidence, not conjecture."

"Noted, your Honor," Aileen said.

As they prepared to leave, Aileen felt the investigation shifting beneath them like tectonically unstable ground. Warren Fletcher's innocence — of murder, at least — had been established, but each answer revealed new questions. The web of connections between Camden, Warren, Vanstone, and Patton now extended beyond Silvergrove to Houston and the Marchesi organization.

And somewhere within that web, the truth about Dana and Camden's deaths remained hidden. Like a garden overrun with invasive species, they'd need to clear away the tangled growth of lies and misdirection before the truth could be coaxed into the light.

"Take extra precautions," Judge Canton said as they reached the door. "All of you. When cases unravel this dramatically, what remains is often more dangerous than what was initially perceived."

Aileen's head dipped, understanding the warning all too well. As they stepped into the courthouse hallway, the afternoon sun cast long shadows through the tall windows. A reminder that even the brightest light created darkness somewhere else.

New Threats

Aileen arrived home to find a certified-mail notice tucked under her doormat, the orange slip indicating she'd missed a delivery. The return address stopped her cold: Lattimore & Crane, LLP. Houston.

She'd never heard of them. She looked up the firm on her phone standing right there on the porch steps.

Corporate litigation. Specializing in defamation and tortious interference.

The voicemail waiting on her home answering machine confirmed what she'd suspected. A measured legal voice, all professional calm: "This message is for Aileen Brannigan of Brannigan's Bloomers. Lattimore and Crane represents Vanstone Capital Group and affiliated interests in matters pertaining to public statements and interference with lawful business operations. You are advised to contact our office at your earliest convenience to avoid further action."

Aileen sat down on the porch step. The evening had gone cool, the first mockingbird calling from somewhere in the live oak, but she barely registered it.

They weren't going to come at her with limousines this time. They were going to come at her through her business. Through the greenhouse permits she'd just filed, through the loan that kept her afloat between seasons, through the name she'd spent years building in this town.

Double drat.

Midnight Confrontation

Billy's Bar and Bowling occupied the lonely stretch of highway between Silvergrove and the county line, its neon sign flickering a rhythmless beat in the misty night air. Inside, country music played at a volume just loud enough to ensure private conversations remained private, while ceiling fans couldn't disperse the cigarette smoke despite state laws against indoor smoking.

Kenyon Vanstone occupied the last booth in the back corner, nursing his third bourbon. His tailored suit looked out of place among the regulars' flannel and denim, but the locals knew better than to comment. Money commanded its own respect, regardless of packaging.

When Raymond Patton entered at half past midnight, several heads turned, then looked away on purpose. The property developer's connection to Vanstone wasn't officially acknowledged, but small towns thrived on unspoken information.

Raymond had barely touched the bench when Vanstone's cold rebuke landed: "You're late."

"There was a situation at my warehouse," Raymond replied, glancing around before continuing. "Break-in. Police are still dragging their muddy boots all over my offices, days later."

Vanstone's expression darkened. "Brannigan?"

"Teenagers, according to the security guard. Her team." Raymond signaled the bartender for a drink. "They were searching the office."

"And what might they have found?" Vanstone asked, his calm tone belied by white-knuckled fingers around his glass.

"Nothing incriminating," Raymond assured him, though perspiration beaded his forehead despite the bar's chill. "Though they seemed particularly interested in some tarps."

"Tarps," Vanstone repeated. "The same tarps you assured me were disposed of four years ago?"

Raymond accepted his whiskey from the approaching server, waiting until they were alone again. "I kept a few. For leverage."

Vanstone's laugh held no humor. "Leverage? You're accumulating evidence against yourself, you fool."

"Insurance," Raymond corrected. "In case you decided I'd outlived my usefulness."

"Like you're doing now?" Vanstone leaned forward. "Your amateur attempts at intimidation have only emboldened that garden witch. The protest was a disaster. And now there's been a break-in at your warehouse?" Vanstone slugged back his whiskey and waved for another.

"Which wouldn't have happened if you hadn't insisted on digging new foundations," Raymond hissed. "Everything was containable until you changed the excavation plans."

"Market conditions changed. The original structure was insufficient."

"Market conditions," Raymond echoed, his bitterness showing. "Always the convenient excuse when you want something."

Vanstone studied him with clinical detachment. "You're becoming unstable, Raymond. A liability."

"Careful," Raymond warned, eyes darting around the almost empty bar. "I'm not the only one with something to lose. Does your board know about your arrangement with Morales? Or the other funds you've diverted to secure this project?"

A flash of genuine surprise crossed Vanstone's face. "You've been keeping records."

"Like I said. Insurance." Raymond's smile didn't reach his eyes. "I'm not the only one who'd face consequences if the truth comes out."

They stared at each other, mutual hostility balanced by mutual vulnerability, at least for the moment.

"You should focus on cleaning up your warehouse situation," Vanstone said, signaling for the check. "And I'll handle the Brannigan woman my way."

"You've tried," Raymond pointed out. "She's still investigating."

"I was being subtle before." Vanstone laid several bills on the table. "Subtlety is clearly wasted in Silvergrove."

As Vanstone stood to leave, Raymond grabbed his wrist. "Don't do anything that would bring more attention. We need to lie low until this blows over."

Vanstone extracted his arm with a look of distaste. "Nothing is 'blowing over,' Raymond. Your arrangement with the mayor bought you four years of silence. That time is ending."

"You don't understand what's at stake for me," Raymond insisted, desperation bleeding into his voice. "I've done everything for her."

"Your obsession with Tamryn Mitchell is your problem, not mine." Vanstone adjusted his cuffs. "Clean up your warehouse. Destroy those tarps. And stay away from Brannigan and her teen detectives."

As the developer departed, Raymond remained in the booth, draining his whiskey before ordering another. In the bar's hazy mirror, he caught sight of his reflection: haggard, aging, the careful façade crumbling under pressure.

Everything he'd done, every compromise and crime, had been for Tamryn. To protect her. To prove his devotion. To earn the place in her life he'd coveted since high school.

Now it was unraveling, thread by thread. And Raymond was beginning to suspect that when the final thread snapped, he would be the one left exposed while others walked away unscathed.

He drained his second whiskey, pulled out his phone, and composed a text to Tamryn: **We need to meet. Our arrangement is changing. Don't trust Vanstone.**

His finger hovered over the send button for a long moment before he pressed it, sealing whatever fate awaited them all.

Chapter Sixteen — Revelations

Rain's End

Morning sunlight spilled through the greenhouse panels, refracting through lingering raindrops to cast prismatic patterns across Aileen's hands as she inspected the repair done by Seaver's C-Thru Glass. Three days of relentless rain had yielded to clearing skies, leaving glistening puddles and mud-slick pathways behind.

"Glass looks good," she told Rick, who was checking the repaired section for leaks. "No sign of weather getting to the seedlings."

"Minor miracle," Rick agreed, climbing down from his stepladder. "Found some standing water in the back corner, but nothing serious."

Aileen shrugged, cataloguing tasks. After the vandalism and rainy interlude, Bloomers needed to regain momentum before summer planting season peaked. The sound of trucks arriving drew her attention outside, where Roy Masters' crew was pulling into the parking lot.

"Right on time," she remarked, heading out to meet them.

Roy Masters himself stepped down from his pickup, clipboard in hand. The construction firm owner's weathered face broke into a smile as he approached.

"Mrs. Brannigan! Thought we'd never see dry weather again." He gestured toward the sodden expansion area. "Gonna need a day for that to drain before heavy equipment, but we can start prep work today."

"Whatever you think is best," Aileen agreed, accompanying him to review the site.

As they walked the perimeter, Roy mentioned several supply delays affecting other projects. "Whole county's backed up. That supermarket development's practically at a standstill."

Aileen paused. "The Piggly Wiggly site? I thought they were just delayed by the investigation."

Roy shook his head. "Nah, more than that. Word at the supply house is Vanstone's pulling resources, redirecting them to a Dallas project. Ernesto's cousin works concrete, says they've seen supply orders cut by half."

"Sounds like they're scaling back," Aileen observed.

"Or pulling out altogether," Roy suggested. "Not that anybody'd mind. That land's got bad juju now."

After arranging the day's work schedule, Aileen returned to the office to find Darwin waiting, tablet in hand and excitement in his eyes.

"New information," he announced without preamble. "Historical property transactions reveal previously obscured connection."

"English, Darwin," Aileen reminded him.

"Stephen Mitchell, Tamryn's late husband, served on the board of Excelsior Group from 2010 to 2017," Darwin explained, displaying corporate records. "The same Excelsior that partnered with Vanstone on the supermarket development."

Aileen shivered and held her jacket closed. "Could be coincidence."

"Possible, but statistically improbable," Darwin countered. "Further investigation reveals Mitchell family trust retains minor ownership stake in Excelsior subsidiaries. And," his voice lowered, "offshore accounts linked to the Mitchell estate show transaction patterns matching payments received by Patton Development."

"You're saying Tamryn has been paying Raymond?" Aileen clarified, struggling to process the implications.

"Indirectly, through complex channels, but yes. The financial patterns suggest regular payments beginning shortly after Dana's disappearance and continuing until recently."

Before Aileen could respond, Jessie entered, her face drawn with emotion.

"I remembered something else," she said, taking a seat beside Darwin. "About Dana, those last days."

Aileen and Darwin waited as Jessie composed herself.

"She called me the night before she disappeared. Said she'd found something in her mom's study. Papers that didn't make sense. Something about her dad's business partner and illegal payments." Jessie twisted her hands together. "I told her to put everything back and forget about it. That it wasn't her business."

Her words refused to dissipate, instead spreading through the office like spilled ink.

"You couldn't have known," Aileen assured her.

"She said they had a huge fight. Her and Aunt Tamryn. Said her mom wasn't who she thought." Jessie's voice dropped to a whisper. "The next day, she was gone."

Aileen absorbed this new information, pieces shifting in her mental puzzle. If Dana had discovered financial irregularities involving her father's business, maybe connecting to Camden Matheson somehow, and then confronted Tamryn...

The office phone rang, interrupting her thoughts. The caller ID showed "VA Hospital, Houston."

"Brannigan's Bloomers," Aileen answered.

"Mrs. Brannigan? This is Sergeant Scruggs." The voice was clearer, steadier than she remembered. "Wanted to thank you for the flowers and to tell you something important."

"I'm listening," Aileen said.

"Been sorting my memories in therapy. That night. The white truck. It came after the other car left. I think I got the order mixed up before."

"What other car?" Aileen asked, pulse quickening.

"Dark sedan. Maybe blue. Someone inside was crying. Then it drove away, and maybe an hour later, the truck with 'Patton' on the door arrived." His voice grew distant, as if following the thread of memory. "Think you might be looking at the wrong person."

After thanking Scruffy and promising to visit soon, Aileen hung up, her resolve hardening. She needed to see Tamryn soon. Not as an investigator confronting a suspect, but as a friend offering one last chance to share the truth.

"I'm going to visit Tamryn tonight," she announced to her team later that afternoon. "Alone."

Their concerned glances spoke volumes, but no one argued. The investigation had reached a point where personal connections mattered more than procedural caution.

"Take care," was all Rick said, his young face serious beyond his years.

Aileen accepted his gesture, hoping her churning uncertainty didn't show. Some truths, once uncovered, could never be buried again.

Shadow Players

Raymond Patton smoothed the photographs with trembling fingers, arranging them in chronological order across his desk. Tamryn at sixteen, her homecoming queen crown the least bit askew and her smile radiant. Tamryn at twenty-two, captured in profile at her college graduation. Tamryn at forty-one, accepting her mayoral oath of office, her husband and daughter flanking her proudly.

The progression of a life, her life, documented through his secret collection. A collection that would be considered disturbing by most, but to Raymond, represented an enduring devotion others couldn't understand.

His office door remained locked, blinds drawn against the mid-afternoon sun. He hadn't slept since the warehouse break-in, since his confrontation with Vanstone at Billy's. The reality he'd maintained for four years was fracturing, fault lines spreading with each new development.

Raymond closed his eyes, transported back to that night against his will. The desperate phone call. Tamryn's voice breaking as she begged him to come right away. His arrival at the Mitchell house, finding her on the hallway floor, hands covered in blood, Dana and Camden's bodies nearby.

"Help me, Ray," she'd sobbed. "I didn't mean to. It was an accident."

He had helped without hesitation, without judgment. Wrapped the bodies in tarps from his truck. Driven to the abandoned Piggly Wiggly property his family had owned. Buried them deep in the soft earth of the overgrown lot, near the old root cellar.

All for her. Everything for her.

Then the arrangement: his protection in exchange for regular payments, channeled through offshore accounts to avoid detection. Not blackmail, he'd told himself. Just compensation for services rendered, for risks taken.

The intercom buzzed, jolting him back to the present.

"Mr. Patton?" His secretary's voice sounded hesitant. "You have a visitor."

Raymond gathered the photographs, sliding them into his desk drawer. "I'm not seeing anyone today, Margaret."

"It's Mr. Vanstone, sir. He says it's urgent."

Raymond's hands moved to his midriff, fingers digging in. "Send him in."

The developer entered without waiting for further invitation, his tailored suit immaculate despite the muggy afternoon. Without speaking, he placed a manila envelope on Raymond's desk.

"What's this?" Raymond asked, not touching it.

"The end of our arrangement," Vanstone replied, frost in his breath. "I'm withdrawing from the Silvergrove project."

Raymond stared. "You can't. We're contractually bound."

"Force majeure." Vanstone gestured in vague fashion. "The unexpected discovery of human remains constitutes extraordinary circumstances. My legal team has prepared the necessary documentation."

"This is about Brannigan's investigation, isn't it?" Raymond's voice rose nearly an octave. "You're cutting losses. Sacrificing me."

"Don't be dramatic." Vanstone straightened his already-perfect cuffs. "This is business. The project's projected ROI no longer justifies the investment given current complications."

"Complications you created by changing the excavation plans!" Raymond's control slipped further. "We had an agreement. Build on the existing foundation. No digging where —" He stopped, aware he'd almost incriminated himself.

Vanstone's smile was cold. "Where the bodies were buried? Yes, that was unfortunate. But perhaps not entirely accidental."

The implication hung in the air between them.

"What are you saying?" Raymond asked, voice hardly above a whisper.

"I'm saying, Raymond, that you've outlived your usefulness. To me, and to Tamryn Mitchell."

Raymond's blood ran cold. "You've spoken with Tamryn?"

"We've had several productive conversations regarding the future of development in Silvergrove." Vanstone moved toward the door. "She's quite pragmatic, once certain... entanglements... are resolved."

After Vanstone departed, Raymond sat motionless, mind racing. He unlocked his bottom drawer, extracting a small key hidden beneath papers. This key opened the safe in his warehouse, the one containing documentation of every transaction, every call, every moment of his arrangement with Tamryn.

His insurance. His leverage.

Raymond dialed Tamryn's number with shaking fingers, reaching her voicemail. "It's Raymond. We need to talk immediately. Vanstone knows everything. Our arrangement is exposed." He paused, emotion overwhelming him. "Everything I've done, I've done for you, Tam. Don't forget that."

He hung up, staring at the framed aerial photograph of Silvergrove on his wall. The town that should have been theirs to shape together. The future that should have been theirs to share.

His gaze drifted to the gun in his desk drawer; a precaution he'd kept since his father's time running the business. Raymond had never fired it, never needed to. But as walls closed in around him, he wondered if that might change.

He reached for the weapon, feeling its weight. The physical manifestation of how heavy his secrets had become.

Community Whispers

Rick maneuvered through the afternoon crowd on Main Street, balancing a stack of plant catalogs Aileen needed from the post office. The afternoon had turned warm, early spring asserting itself after the rain, and Silvergrove residents had emerged to enjoy the sunshine.

Outside Cathy Mueller's Classy Cook Café, a cluster of council members huddled in conversation, their voices dropping as Rick passed. Similar groupings dotted the sidewalk; townsfolk gathered in small knots, exchanging what appeared to be serious updates.

Rick slowed near Barton's Hardware, pretending to examine a display while eavesdropping on two elderly men seated on the bench outside.

"...can't believe they'd just pull out after all that fuss," one was saying.

"Mort at the bank says the financing's been withdrawn," the other replied. "Something about the Mitchell girl's remains causing too much controversy."

"Speaking of Mitchells," the first lowered his voice, "Mabel saw Tamryn crying in her car yesterday. Parked behind town hall for near an hour."

Rick continued walking, pieces of similar conversations reaching him from all directions. By the time he reached the Classy Cook for Aileen's coffee order, his concern had deepened into gloom.

Cathy greeted him with her usual cheerfulness, though Rick detected worry lines around her eyes. "Afternoon, Rick! Aileen's usual?"

"Please. And whatever pastry looks good today."

As Cathy prepared the order, Rick leaned against the counter. "Town seems buzzing today."

"Like a hornet's nest someone kicked," Cathy agreed, glancing around at her packed diner. "Half the council's been in already. Vanstone leaving has everybody talking."

"He's definitely pulling out?" Rick asked.

"According to Councilman Mossberger," Cathy confirmed. "He was in earlier, said Vanstone's lawyer delivered termination notices this morning. Something about 'unfavorable local conditions.'" She lowered her voice. "Between us, I think he got spooked after what y'all found about the old grocery site."

"Maybe," Rick acknowledged. "Guilty conscience?"

"Or business sense. Nobody wants to build a supermarket over a murder site."

As Cathy packaged Aileen's coffee and scone, she leaned closer. "Heard Raymond Patton and Vanstone had words at Billy's Bar the other night. Not friendly ones, according to my cousin who tends bar there."

Rick accepted the bag, adding this to their growing case file of thoughts. "Thanks, Cathy. For everything."

"You tell Aileen to be careful," Cathy added, surprising him. "This isn't about bodies anymore. It's about power in this town. Mayor Mitchell's called an emergency council meeting for tomorrow night."

Outside, Rick noticed Chief Couch engaged in intense conversation with Judge Canton on the courthouse steps. The chief's animated gestures contrasted with the judge's composed listening stance. As Rick passed, Judge Canton caught his eye, motioning him over.

"Afternoon, Judge. Chief," Rick greeted them with the respectful tone he'd learned from Aileen.

"Mr. Malone," Judge Canton smiled. "Running errands for Mrs. Brannigan?"

"Yes, ma'am. Post office and coffee run."

Chief Couch shifted on his feet. "How's she doing after that vandalism business?"

"Focused on repairs and moving forward," Rick replied, not giving anything away.

Judge Canton studied him with shrewd eyes. "Her investigation continues, I take it?"

Rick hesitated, unsure how much to share. "Mrs. Brannigan believes in finding the truth, Your Honor."

"Admirable," the judge agreed. "Though sometimes truth comes an unexpected cost." She glanced at Chief Couch, who was studying his boots. "Particularly when powerful interests are involved."

The warning was subtle but unmistakable. Rick sighed, understanding passing between them without explicit words.

"I'll tell her you asked after her, Judge Canton."

"Please do. And remind her that my chambers are always open, should she require... consultation."

As Rick continued toward Bloomers, he checked his phone to find a text from Aileen: **Going to visit Tamryn tonight. Please close shop. Will update tomorrow.**

Rick's instincts, the same ones that had kept him safe during his father's worst episodes, flared in warning. Aileen was walking into something significant, maybe dangerous. But she was also the most capable person he knew.

He texted back: **Will handle closing. Be careful. Town is talking.**

The afternoon sun cast long shadows as Rick hurried back to Bloomers, the community's whispers following him like ghosts.

The Open Drawer

Tamryn Mitchell's two-story Victorian stood at the end of Magnolia Avenue, its white columns and wraparound porch projecting stability and tradition. Aileen had visited countless times over their three-year friendship, bringing plants for the garden, sharing wine on summer evenings, helping to sort through Dana's belongings after her death.

Tonight, climbing the familiar steps with casserole and wine in hand, Aileen felt like a stranger. Or worse, an intruder.

"Leena!" Tamryn greeted her with her usual warmth, opening the door before Aileen could knock. "You're a sight for sore eyes."

Her friend looked exhausted, her reserves tapped out. Silver more prominent in her auburn hair, shadows beneath her blue eyes. She wore a simple blouse and slacks rather than her usual mayoral tailoring.

"Thought you could use some company," Aileen said, offering the casserole dish. "And real food, not takeout."

Tamryn's smile held genuine gratitude. "You know me too well. Come in, please."

Inside, subtle changes caught Aileen's attention right away. The hallway console table, once crowded with family photographs, now held a single picture of Stephen. Dana's images had been reduced to just one, partially turned away from visitors' line of sight. A new security keypad had been installed near the door.

"Redecorating?" Aileen asked in a conversational tone.

Tamryn's expression flickered. "Simplifying. Too many memories sometimes feels... overwhelming."

She led the way to the kitchen, where she'd already set the table for two. As they settled in with wine and food, Aileen guided the conversation through safe topics; garden center updates, town gossip, Judge Canton's latest community initiatives.

"I hear Vanstone's pulling out of the development," Aileen ventured.

Tamryn bobbed her head in quiet contemplation, eyes on her wineglass. "Official notification came today. Claims the discovery of Dana and Camden creates 'untenable public relations complications.'"

"How do you feel about it?"

"Relieved, honestly." Tamryn took a sip of wine. "The idea of a supermarket there, over where Dana was found... I couldn't bear it."

"And Raymond Patton? How's he taking the news?"

Tamryn's hand tightened almost imperceptibly around her glass. "Raymond is... complicated. He's been calling, but I haven't spoken with him yet."

"You were close once, weren't you?" Aileen pressed. "In high school?"

"Briefly," Tamryn dismissed. "Ancient history."

"He seems to have maintained feelings for you."

Tamryn set down her glass, centering on her folded napkin. "Aileen, what's this about? You didn't come here to discuss Raymond Patton's adolescent crush."

Before Aileen could respond, Tamryn's phone buzzed. She glanced at the screen, frowning.

"I need to take this. Emergency council matter. Help yourself to more wine." She stood, moving toward her study. "I'll just be a minute."

Alone in the dining room, Aileen heard Tamryn's voice rise a bit before the study door closed, muffling the conversation. She waited a moment, then moved to the hallway under the pretense of retrieving her purse.

The antique console table stood against the wall, its single drawer open about two inches. Aileen intended to close it properly, a hostess's instinct to tidy, but hesitated when she glimpsed something inside.

Don't look, her conscience warned. *This isn't why you came.*

But the investigator in her, the puzzle-solver who couldn't leave a mystery unsolved, won out. With a furtive glance toward the study, Aileen eased the drawer open further.

Inside lay an empty pistol holster, nestled beside a partially filled box of .38 caliber bullets. The box lid displayed "Winchester" branding, with ".38 Special" marked in large letters. Fourteen bullets remained in the package designed to hold twenty.

Six missing bullets. Two bodies. Multiple shots.

The sound of the study door opening sent Aileen's heart racing. She pushed the drawer closed and leaned casually against the console, struggling to compose her features as Tamryn reappeared.

"Sorry about that," Tamryn said, approaching. "Council drama never ends —" She stopped, studying Aileen's face. "Is everything alright? You look pale."

Aileen forced a smile, though her hands trembled. "Just remembered something urgent at the shop. I think I left the irrigation system running after testing the repairs."

"Oh." Tamryn's disappointment seemed genuine. "Can't Rick handle it?"

"He's closed up already. I should really check myself." Aileen gathered her purse, movements mechanical as her mind raced with implications. "Rain's finally stopped. Can't risk flooding now."

Tamryn followed her to the door, concern evident. "We barely got to talk. I was hoping for a real visit. Just the two of us, like old times."

"We'll reschedule," Aileen promised, unable to meet her friend's eyes. "Maybe this weekend."

On the porch, Tamryn caught Aileen's arm gently. "Leena, what's going on? You're not yourself tonight."

For a moment, standing beneath the porch light that cast both their faces in golden illumination, Aileen almost broke; almost asked the question burning in her throat: *Did you kill your daughter, Tam?*

Instead, she squeezed Tamryn's hand. "Just tired. The vandalism, the investigation. It's been a lot."

"You're sure that's all?" Tamryn pressed, her blue eyes searching Aileen's face.

Aileen summoned every ounce of acting ability. "Of course. What else would it be?"

As she walked to her car, Aileen felt Tamryn watching from the porch, the weight of her gaze heavy with unspoken questions. Inside her vehicle, hands gripping the steering wheel, Aileen allowed herself to process what she'd discovered.

The gun that killed Dana and Camden had been Tamryn's. Had likely come from that very drawer.

Four years of friendship, of shared confidences and mutual support, crumbled under the weight of this new knowledge. The woman who had welcomed her to Silvergrove, who had helped her rebuild her life after divorce, who had become her closest friend in town; that woman may have murdered her own daughter.

Aileen blinked, trying to focus through the burning in her eyes. The pieces fit together with terrible clarity now, forming a picture she couldn't unsee. The hardest puzzle she'd ever solved, with the most heartbreaking solution.

As she pulled away from the house, Aileen caught a final glimpse of Tamryn in her rearview mirror. A solitary figure on the porch, illuminated against the darkness, watching her drive away.

"I'm sorry, Tam," Aileen whispered to the empty car. "I'm so sorry."

Chapter Seventeen — Hard Truths

Building Foundations

Morning light spilled across the completed greenhouses, their metal frameworks glinting like silver against the Texas sky. Beyond the finished structures, the teens worked with quiet intensity, measuring and marking the foundation lines for the new storage shed. The steady rhythm of shovels biting into earth created a percussive backdrop to their occasional instructions and confirmations.

Aileen stood at the edge of the cleared area, clipboard in hand but attention elsewhere. Before her, two greenhouses stood complete, tangible evidence of progress, of growth. Behind her, Brannigan's Bloomers hummed with the day's first customers. Yet between these visible successes, a hollowness had formed in her chest, expanding with each heartbeat.

"We've got the corners squared now," Rick called, wiping sweat from his brow despite the early hour. "Darwin checked the measurements twice."

"Three times," Darwin corrected, not looking up from his laser level. "And they're accurate to within one-eighth inch."

Verona rolled her eyes. "Is that good enough for shed foundations, Professor?"

"It's perfect," Aileen assured them, forcing a smile. "You've all done amazing work. Especially without Masters' crew here to help."

"Their loss," Gloriano shrugged, leaning on his shovel. "Though I bet that 'emergency project' in Houston is connected to our friends in the white limo."

Jessie nodded, blonde hair escaping her practical ponytail. "Too coincidental otherwise."

Aileen watched them work, pride mixing with a growing heaviness. They had evolved from a loose collection of teens into a cohesive team: observant, thoughtful, capable. Their theories about Vanstone and Patton were solid, their evidence well-researched. Yet she'd noticed how they avoided mentioning another name in her presence.

Tamryn.

The evidence pointed toward her possible involvement, yet they skirted the topic like a pothole in a familiar road. They were protecting her feelings, Aileen realized. They knew how close she was to the mayor, how that friendship had sustained her when she first arrived in Silvergrove. They didn't want to hurt her by stating the obvious.

Tamryn's house stood on the street where Dana and Camden were last seen together. Tamryn had steered the investigation toward Warren, then Patton. Tamryn had called an emergency council session the moment Warren was cleared.

Each fact landed like a stone in Aileen's consciousness, building a wall she could no longer ignore.

"Mrs. B?" Rick's voice broke through her thoughts. "We need more marking stakes."

"Of course." She said, returning to the present moment.

The physical labor around her continued. Honest, straightforward work. Measuring lines that formed perfect right angles. Digging holes to consistent depths. Checking levels against objective standards. So unlike the investigation with its tangles of relationships, half-truths, and emotional complications.

Dirt under fingernails. Sweat beading on foreheads. The scrape of shovels against rocks. The mundane reality of building something solid anchored Aileen for the moment, providing respite from the circling thoughts.

A customer's voice called from the main building, asking about roses. Aileen hesitated, then made a decision.

"I'm closing early today," she announced, surprising them all. "We need uninterrupted time to finish this foundation before the concrete arrives tomorrow."

"But it's only ten-thirty," Verona pointed out.

"Sometimes foundations require our full attention," Aileen replied, the double meaning clear to herself if not to them.

As she walked away to handle the customer and close the shop, she felt herself separating, physically and emotionally, from the team. The distance necessary to face what she'd been avoiding. To build a foundation strong enough to support the weight of truth, even when that truth might destroy a friendship she cherished.

Behind her, the teens exchanged concerned glances, their shovels stilled. They knew something had shifted. What they couldn't know was how completely their mentor's world was about to tilt on its axis.

Photographs and Memories

The afternoon sun slanted through Aileen's home office window, illuminating dust motes that danced above the scattered case files. She sat alone at her desk, photograph after photograph spread before her like tarot cards foretelling an unwanted future. Her finger traced the edge of one image: Tamryn and Dana at the town's Fourth of July celebration five years earlier, their arms around each other, smiling.

Dana's eyes sparkled with youth and possibility. Tamryn's held something Aileen now recognized as fear.

"I should have seen it," she whispered to the empty room.

She reviewed the timeline she'd constructed, paying particular attention to Tamryn's statements and actions. Yellow sticky notes marked contradictions she'd previously overlooked or rationalized away.

Tamryn claiming Dana had been restless and unhappy for months, contradicted by Dana's teachers and friends.

Tamryn insisting Dana must have run away with Camden, despite leaving behind her phone, wallet, and beloved camera.

Tamryn steering conversations away from the actual crime scene, focusing instead on Camden's character and Warren's suspicions.

Aileen opened a folder she'd deliberately set aside earlier in the investigation: phone records obtained through Judge Canton's warrant.

A single line highlighted in blue: a twenty-minute call from Tamryn Mitchell to Raymond Patton at 11:43 PM the night Dana disappeared.

The evidence she'd ignored stared back at her, damning in its simplicity.

A memory surfaced. Tamryn's behavior when Dana was first reported missing. Not the hysterical concern of a mother whose child hadn't come home, but the wooden calm of someone performing grief rather than experiencing it. At the time, Aileen had attributed it to shock or stoicism. Now she recognized it as something else.

The knowledge that she knew where Dana was.

The realization crashed over her with physical force, driving the air from her lungs. She'd been blind by choice to Tamryn's involvement because of their friendship, because of the support Tamryn had offered when she needed it most, because of her own unwillingness to believe that someone she trusted could hide such darkness.

"Some detective," she muttered, ashes of failure filling her mouth. The grandfather clock in the hallway ticked with merciless precision, marking the passage of time she'd wasted following false leads.

Photographs blurred through unshed tears as Aileen gathered them together. The silence of the empty house pressed against her ears, broken only by the occasional creak of settling wood and her own unsteady breathing. The weight of truth settled on her shoulders like a physical burden, compressing her spine, making her feel decades older than her fifty-one years.

With hands that trembled in spite of her attempts at control, she rose and approached the evidence board that hung on her office wall. A photograph of the excavation site held position in the board's center. Slowly, deliberately, she unpinned it and replaced it with Tamryn's official mayoral portrait.

The act was painful, as if she were betraying her friend by acknowledging the possibility of her guilt. Yet as the pin secured the photo in place, Aileen felt something shift inside her: the first step toward whatever painful resolution awaited.

So much still unclear. When, exactly? Where? Who pulled the trigger?

"I'm sorry, Tam," she whispered to the smiling image. "But I need to know the truth."

Outside her window, clouds gathered on the horizon, promising an evening storm. Inside, the storm had already begun.

Night Reflections

Darkness had fallen by the time Aileen settled into the Adirondack chair on her back porch. The wooden slats pressed against her spine, unyielding yet somehow comforting in their solidity. Her garden stretched before her, visible in vague outlines against the night sky where stars punctuated the blackness like distant questions. Beside her, a cup of chamomile tea had gone cold, untasted, forgotten. Lightning from the gathering storm flashed across her back fence like broken Klieg lights.

The phone call with Mavourneen kept replaying in her mind: stilted and formal, both of them navigating the minefield of their estrangement. Mav had called to discuss her upcoming graduation, duties performed rather than emotions shared.

"I'm not sure if you'd want to attend," Mav had said, voice neutral, flat.

"Of course I want to," Aileen had replied, heart cracking at the uncertainty in her daughter's voice.

"Well, it's three weeks from Saturday. I'll email the details."

And then pleasantries, promises to talk again soon, the call ending with wounds still unaddressed, healing still postponed.

So like her conversations with Tamryn lately. Surface communications obscuring deeper truths. The parallel struck her full force now as she stared into the darkness. How similar they were, these relationships between mothers and daughters. Tamryn and Dana. Aileen and Mav. Different circumstances but the same fundamental fractures.

A soft weight pressed against her ankle. Bosco had emerged from the shadows, the orange tabby kitten settling against her bare feet with complete trust. Moments later, the smaller form of Lotus appeared, leaping gracefully into her lap with a questioning chirp. Aileen stroked the blue kitten's fur without thinking, finding comfort in its silky warmth.

"How do we justify ourselves?" she asked the night air. "How did Tamryn explain away whatever happened with Dana?"

The crickets offered no answers, their rhythmic chirping neither acceleration nor pause. Wind rustled through her garden, carrying the scent of impending rain and late-blooming jasmine.

Aileen wondered what desperate rationale Tamryn had constructed. Protection of reputation? Fear of legal consequences? Or something deeper: the terror of acknowledging an unforgivable action? Whatever had happened that night, Tamryn had chosen concealment over truth, had enlisted Raymond Patton in her deception, had built her continuing life on the foundation of that buried secret.

Just as Aileen had built her own life on avoiding difficult truths with Mavourneen. She'd never forced the conversation about her ex-husband's manipulation, about the economic realities of caring for a dying parent, about the impossible choices that strained their relationship to breaking. She'd allowed Mav's anger and distance rather than demanding honesty between them.

In her lap, Lotus kneaded tiny paws against her thigh, purring with contentment. At her feet, Bosco had fallen asleep, his small body warm against her skin. These creatures needed her for food, shelter, protection. Just as Scruffy needed his rescued kittens to anchor him to reality and purpose.

"Justice and mercy," Aileen whispered to the darkness.

Could there be a balance between exposing Tamryn's actions and understanding the human frailty behind them? Between truth and compassion? Between fulfilling her obligation to the dead while acknowledging her friendship with the living?

The ethical tangle seemed impossible, until she realized that true friendship required honesty, even when painful. That she owed Tamryn the truth as much as she owed it to Dana and Camden. Allowing her friend to continue living inside a prison of secrets wasn't kindness; it was complicity.

Something shifted inside Aileen's chest, the weight of despair transforming into determination. The path forward would be painful, perhaps devastating, but necessary. For Dana. For Camden. For Tamryn herself, who had lived four years carrying whatever terrible knowledge she possessed.

For the first time since confronting her suspicions, Aileen took a deep, cleansing breath. Her spine straightened despite the day's exhaustion. The night sounds intensified around her: crickets, distant thunder, the rustling of leaves. Life continuing despite human tragedy.

Lotus looked up at her with luminous green eyes, a silent witness to her decision. Carefully gathering the kitten against her chest, Aileen stood. Bosco protested at the disruption before resettling on the warm wooden planks.

"Come on," she murmured to the kitten. "We have work to do."

Inside, she moved through the darkened house, switching on lights: in the hallway, the kitchen, her office. Symbolic illumination against the gathering shadows, both literal and figurative.

With Lotus curled beside her keyboard like a small sentinel, Aileen reached for her phone. First, she would call Roland. Then Judge Canton. Next steps taking shape with increasing clarity.

The rain began outside, gentle at first, then strengthening. A ritual cleansing, renewing, revealing what lay beneath the surface. Aileen felt a corresponding resolution wash through her. Tonight might be her darkest hour, but tomorrow would bring light. And with it, however difficult, the truth would emerge, unbidden until now.

Chapter Eighteen — Breaking Tangled Webs

Indoor Investigation

Rain drummed against the windows of Brannigan's Bloomers, transforming the morning light into a watery penumbra in the workroom. Aileen had cleared the central table of its usual gardening supplies, replacing them with evidence boards, folders, and laptops. The team gathered around, their expressions a mix of purpose and concern.

"No outdoor work until the rain stops," Aileen announced, though everyone had already figured that out. "Which gives us time to organize what we know about Vanstone, Patton, and the supermarket project."

Darwin adjusted his laptop screen, his fingers moving with practiced efficiency. "I've been tracking the financial connections between Vanstone's development company and the town council."

"We know he bribed Abel Morales," Jessie said, gesturing toward a photograph of the councilman pinned to their makeshift evidence board.

"Yes, but it goes deeper." Darwin turned his screen so everyone could see the spreadsheet he'd created. "At least two other council members received payments through shell companies that trace back to Vanstone's primary holding company."

"Which ones?" Verona leaned forward, squinting at the screen.

"Elmer Sellers received three payments totaling $25,000 through a landscaping company that doesn't exist." Darwin highlighted the relevant rows. "And Meghan Cacciatori received $30,000 through a 'consulting fee' for services never rendered. I guess to be sure she didn't change her Yes to a No."

"That explains the sudden shift in the council vote," Rick observed. "From a 4-4 deadlock to 5-3 in favor."

"Exactly," Darwin said. "When he wasn't sure Abel's vote was enough, Vanstone expanded his strategy."

Gloriano whistled low. "Man, this guy doesn't mess around."

Aileen studied the evidence with growing certainty. The corruption web was extensive, calculated, and well-documented, thanks to Darwin's meticulous research and Felicity's financial expertise.

"There's more," Darwin continued, flipping to another document. "The development plans filed with the county differ in detail from what was presented to the town council. The 'supermarket' is phase one of a much larger development, including a hotel, conference center, and upscale housing tract."

"Which explains why they've been so aggressive," Aileen concluded. "The profit margin on the complete project would be massive."

"And why Marchesi's people got involved," Jessie added. "This isn't about groceries; it's about transforming Silvergrove itself."

Aileen gathered the printed documents, sliding them into a manila folder with practiced efficiency. "This is enough. We're taking it to Roland and Judge Canton immediately."

"What about Tamryn?" Verona asked, her voice cautious. "She's been pushing for this project from the beginning."

A momentary silence fell over the room. The question they'd all been avoiding.

"One thing at a time," Aileen replied, her tone making it clear the subject was closed for now. "First, we deal with the immediate corruption. Roland needs to arrest Vanstone before he tries to leave town."

She stepped away from the table, phone already in hand. The call connected after two rings.

"Roland? It's Aileen. We have everything you need on Vanstone, Patton, and three council members... Yes, definitive evidence... No, you need to move now. Bring Vanstone to the courthouse for an emergency hearing... Patton too, if you can find him... Abel Morales is already at the courthouse for a budget meeting; Judge Canton can handle him."

She listened for a moment, then added, "There's more, but this has to happen first... Yes... I'll be there within the hour."

Ending the call, Aileen turned back to the team. Their faces reflected a mix of triumph and uncertainty. The satisfaction of solving one mystery shadowed by the looming revelation they all sensed was coming.

"Rick, you're in charge until I return," she instructed, gathering her purse and car keys. "Keep everyone working inside. We'll reassess the outdoor schedule when I get back."

"You have to do this," Rick whispered, his eyes communicating understanding beyond his years.

Aileen paused, unable to speak past the tightness in her throat. The corruption case was straightforward: bribery, fraud, conspiracy. The evidence was clear, the consequences predictable.

What would come next would be infinitely more complex and painful.

The rain continued to fall as she left Bloomers, nature's steady rhythm contrasting with the chaotic beating of her heart. The windshield wipers swept back and forth as she drove toward the courthouse, matching the thoughts that oscillated in her mind.

Justice and mercy. Truth and compassion. Duty and friendship.

The impossible balance she would somehow have to find.

Vanstone Exposed

Late afternoon sun slanted through Judge Canton's office windows, emphasizing the grain in the polished oak conference table. The judge sat at the head, her dark eyes watchful. Aileen stood near the windows, while Vanstone and Abel Morales sat opposite each other, tension visible in their postures.

"Mrs. Brannigan," Judge Canton spoke with her usual quiet authority, "you have evidence to present?"

Aileen breathed to calm her jitters, opening her notebook. "Three sets of evidence, Your Honor. First, financial records showing irregular payments from Vanstone Development to accounts controlled by Mr. Morales."

"Business consulting fees," Vanstone interrupted, his fake smile slipping at the corners.

"Second," Aileen continued, "sworn statements from four council members about attempted bribes."

Abel's hands clenched the armrests. Sweat beaded on his forehead.

"And third, documentation of shell companies used to launder funds, connecting both men to organized crime figures in Houston."

"This is absurd," Vanstone stood, straightening his tie. "Your Honor, this amateur detective —"

"Sit. Down. Mr. Vanstone." Canton's voice cracked like a whip.

"I can't —" Abel broke. "I won't go to prison alone, Kenyon! You promised to protect me!"

Vanstone's facade crumbled. "You stupid —" He caught himself. "It wasn't just us! Raymond Patton orchestrated everything! Ask him about the bodies at the site. Ask him about Mayor Mitchell's secrets!"

Judge Canton leaned forward. "Bodies, Mr. Vanstone?"

"The ones Patton helped bury!" Vanstone's eyes held a desperate gleam. "Why do you think he was so interested in that property? Ask your precious mayor about her daughter! Ask about —"

Abel lunged across the table, grabbing Vanstone's collar. "You promised!"

The two men grappled, knocking over chairs. Judge Canton's hand moved to the panic button under her desk.

Aileen grabbed a wooden chair, testing its weight. As Abel threw a wild punch at Vanstone, she brought the chair down across their shoulders. The chair splintered, and both men collapsed in a groaning heap.

Officers burst through the door, weapons drawn, finding Aileen standing over the moaning men, holding the chair's broken legs.

"Perfect timing," she said dryly, dropping the makeshift weapons.

Judge Canton's lips twitched. "Mrs. Brannigan, remind me never to challenge you to a duel."

"Your Honor," Aileen's voice was quiet, "what Vanstone said about Raymond Patton..."

"Later." Canton pointed to the officers securing Vanstone and Abel. "First, let's process these two. Then we'll discuss Mr. Patton's... interesting connection to recent events."

As the officers led the suspects away, Aileen stared out the window at the storm-induced gloom. Vanstone's desperate accusations had confirmed her growing suspicions about Raymond Patton. From there, Aileen's mind jumped to Patton's ties to Tamryn. In one brilliant flash, Aileen knew all the answers. Now she just had to prove it.

The Truth is Clear

The main lights of Brannigan's Bloomers had been switched off, leaving the security fixtures and the small lamp on Aileen's office desk as the only light in her quiet space. Outside, the rain had given up, leaving puddles that reflected the emerging stars like scattered silver coins. The scent of damp earth and green growth permeated the air, life continuing despite human drama.

Aileen sat behind her desk, silent tears tracking down her face. The folder containing tomorrow's evidence lay before her, its contents both damning and heartbreaking. She'd reviewed each item a dozen times, searching for some alternate explanations, some paths that didn't lead where she knew they must.

There were none.

The sound of the back door closing startled her. Footsteps approached; Rick's distinctive stride, steady and purposeful even when exhausted.

"Greenhouses are locked up," he called, voice echoing in the empty building. "Everyone else headed home after we finished the inventory."

Aileen wiped her eyes, but not quickly enough. Rick appeared in her doorway, his expression shifting from routine reporting to concern when he saw her face.

"Mrs. B? What's wrong?"

She attempted a smile that failed before it formed. "Just tired, Rick. It's been a long day."

He didn't move from the doorway, neither accepting her explanation nor challenging it directly. After a moment, he asked, "The hearing didn't go well?"

"No." Aileen shook her head. "Actually, it went better than planned. Vanstone and Patton are in custody. Abel has been removed from the council pending further proceedings."

"Then why..." Rick gestured toward her tear-stained face.

Aileen looked at the young man before her. Seventeen, already carrying adult responsibilities, facing life's complexities with uncommon grace. She'd mentored him, trusted him, allowed him into the investigation despite the risks. He deserved honesty now.

"Because we solved one mystery only to confirm another," she said, almost too low to be heard. "And tomorrow I have to do something terrible."

Rick stepped into the office then, taking the chair across from her desk. "The meeting at Mayor Mitchell's?"

Aileen struggled for breath, fresh tears threatening. "I need you to be strong for me, Rick. I'm about to destroy something precious."

Alarm flashed across his face. "What can I do to help? What should I expect?"

"Just be there." Her voice caught. "I'm going to unmask a murderer."

Rick absorbed this, his natural protective instinct battling with his commitment to truth. "Can I... could I do this for you?" he asked He breathed in, then exhaled. "Present the evidence, I mean?"

The offer touched her heart. This boy-becoming-man willing to shoulder her burden. Aileen gave a watery chuckle through her tears.

"No, but thank you for offering. This is my responsibility." She wiped her eyes again. "I would have you hold my hand, but tongues would wag."

The small attempt at humor broke through the heaviness. Rick smiled, though his eyes remained worried.

"You were there for me when I was hospitalized after my beating..." he trailed off, the memory of the gang's brutality still raw. "I'll do whatever you need. Just tell me."

"Bring your courage and strength," Aileen said. "I'll need it."

The chairs scraped back in unison, their timing perfect without trying. When Rick wrapped his arms around her, it felt like the most natural conclusion to their conversation. Aileen hugged back fiercely, thankful for this unexpected alliance that had grown into something so much more than its professional roots - a bond that defied easy categorization.

When they separated, both pretended not to notice the other's damp eyes.

"Tomorrow at eight-thirty?" Rick confirmed as they gathered their belongings.

"The Mayor's house. Judge Canton is arranging for everyone to be present."

"I'll be there," he promised.

As they left Bloomers, locking the door behind them, the night sky had cleared to a tapestry of midnight blue. Stars sparkled overhead, indifferent to human suffering yet somehow comforting in their constancy. Tomorrow would bring pain, revelation, and the end of certain illusions. But it would also bring truth, and with it the possibility, however distant, of healing.

For now, that possibility would have to be enough.

Chapter Nineteen — Buried Secrets

Pictures and Memories

The night before, Aileen sat at her kitchen table long past midnight. The evidence folder lay open in front of her, though she'd been through it twice already that evening. A third time wouldn't change what it said. She did it anyway. Habit, or dread, or maybe just the need to do something with her hands while her mind ran its own circles.

The chamomile tea she'd made herself around ten had gone cold. She'd forgotten to drink it.

The photographs were the hardest part. Dana Mitchell at sixteen, wide-eyed and smiling the way a girl smiles before the world makes her careful. Camden Matheson at a school arts fair, a pen behind his ear. And Tamryn. Aileen kept coming back to Tamryn. Ribbon-cuttings and church potlucks and food pantry drives. The easy laugh Aileen had known across coffee mugs and back fences for twenty years.

She got up just past one and walked through the dark house to the back porch. The yard lay silver and quiet under a half-moon. Phil's wind chimes hung motionless, the night too breathless to move them. She'd been meaning to take those chimes down for three years now. She still hadn't.

"Whatever you need me to do," she thought, more at Phil's memory than at the moon, "I could use a little more courage than I currently have."

The moon said nothing. The Bradford pear at the fence line stirred once in a ghost of a breeze and went still.

She went back inside and slept three hours.

Grasping the Sword

Morning sunlight streamed through Aileen's kitchen window, casting golden rectangles across her polished oak table. Outside, birds chirped in cheerful ignorance of human tragedy. The day promised warmth and clarity, nature's cruel contrast to the darkness Aileen carried within.

She sat dressed in a navy linen suit she reserved for funerals and bank meetings. Her fingers tapped an indeterminate rhythm against the manila folder before her, its contents now committed to memory after countless reviews. A half-empty coffee cup had gone cold beside her right hand, forgotten as her mind rehearsed the terrible narrative she would soon deliver.

The clock on her microwave blinked 7:45. Forty-five minutes remained before she would destroy a friend, expose a killer, and forever alter Silvergrove's understanding of itself.

Her phone rang, Judge Canton's direct line.

"Aileen," the judge's voice came through clear and steady. "Are you ready?"

"As I'll ever be," Aileen replied, surprised by the calmness in her own voice. "Is everything arranged?"

"Yes. Chief Couch is transporting Raymond Patton from county lockup. Mayor Mitchell is expecting us for what she believes is an update on yesterday's corruption hearing. Everyone else will arrive at 8:30."

"And Rick?"

"He's meeting us there," Judge Canton confirmed. A pause, then, "Are you certain about this, Aileen? Once started, there's no turning back."

Aileen's gaze fell on a photograph propped against her fruit bowl: Dana Mitchell's senior portrait from the previous investigation files. Young, vibrant, forever seventeen.

"I'm certain," she said. "Dana and Camden deserve justice, even after four years."

"And Tamryn?"

"She deserves the truth, however painful." Aileen's voice stumbled over erratic breathing. "Living with secrets this dark is its own punishment."

They finished their conversation with logistical details, and Aileen ended the call. Rising from the table, she gathered the folder and her purse. Her reflection in the hallway mirror showed a woman she couldn't recognized; composed on the surface but with eyes that had aged years in days.

"I didn't ask for this," she told her reflection. "But I can't walk away from it either."

Outside, her garden bloomed in riotous color, oblivious to human misfortune. The transplanted perennials she'd set out just last week had taken root, their stems reaching toward the sky. Life continuing, growing, regardless of what secrets lay buried beneath the soil.

Aileen straightened her back, squared her shoulders, and walked to her car. The folder on the passenger seat seemed to weigh as much as a gravestone. In forty minutes, the weight would shift from her shoulders to Tamryn's conscience.

She hadn't sought this burden, but she would carry it to its conclusion. For Dana. For Camden. For justice that was four years overdue.

The Drive

Traveling across Silvergrove took eleven minutes at that hour. Aileen made it fifteen, taking the long way without quite deciding to.

Past Second Baptist, its white clapboards pale in the early light. Past the corner lot where the Vanstone development sign had been standing since April, its edges beginning to curl in the summer heat. Past the library. Past the loose gravel patch on Pine Street she always took slow. Past the redbud at Third and Sycamore, past its April glory now, reduced to plain green.

Four years in Silvergrove. Long enough to know the morning smell of it: cut grass and damp concrete and someone's breakfast bacon two blocks over. Long enough that the grief of what she was about to do felt real and particular, not theoretical.

She turned onto Mitchell Drive.

Chief Couch's cruiser sat at the curb. Judge Canton's gray Buick nosed up close to the mailbox. Rick's truck was pulled to the far edge of the drive, the way he always parked so as not to block anyone in.

Aileen pulled up behind the Buick and sat for a moment, hands loose on the wheel, the folder on the passenger seat.

A pair of cardinals was arguing in the live oak overhead. The male urgent and insistent; the female answering in a lower, steadier key.

She picked up the folder and got out of the car.

The Final Reveal

Morning shadows crept across Tamryn Mitchell's living room. The familiar space felt different, charged with unspoken tension. Aileen stood near the fireplace, where family photos showed happier times. Judge Canton sat in a wingback chair near the entrance, while Chief Couch positioned himself by the French doors. Delilah hovered nearby, a mixture of concern and curiosity on her face.

Tamryn perched like a mannikin on her antique settee, clearly confused by all the unexpected visitors in her room. Raymond Patton stood behind her, offering protection, however unwanted.. Rick leaned against the wall near Andy Burrell, both men focused on the tableau unfolding in the room. Jessie sat alone in a corner chair, her reddened eyes fixed on a photo of Dana.

"Thank you all for coming," Aileen began, her voice steady. "We're here because four years of lies need to end. Now."

"Aileen, please..." Tamryn's whisper held a note of desperation.

"Let me tell this story, Tam. The whole story." Aileen moved to the center of the room. "It begins with Camden Matheson, a predator who'd moved from school to school. But this time was different, wasn't it, Andy?"

Andy spoke in low, measured tones. "He'd resigned. Said he was leaving town."

"Because Dana rejected him," Aileen continued. "She was smarter than he expected. Stronger."

Jessie's soft soprano reached across the room. "She told me she was scared of someone. I thought she meant Camden."

"No." Aileen turned to Tamryn. "She was scared of you, Tam. Of what you might do when you found out about Camden's advances."

Raymond shifted, his breath gone rapid, knees locked. Couch's hand moved to his weapon. Delilah closed off a look of shock and moved to block the doorway.

"That night," Aileen continued, "Camden came here. Not to take Dana away, but to threaten exposure. He'd lost his power over her, so he tried to use her to save himself."

"Stop this!" Raymond's voice cracked. "You don't understand!"

"I understand it all." Each word a hammer blow. Aileen picked up Dana's silver cross from the mantel. "This cross, Tam. The one you always made her wear to church. The one that identified her body."

Tamryn's composure cracked. "I just wanted to protect her..."

"From what, Aunt Tam?" Jessie's voice trembled.

"From becoming me. From my mistakes." Tears rolled down Tamryn's cheeks. "Camden chased her into the hall. He had Dana's arm. She was screaming. I got Stephen's gun from the console..."

"And you fired." Aileen's voice was gentle. "But you hit Dana instead of Camden."

"My baby..." Tamryn's sob filled the room. "My precious baby..."

Raymond lunged forward. "She doesn't have to tell you anything!"

Couch intercepted him, but Raymond fought like a wild bear. "I protected her! I cleaned it up! I kept her safe!"

"Because you thought she'd be yours," Aileen said. "Your obsession with Tamryn led you to hide two bodies, Raymond. To lie to an entire community."

"You don't understand love!" Raymond broke free, charging toward Aileen.

Rick moved to protect her, but Couch and Delilah tackled Raymond first. The crash knocked over an end table, sending Dana's framed graduation photo shattering to the floor.

In the sudden silence, Tamryn's voice croaked, a rough whisper. "I killed them both. Camden was trying to save her, and I... I couldn't stop firing. The gun just kept..." She covered her face with trembling hands.

Judge Canton stood. "Tamryn Mitchell, as an officer of the court, I need to warn you of your rights."

As Couch and Delilah secured Raymond, Jessie crossed to Tamryn's side. She knelt beside her aunt, taking her hands. "I don't understand, but I forgive you," she whispered. "Dana would want me to forgive you."

Tamryn collapsed into Jessie's arms, years of buried grief breaking free at last.

Aileen felt Rick's steady presence beside her. Through the French doors, she could see strong, cleansing sunlight pushing away the darkness. Another secret revealed, another truth faced. But the cost... the cost was too much to bear.

Aileen Confesses

The elegant living room of the Mitchell home had transformed into something between a crime scene and a funeral parlor. The space where Tamryn had sat now stood empty, her absence louder than any words. Patton's absence noted in the broken table and photos. Through the large front window, Aileen watched Chief Couch and Delilah escort them to separate patrol cars, Tamryn's head bowed, Patton's face impassive.

Aileen moved to the settee, her body too heavy for her legs to support. Rick stood behind her, his presence a silent support. Jessie sat on the Persian rug beside Aileen's feet, her face tear-streaked, one hand clutching Aileen's ankle as if anchoring herself against a hurricane.

Judge Canton remained in the wingback chair, her judicial composure intact despite the emotional devastation they'd all witnessed, experienced. Andy Burrell paced near the fireplace, bow tie askew, hands moving from his pockets to gesture without meaning.

"I still can't believe it," Andy murmured, breaking the heavy silence. "Tamryn Mitchell. Our mayor."

"The evidence is incontrovertible," Judge Canton replied, her quiet, even tones soothing jangled nerves. "The gun registration. The phone records. The timeline."

"But how did you put it together?" Andy turned to Aileen. "When did you know it was her?"

Aileen shook her head, unable or unwilling to relive her investigative process. The tears she'd managed to suppress during her clinical presentation now threatened behind a fragile dam of composure.

"It wasn't one thing," she said at last. "It was everything together. Patterns that didn't match our theories about Warren or Vanstone. Questions Tamryn deflected. Reactions that seemed... rehearsed."

Jessie looked up, her young face streaked with mascara. "My cousin. All this time, buried in that field." Her voice broke on the final word.

Aileen placed a gentle hand on the girl's head. "I'm so sorry, Jessie."

Judge Canton leaned forward, her dark eyes studying Aileen. "There's more, isn't there, Aileen?."

The perceptiveness of the question startled Aileen, who paused for a long minute. She met the judge's gaze, then dropped her chin.

"This case..." she began, her voice roughening. "Watching Tamryn and everything that happened with Dana... it's like looking into a mirror."

Rick's hand came to rest on her shoulder, steadying her.

"My daughter Mavourneen and I. We're estranged," Aileen continued. "Different circumstances, of course. No crime. Just... failure. My failure to demonstrate what mattered."

"When her grandmother was dying," Rick explained in soft words to the others, protective even now of his mentor's privacy.

Aileen sighed. "I lost myself in caregiving, then in grief. My marriage collapsed. And Mav... she couldn't understand why I wasn't there for her when she needed me."

"That's hardly comparable to murder," Andy protested.

"No," Aileen agreed. "But the distance between mother and daughter, that's the same. The silence that grows into something impenetrable. The inability to reach across it."

She looked down at Jessie, whose tears had quieted as she listened.

"Tamryn lost Dana long before that night," Aileen continued. "Lost her to silence and misunderstanding. To unheeded grief. I can't let that happen with Mav. I can't let my unprocessed grief continue to hurt my daughter. I won't."

Judge Canton considered her words with an incline of her head. "So what will you do?"

"Whatever it takes," Aileen said with sudden clarity. "I'm going to North Carolina for her graduation. I'm going to speak the truths I've avoided. And I'm going to invite her to Silvergrove. I don't expect anything, but I'll offer everything.."

Rick squeezed her shoulder. "She'll come."

"I hope so," Aileen whispered. "I hope it's not too late."

As the group sat in contemplative silence, sunlight shifted through the windows, illuminating dust motes that danced like memories in the air. Outside, Silvergrove continued its daily rhythms, unaware that its leadership and history had been shifted, never to go back.

Within these walls, something had shifted too. Justice had been served, however painfully. And in the serving, Aileen had found a path toward healing her own deepest wound, one she'd traveled to Texas to escape but would now have to face.

"It's never too late," Judge Canton said with sympathetic finality, rising from her chair. "Not while there's still life and love."

More Secrets Unearthed

The noon sun beat down on Aileen's shoulder as she drove back to Brannigan's Bloomers with Rick beside her. The emotional exhaustion of the morning had left them both silent, the car radio turned off, windows down to let the warm Texas air flow through the vehicle.

"You did the right thing," Rick said as they pulled into the garden center's parking lot.

Aileen paused, unable to find words that encompassed the complexity of what had transpired. Her navy suit was wrinkled now, a coffee stain marking the cuff where her hand had trembled during her presentation.

"Let's check in with the team. Then I'm going home," she said, gathering her purse and the now-empty evidence folder.

The main building stood quiet, the CLOSED sign visible in the window despite the posted business hours. Aileen had given everyone the option to take the day off, knowing the news would spread like fire through Silvergrove's efficient grapevine.

They heard the sound of someone running just as Aileen's fingers brushed the doorknob of the office. Darwin and Verona burst through the supply room door, faces flushed with excitement.

"There you are!" Verona exclaimed. "Come quick!"

Darwin's eyes were wide behind his lenses. "We found something! You won't believe it!"

"Found what?" Rick asked, as Aileen stood, bewildered by their enthusiasm.

"In the foundation dig! Come see!" Verona grabbed Aileen's hand, pulling her toward the back lot.

Too shocked to resist, Aileen followed, Rick close behind. They emerged into the cleared area where the storage shed foundation had been marked. The entire teen team was there: Jessie having come directly from the Mitchell house, Gloriano and Garrett on their knees in the dirt.

"Look!" Darwin pointed to what appeared to be a large canvas bag, the top exposed in the excavation.

Garrett looked up, his face smudged with wet soil. "We think there's another one too, about four feet over that way."

Without hesitation, Aileen kicked off her sensible pumps and knelt beside the boys, navy suit be damned. "When did you find this?"

"About an hour ago," Darwin explained. "We were digging the holes deeper after the rain and hit something solid."

Working together, they gently exposed more of the canvas. Garrett used a small garden trowel with surprising delicacy, scraping away dirt to reveal what appeared to be a waterproof shipping bag.

"There's something hard inside," he reported. "Multiple items, I think."

As they worked, Verona and Rick focused on the second location, confirming another bag buried at about the same depth.

"Got it!" Garrett announced, easing the first bag free from its earthen prison. With care that belied his big fingers, he unzipped the outer covering to reveal decomposing bubble wrap and what appeared to be tissue paper.

Inside, nestled like a precious gem, sat a figure of smooth, gleaming red stone. A cat in seated position, its carved eyes watching them with ancient amusement.

"The jade cat," Aileen breathed, recognition immediate despite having never seen it before.

"From the Boucheron case," Darwin whispered. "But there's more."

Indeed, as they unwrapped additional items it became clear they'd discovered far more than just the notorious red jade cat. Small sculptures, miniature paintings, carved precious stone figurines. Piece after piece of a valuable collection of art.

"Sixty-four pieces in total," Darwin counted rapidly. "Plus the cat makes sixty-five."

Aileen sat back on her heels, navy suit now thoroughly ruined with Texas soil, her hands dirty but carefully cradling a small jade horse. Around her, the teens exclaimed over each new discovery, their earlier somber mood transformed by this unexpected treasure.

"The Boucheron art collection," she said wonderingly. "Hidden here all along."

Rick straightened, grasping the significance. "One mystery solved earlier today. And now another one closed."

As sunlight glinted off the red jade cat's polished surface, Aileen straightened her shoulders, a different tension replacing the weight she had carried. Beneath the soil of Silvergrove, terrible secrets had been buried: bodies, evidence, treasures. But with persistence and courage, truth found its way to the surface.

Perhaps her relationship with Mavourneen could follow the same path.

Justice Prevails

Darwin's phone buzzed in his pocket. He checked the screen and looked up, blinking behind his glasses. "It's Felicity."

He put her on speaker. The accountant's voice came through brisk as ever, though with a warm overlay. "I thought you'd want to hear this. The Texas Rangers picked up Kenyon Vanstone at Houston Intercontinental forty minutes ago. He had a flight to Zurich booked for this evening."

Nobody said anything for a moment.

"The Eastern Pine account is frozen," Felicity continued. "The DA is working with federal prosecutors. Wire fraud, on top of the state charges. He won't be developing anything for a long while."

Darwin lowered the phone. The jade cat sat in Aileen's soil-blackened hands, catching the afternoon light.

"That's it, then," Rick said. Not quite a smile, but something in his face had let go of a tension that had been there for weeks.

"Most of it," Aileen said.

The word most carried weight she didn't try to hide. There would still be hearings, lawyers, a community looking for its footing. Still a Jessie who'd lost her cousin twice: once to the earth, and once again to the truth.

But the people who'd done the harm were in custody. The evidence was in the open.

She set the jade cat carefully in Darwin's hands and wiped the Texas clay from her palms on what was left of her ruined navy suit.

Close enough to justice, for today.

Chapter Twenty — Community Healing

New Beginnings

The limestone steps of the Silvergrove courthouse gleamed in the morning sunlight, scrubbed clean after the previous day's rain. A small podium had been set up, adorned with the town seal and a modest bouquet of local wildflowers. Chairs for the press, mostly regional newspapers and a lone television crew from KTRE in Lufkin, faced the steps in neat rows.

Dahlia Bresslin, now mayor pro tem, stood at the microphone, her silver-streaked hair pulled back in a professional chignon, her posture regal despite the circumstances that had elevated her to this position. Behind her, Aileen and her team of teen investigators formed a supportive semicircle.

Jessie stood tall, her blue eyes clear despite the emotional toll of recent days. Darwin fidgeted while Verona toyed with a silver bracelet. Rick maintained his constant presence, pride evident in his stance. Garrett, handsome in a pressed Western shirt, and Gloriano, for once without disguise or antics, completed the teen contingent.

Most surprising was the figure at parade rest beside Aileen: Sergeant Scruffy Scruggs, transformed beyond recognition. His military dress uniform fit him like a second skin, medals and ribbons creating a tapestry of service across his chest. His beard trimmed, his hair cut short, his eyes clear and focused.

"Thank you all for coming," Dahlia began, her voice reaching the last row. "The events of the past weeks have tested our community in unprecedented ways. We've faced corruption, witnessed arrests of trusted officials, and confronted painful truths about our town's recent history."

A solemn nod rippled through the audience.

"But adversity reveals character," Dahlia continued. "And the character of Silvergrove has proven resilient, compassionate, and committed to justice. Today, we begin healing."

She turned her shoulders, gesturing toward Aileen and the teens.

"We owe an immeasurable debt to Aileen Brannigan and her extraordinary team of young investigators. Through their diligence, courage, and refusal to accept easy answers, they uncovered not only the corruption that threatened our town's development but also brought closure to two families who have waited four years for answers."

One by one, Dahlia recognized each teen by name, acknowledging their specific contributions. Darwin's analytical brilliance. Jessie's emotional strength despite personal connections to the case. Rick's steady leadership. Verona's attention to detail. Garrett's community connections. Gloriano's street-smart observations.

With each acknowledgment, the teens stood a little straighter, their expressions reflecting pride tempered by the seriousness of what they had uncovered.

"Regarding the supermarket development project," Dahlia continued, "I'm pleased to announce that a new investor group has proposed a more appropriate plan for our community. Rather than one massive supermarket, they will build two smaller markets in underserved areas, partnering with existing local grocers to ensure fresh food at fair prices for all Silvergrove residents."

A murmur of approval spread through the gathered crowd.

"The former Piggly Wiggly site." Dahlia paused, acknowledging with her silence the tragic discoveries made there, "The site will be transformed into a memorial peace garden honoring Dana Mitchell and Camden Matheson. This garden will be designed and maintained by Brannigan's Bloomers."

She turned toward Aileen with a genuine smile. "In addition, the recently recovered Boucheron art collection, including the famous Red Jade Cat, will be displayed in our town museum, bringing visitors and recognition to Silvergrove for something positive and beautiful. I want to acknowledge the Boucheron Estate for their kindness, and for their reward of 10% of the treasure's value, awarded to Mrs. Brannigan."

The crowd's agitated responses showed their surprise.

After a few more announcements regarding interim government arrangements, Dahlia invited Aileen to the podium. Aileen's posture showed her own understanding of the gravity of the moment, her expression composed despite the emotions of recent days.

"Thank you, Mayor Bresslin," she began, her voice steady. "Before I speak about our community's path forward, I'd like to invite Sergeant Scruggs to join me."

A ripple of surprise moved through the audience as the transformed homeless veteran stepped forward.

"Many of you know Scruffy as a fixture on our streets," Aileen said. "What most don't know is that Staff Sergeant James Earnest Scruggs earned the Bronze Star with Valor in Iraq, and has helped dozens of fellow veterans in our community."

Scruggs remained at attention, his weathered face impassive except for a slight softening around his eyes. He stared over the heads of the assembly as if reporting to a new commanding officer.

"The peace garden will include a special plaque honoring all Silvergrove residents who served our country," Aileen continued. "Because remembering all our community members, even those we sometimes overlook, is essential to true healing."

Scruggs gave a nearly imperceptible nod of appreciation.

"As we move forward," Aileen said, scanning the crowd, "we do so with both accountability and compassion. What happened in our town was tragic. Lives were lost, trust broken. But Silvergrove is more than its worst moments. It's also its response to those moments."

"I feel obliged to respond to the generous finder's fee Mayor Bresslin mentioned." The crowd stilled to a frieze in the Texas heat. "Dana Mitchell's name will live on a foundation, funded by the full award, to provide scholarships for our brightest students in need."

The crowd cheered, hats tossed in the air. Aileen waited for decorum to return.

She smiled, the expression genuine if still touched with sadness. "To celebrate, Brannigan's Bloomers will host an ice cream social this evening at six o'clock. Everyone's invited. Music will be provided by our own Garrett 'Garth' Herbers, with special guest Iris Leigh from Cedar Springs."

The announcement lightened the mood, heads nodding in approval at the gesture to the community.

"Because sometimes," Aileen concluded, "healing begins with celebrating together, acknowledging what we've been through and choosing to move forward. One scoop of ice cream at a time."

As she stepped back from the podium, Scruggs executed a perfect military turn and extended his hand to her. The handshake they exchanged symbolized something profound: two people who had found their place in Silvergrove despite difficult beginnings, now working together to help the town heal.

Behind them, the teens stood tall in the Texas sunshine, their young faces reflecting both the weight of what they had uncovered and the pride in how they had served their town. They had entered the investigation as children playing at being detectives. They emerged as something more: trusted partners in the pursuit of truth and justice.

Sweet Closure

Twilight had deepened into moonlit evening by the time the last notes from Garrett's guitar faded across the garden center's parking lot. Strands of white lights twinkled above the crowd, strung between recently constructed greenhouses whose plastic walls glowed like paper lanterns. The scent of night-blooming jasmine mingled with the sweet perfume of melting ice cream and freshly watered plants.

"That's a wrap, folks," Garrett announced, his voice carrying without the microphone he'd used earlier. "My thanks to Iris, our own Iris Blue, for helping us out with her beautiful vocals. And thanks to you all for coming out tonight."

Applause rippled through the remaining crowd, perhaps thirty people lingering after the larger gathering had dispersed. Empty ice cream containers, stacked cups, and scattered napkins provided ample evidence of the event's success. Several teens worked in teams, collecting trash and folding chairs.

Aileen leaned against a potting table, exhaustion evident in her posture, satisfaction in her eyes. Around her, a tableau of community played out in miniature: Darwin explaining some scientific principle to

Judge Canton, who listened with genuine interest. Verona helping Scruffy Scruggs load leftover ice cream into containers, supplies for his veteran network. Jessie and her mother embracing next to the foundation of what would become the storage shed, their relationship strengthened through shared grief.

"This event will be remembered for years," Rick said, appearing beside Aileen with a broom in hand. "The night Bloomers hosted half the county."

Aileen laughed, a genuine, unforced sound that startled even herself. "Is that what we did? It felt like feeding an army."

"A very appreciative army," Andy Burrell added, approaching with two cups of coffee. He handed one to Aileen, his bow tie askew after hours of helping serve ice cream. "I think the final count was twenty-three gallons."

"And worth every sticky spoon," Aileen replied, accepting the coffee with thanks.

Rick gestured toward the scattered cleanup efforts. "I should help with —"

"Lock it up and leave it until tomorrow," Aileen interrupted with a dismissive wave. "We've all earned a night off."

Rick's eyebrows rose in surprise. "Are you feeling okay, Mrs. B? You never leave messes overnight."

"Consider it my prescription for community healing," she replied, the lightness in her voice a welcome change from recent days. "Some things can wait."

As the remaining guests said their goodbyes, Aileen found herself surrounded by her teen team one final time that evening. Each face reflected a mixture of fatigue and accomplishment.

"Get some rest," she told them. "The new greenhouses need filling tomorrow, and I expect you all bright-eyed and capable."

"Will you be here?" Darwin asked. "Or are you leaving for North Carolina?"

"My flight's not until Thursday," Aileen answered. "Three more days to get you all organized before I go see Mav."

Something in her tone, the absence of anxiety when mentioning her daughter, made Rick smile. "You're ready," he observed.

"As I'll ever be," Aileen agreed. "Some conversations can't wait any longer."

One by one, the teens departed with parents or in their own vehicles, until only Andy remained with Aileen in the illuminated garden center. Behind them, the new greenhouses stood complete but empty, waiting to be filled with growing things.

"I should get you home," Andy offered. "You look ready to fall asleep standing up."

"That obvious, is it?" Aileen smiled, gathering her purse.

As they walked to Andy's sensible sedan, Aileen found herself speaking about her upcoming trip with unexpected optimism. "I've booked a hotel near campus. Graduation is Saturday morning, but I'm arriving Thursday to give us time to talk before the ceremony."

"Good plan," Andy said, opening the passenger door for her. "Having neutral territory might help."

"That's what I thought. And I've found a small garden center near her apartment. I thought maybe we could visit together if the conversation goes well." Aileen settled into the seat as Andy closed the door.

When he joined her in the car, he hesitated before starting the engine. "You know, whatever happens with Mavourneen, you've built something special here."

Aileen followed his gaze back toward Brannigan's Bloomers, where the white lights continued to twinkle against the night sky. Two completed greenhouses. A thriving business. A team of remarkable young people. A community that trusted her judgment and valued her contributions.

"I have, haven't I?" she said.

"You said earlier that healing begins with being together," Andy continued. "I think it also comes from building something worthwhile together."

He started the car, its headlights illuminating the road ahead. As they pulled away from Bloomers, Aileen looked back once more at the garden center, her garden center, then forward toward the path ahead.

Two directions, both now filled with possibility rather than fear. Whatever happened with Mavourneen, no matter what challenges awaited Silvergrove as it processed recent revelations, she had found solid ground. She had built foundations that would last.

The car turned onto the main road, leaving Bloomers behind but carrying its promise forward. In the passenger seat, Aileen Brannigan closed her eyes, allowing herself, finally, to rest.

The End of

Forget-Me-Nots and Forgotten Graves

Other Tales from White Jade Books

Brannigan Mysteries

Secrets of Silvergrove

Forget-Me-Nots and Forgotten Graves

Blue Iris, Blood Morning

Lotus, Lilies, and Last Courses (Fall 2026)

Roses are Red, Violets are Murder (Winter 2026)

Summers Rose Investigations

End in a Dead Heat

So Easy It's Criminal

Tacos, Sunsets, and Murder

The Drowned Duck (Summer 2026)

Cascade Agency Thrillers

Warm Taipei Rain

New Delhi Monsoon (Late 2026)

Mel Hunter Mysteries

Dead to Rites (Summer 2026)

Canned and Buried (Winter 2026)

Science Fiction

Samarqand: Prelude

Samarqand

Blue Stone, Black Water

The Other Side of the Sky (Summer 2026)

Redeeming Lost Pegasus (Fall 2026)

Lost and Fallen (Winter 2026)

ABOUT THE AUTHOR

Dr. Mitchell R. White, Ph.D.

Mitch White writes murder mysteries, cozy and otherwise, as well as science fiction and fantasy novels. His works can be read via the Kindle platform (tablets and computers), and now in print.

Mitch White grew up reading the greats of his time in science fiction, fantasy, action and mystery. These stories encouraged Mitch to try his hand at writing while in graduate school, where he was fortunate enough to take creative writing courses led by Orson Scott Card. The demands of school and family prevented Mitch from publishing, though the "writer's bug" never left his soul.

Working through school found Mitch in roles from ditch-digging to nuclear non-destructive testing, mixologist to prep cook for a dorm of 1,200 students. All these experiences provided incentive to finish a doctorate in chemistry, with other degrees gathered along the way.

A rewarding career in science and technology, and a gratifying family life, left little time to write until retirement appeared on the horizon. Traveling the world as a consultant scientist and engineer provided exposure to and appreciation of many cultures. Nothing broadens one's perspective quite like travel, and Mitch's experiences in other lands informs his interests and prose.

Mitch also taught as visiting professor in the sciences at several universities. He provided technical training in semiconductor and computer manufacturing, process optimization, quality improvement, and statistics to over 20,000 attendees on five continents.

Avocations pursued through the years include cooking, mixology, chess, travel, photography, fostering Golden Retrievers, and recreational computing.

Somewhere in all this chaos, Mitch found time for family, raising a daughter and now spoiling a granddaughter.

During retirement, Mitch performs as a professional musician when not writing. Mitch finds that the two avocations cooperate well, and he looks forward to years of fun, creative endeavors.

He lives in the suburbs of Austin, Texas, very close to the center of the universe.

www.ingramcontent.com/pod-product-compliance
Lightning Source LLC
LaVergne TN
LVHW090600110826
845146LV00001B/203